On Her Majesty's Frightfully Secret Service

Berkley Prime Crime titles by Rhys Bowen

Royal Spyness Mysteries

HER ROYAL SPYNESS
A ROYAL PAIN
ROYAL FLUSH
ROYAL BLOOD
NAUGHTY IN NICE
THE TWELVE CLUES OF CHRISTMAS
HEIRS AND GRACES
QUEEN OF HEARTS
MALICE AT THE PALACE
CROWNED AND DANGEROUS
ON HER MAJESTY'S FRIGHTFULLY SECRET SERVICE

Constable Evans Mysteries

EVANS ABOVE
EVAN HELP US
EVANLY CHOIRS
EVAN AND ELLE
EVAN CAN WAIT
EVANS TO BETSY
EVAN ONLY KNOWS
EVAN'S GATE
EVAN BLESSED

Anthologies

A ROYAL THREESOME

Specials

MASKED BALL AT BROXLEY MANOR

On Her Majesty's Frightfully Secret Service

RHYS BOWEN

BERKLEY PRIME CRIME
New York

BERKLEY PRIME CRIME
Published by Berkley
An imprint of Penguin Random House LLC
375 Hudson Street, New York, New York 10014

Library of Congress Cataloging-in-Publication Data

Names: Bowen, Rhys, author.
Title: On her majesty's frightfully secret service / Rhys Bowen.
Description: First edition. | New York : Berkley Prime Crime, 2017. | Series: A royal spyness mystery ; 11
Identifiers: LCCN 2016057174 (print) | LCCN 2017004278 (ebook) | ISBN 9780425283509 (hardcover : acid-free paper) | ISBN 9780698410251 (ebook)
Subjects: LCSH: London (England)—History—20th century—Fiction. | Aristocracy (Social class)—England—Fiction. | Women spies—Fiction. | BISAC: FICTION / Mystery & Detective / Historical. | FICTION / Mystery & Detective / Women Sleuths. | GSAFD: Humorous fiction. | Mystery fiction.
Classification: LCC PR6052.O848 O5 2017 (print) | LCC PR6052.O848 (ebook) | DDC 823/.914—dc23
LC record available at https://lccn.loc.gov/2016057174

First Edition: August 2017

Printed in the United States of America
1 3 5 7 9 10 8 6 4 2

Cover art by John Mattos
Cover design by Rita Frangie

This book is dedicated to Minerva's Muses, the delightful and talented women who were my students at a writing workshop in Tuscany last summer and whose first published novel I eagerly await!

And thanks also to my lovely new editor, Michelle; all the publicity folk at Berkley; Meg, Christina and everyone at Jane Rotrosen and last but not least my husband, John, who is always my most demanding and picky editor!

On Her Majesty's Frightfully Secret Service

Chapter 1

Monday, April 8, 1935
Kilhenny Castle, Ireland

Darcy has gone. Not sure what to do next.

I should have known it was too good to last.

I had spent the last two months at Kilhenny Castle, Darcy's ancestral home. I had experienced the merriest Christmas I had ever known, with Darcy, his eccentric family and the Polish princess Zou Zou Zamanska. We had fought hard to prove Lord Kilhenny's innocence when he was wrongly accused of a crime and had managed to gain back his castle. The next month was spent making it habitable again. It had been a wonderful, almost miraculous time to be close to the man I loved, to actually be planning our wedding in the summer. Darcy had also been helping his father to restore the racing stable, now owned by the princess, to its former glory and they had succeeded in winning the gold cup at the Punchestown races.

But all good things must come to an end. Darcy had never been the sort to stay in one place for long. Neither had the princess. She had flitted between Ireland and London in her little aeroplane as casually as if she was going down to the corner shop for a loaf of bread. Then one day in March she announced that she was leaving to enter a round-the-world air race. Darcy's father, usually never one to let his feelings show, had stomped around miserably for days after she had gone. They were clearly fond of each other, but as far as I knew he hadn't declared his love for her. Perhaps his stupid pride made him think that he didn't have enough to offer her, either in rank or in fortune. Not that she would have cared. Zou Zou, as she liked her friends to call her, was one of the most open and generous people I have ever met. And I think she had definitely fallen for the roguish Lord Kilhenny. Who wouldn't? He had the same rugged good looks and wicked twinkle in his eye as his son!

Then shortly after Zou Zou flew off in her tiny plane, Darcy came to me and said he'd have to leave for a while. He had an assignment that he couldn't refuse. Even though we were engaged to be married he had never revealed to me for whom he was actually working, although he had dropped hints that it was the British secret service.

"How long will you be gone, do you think?" I asked, trying to look light and cheerful.

"I have no idea," he said.

"And I suppose you can't tell me where you'll be going or what you'll be doing?"

He grinned then. "You know I can't. And actually I don't know myself yet."

I stood there, looking at him, thinking how incredibly handsome he was with those wild dark curls and alarming blue eyes. I took his hands. "Darcy, will it be like this when we're married?" I asked and heard a little catch in my voice. "Will you always be going off somewhere and leaving me at home to worry about you?"

"You don't need to worry about me," he said. "I'm a big boy. I can take good care of myself. But as to what I do when we're married, we'll just have to play it by ear. Maybe we'll move back here to the castle and raise our children the way I was raised. But I want to make enough money to provide for you. You know that."

"Yes, I know," I said, fighting back an embarrassing tear, "but I'll miss you."

"I'll miss you too, you silly old thing." He stroked back a curl from my cheek. "I'll be in London first," he added. "I'll make an appointment to see the king's private secretary and see how things are progressing."

He was talking about our wedding, of course. In case you don't know, I am the daughter of the Duke of Rannoch, great-granddaughter to Queen Victoria and second cousin to the king. As such I am part of the line of succession—currently thirty-fifth in line to the throne. And members of the royal family are not allowed by law to marry Catholics. Darcy was a Catholic so the only way to be allowed to marry him was to renounce my claim to the throne. This was all rather silly as there was little likelihood that I'd find myself crowned Queen of England (not unless there was a plague or flood of biblical proportions). But the whole thing had to be done properly. Darcy had presented a petition on my behalf. Then it had to be approved by Parliament. The petition had been presented, but we had heard nothing. So the wedding date was in limbo and it was most unsettling. I rather wished we had managed to reach Gretna Green, as Darcy had once tried to do, and been married in secret.

But left alone in the Irish countryside, now doubts crept into my mind. What if Parliament refused to let me renounce my claim? Could we defy them and marry? We'd have to leave England and live abroad if necessary because I was going to marry Darcy. Nothing was going to stop me. But it was an unsettling time, suddenly finding myself alone at Kilhenny Castle with Darcy's father. He had never been the most genial of men. Now he was clearly worried about Zou Zou so he went around with a scowl on his face and became annoyed by the smallest of things—much the way he had been when I first arrived there in December.

I, in turn, was worried about Darcy, about the future of our marriage and to what dangerous part of the globe he might be sent. More than anything I wondered what I should be doing next. I sensed that Lord Kilhenny welcomed my company and would sink into deeper gloom if I left. And yet I felt lonely, unsettled and out of place in Ireland. I enjoyed visits to Darcy's eccentric great-aunt and great-uncle, who lived in a rambling old house nearby, as well as walks through the countryside, where roadside hedges were now blooming with spring flowers and the air smelled of spring. But I wanted to be gone.

My thoughts often turned to my friend Belinda who had fled to Italy to have a baby that no one should know about. Was she feeling equally lonely? She had suggested when I last saw her that I come and stay with her in Italy, but I had heard nothing since and had no address in Italy to write to. I hoped she was all right. I also worried about my grandfather in London. I had written to him several times, but had heard nothing in return since Christmas, when I had received a rather lurid card and a box of Quality Street chocolates. I knew he wasn't much of a writer, but I was concerned about his health. He had a weak chest and the London fogs were often brutal in winter. I would have gone to London to visit him, but I had nowhere to stay. My brother, the current duke, owned our family home, Rannoch House on Belgrave Square, but he and my dreaded sister-in-law, Fig, had gone to the south of France for the winter and Fig had made it clear to me that I was not to use their house while they were gone.

Zou Zou had also said that I was always welcome to stay with her when I was in London, but she was on a round-the-world race, which might take months. So I stayed on in Ireland, rushing to the post every morning in the hope of news from somebody. And then one morning I went out for an early walk. It was a perfect spring day. Daffodils were blooming all over the castle grounds. Birds were singing madly in the trees, which now sported new buds. The air smelled fresh and fragrant. It was the sort of day to go for a long ride, but the only horses at Kilhenny these days were at the racing stable and I didn't think Darcy's father would trust me with one of his prized mounts.

I was halfway down the path to the front gate when I met the postman, coming toward me on his bicycle.

"Top of the morning, my lady," he said, coming to a halt beside me. "'Tis a grand day, is it not? And a letter for yourself from London, no less."

He handed it to me. A fat envelope. I looked for Darcy's black, impatient scrawl, but instead I saw my brother's handwriting. So they were home in England again.

"I see there's a crest on the back of that envelope," the postman said, eyeing it curiously. "So it's from some lord or lady, is it? I expect it's important, then."

He was hovering, waiting for me to open it. Although I was dying to know why my brother might be writing to me after such a long silence, I certainly wasn't going to open it with the postman peering over my shoulder, ready to spread the news to the rest of the village.

"Thank you very much," I said. "I'd better go indoors and read it, hadn't I?"

I saw him watching me with disappointment as I went back up the path to the castle. Once inside I went into the dining room and poured myself a cup of coffee. There was no sign of Darcy's father. He went to the stables at the crack of dawn most mornings and I had become used to eating breakfast alone. I had just sat down when the housekeeper, Mrs. McCarthy, came into the room bringing a dish of smoked haddock.

She started when she saw me. "Oh, your ladyship, I didn't know you were already up, and me with no breakfast ready for you."

"Please don't worry, Mrs. McCarthy," I said. "I was going out for a walk and then I met the postman and he had a letter for me, so I wanted to come inside and read it right away."

"Oh, how lovely. A letter for you." She beamed with pleasure. "It's not from Mr. Darcy himself, is it?"

"Unfortunately, no," I said.

"My, but that's a grand crest on the envelope," she said, hovering behind me with the dish of haddock still in her hands.

"It's from my brother, the Duke of Rannoch," I said.

"Oh, your brother. Well, isn't that grand." She showed no sign of moving away. I was beginning to think that curiosity was a local trait. "No doubt he's got some news for you. That looks like it could be a long letter."

"Well, he's just come back from the south of France," I said. "I expect he's giving me a full report on his time there."

"Oh, the Riviera. Now, isn't that grand? I expect they had a lovely time there. All those yachts and things."

It was quite clear she didn't plan to move.

"Don't you think you should put the dish of haddock onto the warming tray or it will get cold?" I said.

She chuckled. "Would you look at me. I'd quite forgotten I'd got the thing in my hands."

As she headed for the sideboard with the various breakfast dishes on it I opened the envelope. Two more letters fell out as well as one page of writing paper with the Rannoch crest on it. I read that first.

My dear Georgiana,

I hope this finds you in good health. We were not sure where to send the enclosed, but I'm mailing them to O'Mara's address in Ireland in the hope that you might still be there. We did read in the English newspapers about the amazing turn of events concern-

ing Lord Kilhenny and I must say I am very glad for you that he was cleared of any wrongdoing.

We arrived back from Nice to find the enclosed letters waiting on the hall table. It appears they had been posted some time ago, but the house had been shut up with no servants until we returned home. I see one of the letters comes from Buckingham Palace. I do hope it was nothing urgent. I took the liberty of dropping a line to Their Majesties' private secretary to say we had all been out of the country and I was forwarding the letter to you.

We all had a splendid time at Foggy and Ducky's villa—well, not exactly splendid. It was a trifle crowded. The term "villa" is actually somewhat of an overstatement. It's an ordinary small house on a backstreet in Nice, but is within walking distance of the sea. The water was too cold for bathing, but we took some nice walks. Podge was disgusted that the beach was not sandy, but he's a good little chap and amused himself well.

We'll be in London for a couple of weeks before we head back to Scotland and look forward to hearing from you.

Your affectionate brother,
Binky

I looked up. Mrs. McCarthy had now deposited the haddock on its warming tray and had returned to hover behind me.

"All is well, I trust, your ladyship?" she asked.

I folded the letter. "Thank you, Mrs. McCarthy. All is indeed well. And I think I'll leave the other letters until I've enjoyed your delicious smoked haddock."

I think I heard her sigh as she admitted defeat and went back to the kitchen.

When I had finished my breakfast I retreated to my bedroom and opened the other letters. The royal one first, naturally. It was from the queen, not dictated to a secretary but written with her own hand.

> *My dear Georgiana,*
>
> *I trust you are well. I understand from the king's secretary that your young man has indicated that you wish to marry him and, given his Catholic faith, have expressed yourself willing to abandon your place in the line of succession.*
>
> *This is indeed a big step, Georgiana, and one not to be undertaken without a great deal of thought. I would expect to hear from your lips that this is indeed your intention and that you are quite sure of the ramifications. To that end I hope you will come to the palace and we can discuss your situation over tea. Please let my secretary know when might be a convenient date for you.*
>
> *His Majesty sends you his warmest wishes, as do I,*
>
> *Mary R.*

(You'll notice that even in an informal letter to a cousin she was still Mary Regina. One never stops being a queen.)

I stared at the letter for a long time while my stomach twisted itself into knots. Did this mean that they might not approve the marriage, nor give me permission to abandon my claim to the throne? It all seemed so silly. They had four healthy sons and already two granddaughters, with the promise of many more grandchildren to come. I should go to London immediately and sort things out with her. Let her know that I intended to marry Darcy no matter what. I felt my stomach give an extra little twist when that thought popped into my mind. Queen Mary was a rather terrifying person. I had never crossed her in my life before. I don't believe many people have dared to do so. The only exception being her son and heir, the Prince of Wales. She had let him know quite clearly that she did not approve of his friendship with the American woman Mrs. Simpson. Not only was that lady currently married to someone else, but she had already been divorced once. The Church of England, of which the king is the head, does not countenance divorce. I don't think the queen ever believed that her son would contemplate marriage to such a person. She trusted that he would do the right thing when the time came and make a suitable match, like his younger brother George, whose wedding to the Greek princess Marina I had just attended.

I put that letter on my dressing table, then opened the other. It bore Italian stamps and I noticed the date on the postmark. January 21, 1935. Poor Belinda—she had written to me in January and I hadn't replied.

My dear Georgie,

Well, I have done it! I have fled to Italy as I promised and have rented an adorable little cottage on the shore of Lake Maggiore, just outside the town of Stresa. The views are spectacular. I have oranges growing on my back terrace. I have engaged Francesca, who comes in daily to cook and clean. She is determined to fatten me up and cooks the most divine pastas and cakes. So everything is going as smoothly as one could hope at this moment. Except for the loneliness. You know me—I like to be in the middle of things, out dancing, having fun. And here I am shut away from my own kind, reading books and even knitting during the long evenings. I'm not a very good knitter, I have to confess, and the poor child would be naked were it not for Francesca and her sisters, who have knitted little garments with lightning speed for me.

As to the question of the poor child—I am still in an agony of indecision. I cannot be saddled with a baby. How could I? If word got out I should be spoiled goods for life with no hope of ever marrying well. To be honest, with my past I have little hope of securing the son of a duke or earl, but an American millionaire would do quite well! But what to do with the baby? At least I have made inquiries about a clinic where I can give birth. Not in Italy, definitely. All those Francescas fussing around me!

Fortunately Lake Maggiore lies half in Italy and half in Switzerland. So all I have to do is take the steamer to the top end of the lake and admit myself to a lovely clean, sterile and efficient Swiss clinic in good time for the birth. Golly, when I write that word I feel most apprehensive. One hears such horror stories.

I sit here on my terrace, watching the ships going up and down the lake, and I think of you. I hope you are with your dear Darcy and all is finally well. I did read in an English newspaper that his father was found to be innocent. Jolly good for you and Darcy, finding out the truth. I'm glad one of us is going to be happy. Do let me know when the wedding will be, won't you?

Or better yet come over to stay for a while, if Darcy can spare you. You'd love my sweet little house and we'd pick oranges and gossip and laugh just like we did when we were in school together. Please say yes, even if it's only for a week or two. I will happily pay your fare. To be completely honest I wish you could be with me around the time of the birth. It's rather frightening to know that I'll be alone with no relative to hold my hand. Of course my family cannot be told under any circumstances. Can you imagine my stepmother crowing with delight over my downfall and shame? She would probably try to stop me from inheriting Grandmama's money if she knew.

So do write back, dear, dear Georgie. I long to get a letter and long even more to see your smiling face.

Your lonely friend,
Belinda

I put that letter to join the queen's on my dressing table and sat staring out of the window. White clouds raced across the sky. Seagulls wheeled in the strong spring breeze. I pictured Belinda's lake with the orange tree on her terrace and poor Belinda sitting all alone, dreading what lay ahead of her, hoping for a letter or a visit from a friend.

I should go to her, I decided. I'd want my friend to come to my aid if such a thing had happened to me. There was nothing to stop me from going out to Italy if Darcy was away. He hadn't told me how long he'd be gone. I don't suppose he knew it himself. In the past he'd been in such far-flung regions as Australia and Argentina. This time it might be China or Antarctica for all I knew. And Belinda had offered to pay my fare. I now had a small savings account so I could afford to buy the ticket, but that money was for my wedding . . . if it was allowed to happen.

I went over to the wall and tugged on the bell pull. Now that I had come to a decision I wanted to leave on the next boat before I got cold feet about crossing the Continent alone.

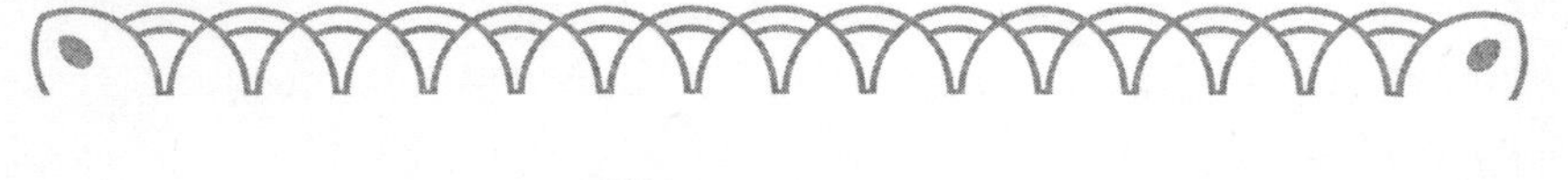

Chapter 2

Monday, April 8
Kilhenny Castle

At last I have a plan and a mission in life. Can't wait to see Belinda and her orange trees!

Almost immediately I heard the patter of little feet running down the corridor toward me. My door opened and a little freckled face, topped with the brightest red hair you have ever seen, poked around my door.

I smiled at the eager little face, thinking how different she was from my former maid, Queenie. I would have had to ring at least three times before she showed up and then the whole room would shake with the clomp of her approaching feet. But Queenie was now happily installed as undercook with Darcy's great aunt and uncle. Either she had improved or they simply didn't notice when she burned down their kitchen but I had heard no complaints about her. I rather suspected that their house was so eccentric and chaotic that they'd only laugh if her puddings wound up on the ceiling.

"You rang, my lady?" my new maid asked, dropping a curtsy.

"I did, Kathleen," I said. She was a girl from Kilhenny village, the daughter of the baker, and had proved herself a quick learner and so eager to please it was almost embarrassing. She was like a devoted spaniel, not leaving my side for a second. Of course, she was not without her share of mistakes, as she had never had to wash silk stockings, press velvet or handle any other delicate fabrics. Fortunately I did not possess much of the above and most of my wardrobe had been left at my brother's house in London. But I have to say she learned from her mistakes and never repeated them.

"Please go up to the box room and bring down my suitcases. You'll find my labels on them. And then pack all my things, the way I showed you, between tissue paper."

Her forehead wrinkled and she looked as if she might be about to cry. "You're going away, my lady? You're leaving us?"

"We're going to London and then maybe to Italy."

"We?" she asked in a horrified voice.

"You're coming too, of course."

She had wide blue eyes to start with. These now became impossibly large with alarm.

"Holy Mother of God!" She crossed herself. "London? And Italy? Me? Oh no, my lady. I could never go to foreign parts."

"But a lady's maid always accompanies her mistress when she travels," I said. "Who else would look after the luggage and help me dress on the train?"

She had backed away now until she was pressed against the door.

"But, my lady, when I took on this job as your maid, I thought it meant looking after you here, at Kilhenny Castle, not tripping off to foreign parts. My mother would never let me go and be among all those heathens and wicked men."

I tried not to smile. "Actually they are not heathens, Kathleen. In Italy they are all Catholics like you." It did cross my mind that they pinched bottoms in Italy, but I added, "Your pope himself lives in Italy."

Her face brightened a little. "The pope? That's right. Rome is in Italy, isn't it? And the pope lives in Rome. Will you be seeing him, then, your ladyship?"

"I think that's highly unlikely," I said. I realized as I said it that I could have bribed her with a possible visit to the Vatican, but I couldn't see how I would fit Rome into a stay on the Italian lakes on the Swiss border. "The place I'm staying is far from Rome, I'm afraid," I added.

Her face fell. "No matter," she said. "Me mother wouldn't let me go even if it was to see the Holy Father himself. She'd die of worry and grief."

"It would only be for a few weeks at the most, Kathleen," I said. "And what about when Mr. Darcy and I get married? We will probably decide to live in England most of the time."

"England?" she echoed, making it sound as if I had just said Zululand. She shook her head violently. "I'm sorry, my lady. I'm proud and happy to be your maid when you're here at the castle, but don't go asking me to travel with you to heathen parts, because I couldn't desert me mother like that."

It seemed that even London counted as heathen parts to Kathleen. I was afraid she had made up her mind. I was either going to travel maidless back to England or I was going to have to reclaim Queenie. Oh golly. The thought of bringing Queenie back to Rannoch House was almost more than I could bear. My sister-in-law hated her so violently that I'd have to endure a constant tirade. And then Queenie would probably prove my sister-in-law's point by clogging up the loo and flooding the bathroom or burning my best velvet dress.

I sent Kathleen up to retrieve my suitcases and tried to think of a way around this. I could travel without a maid, I supposed. Many modern women did. Even Princess Zou Zou had flitted between here and London with no maid for the first month before she sent for her maid from Eaton Square. The problem was one really needed a maid to assist in dressing and undressing. So many dresses and blouses were made with tiny buttons down the back, impossible to do up alone. And frankly I had little idea of the correct way to clean the various items I wore. I tried to recall how awful Queenie had been. Did I have an exaggerated memory of her disasters? She hadn't been too bad most of the time. And she had been jolly brave on a couple of occasions, helping to save me from dire predicaments. And she loved going abroad. So did I owe it to her to give her the chance to accompany me to Italy? I realized that it would not be the right thing to sneak away without telling her.

I waited until Kathleen, now rather weepy at the thought of losing me, had reappeared with my bags, then I went downstairs and found Mrs. McCarthy in the kitchen.

"If his lordship comes back, please tell him that I've borrowed the estate car for a few moments," I said. "I'm going to see his great-aunt."

"I will do that, my lady," Mrs. McCarthy replied. "So I'm hoping it was good news that you had in all those letters?"

"It was, thank you," I replied. "It appears I have to return to London immediately to meet the queen."

"Fancy that." A look of awe crossed her face. "Never did I think that I'd hear those words spoken in a house where I was working. But then I'm forgetting that you're related to His Majesty yourself, aren't you? Mr. Darcy told us about you being so highborn and quite pally with royalty."

"So you'll tell Lord Kilhenny, will you?"

"That you're going to be meeting the Queen of England?" she asked.

"No, that I'm borrowing the estate car. I won't be long."

Then I hurried out before she could prolong the conversation.

As I drove through the village I looked at it quite fondly. It was comforting to know I would be back, that Darcy and I would visit his father and share festive occasions with him. At last a place where

I would belong and be welcome. If I was ever allowed to marry Darcy, that is. I felt a knot in my stomach when I thought of meeting the queen. I could just imagine her smooth, imperious voice saying, "No, Georgiana, it is quite out of the question. You may not be permitted to marry him and that's that."

Maybe I was reading too much into that letter, I told myself. Maybe the queen just wanted to hear from my own lips that I wanted to marry Darcy. I negotiated the steep hill beyond the village and crossed over the little bridge. The stream was running high after so much rain. Then I turned in at the gate leading to Mountjoy, home to Sir Dooley and Lady Whyte, Darcy's great-uncle and great-aunt. In spite of its name Mountjoy was not on a hillside, nor did it look joyful. It was a large ramshackle building with gables and a turret at one end. Chickens and ducks wandered across the forecourt. A few sheep and a cow looked over the fence from the field to my left. At the sound of the motor a pack of dogs emerged from the front door and jumped around me, barking wildly. As I came to a halt the owner of the house came out. Great-Aunt Oona was a large woman with many chins. She always wore an odd assortment of clothing and today she was wearing a purple silk tea dress with a fringed shawl over it, a flowery apron over that and to finish off the whole outfit gum boots.

"What in the name of goodness is all that row about?" she demanded. Then she saw me and a smile lit up her face.

"Well, aren't you a treat to behold?" she said. "I was just saying to Dooley last night that we should go over and rescue you, now that Darcy has flown the coop. I expect it's pretty bloody with just Thaddy there. Has he reverted to his old bad-tempered self?"

"He's a bit grumpy sometimes," I admitted. "He's missing Zou Zou."

"Well, of course he is. And worried about her, I don't doubt. A round-the-world air race indeed! And that little contraption she's flying is little more than paper and string. Still, it's Thaddy's own fault. I told him he should make his intentions known. Snap her up before some other man does. But you know him."

I nodded. "Too proud," I said. "Doesn't think he has enough to offer her."

"Absolutely right. Well, you'd better come inside, hadn't you?" She led the way, shouting to the dogs, "Out of the way, you great stupid beasts," and then bellowing, "Dooley, come down here on the double. It's your favorite young lady come to see you."

We went through into a sitting room where there was, as usual, nowhere to sit. Every surface was piled high with papers, books, a violin, a basket of eggs, a summer hat and a large tabby cat. Oona lifted the eggs from an armchair and motioned for me to sit.

"You're in luck," she said. "That girl of yours baked shortbread this morning. Got a deft hand with baking, I'll say that for her. She's a gem, she is. And Treadwell's getting past it, although he won't admit it."

It was astonishing to hear Queenie described as a gem. "Disaster" and "hopeless" were more usual descriptions. It really did seem that she might have found her niche at last.

"So she hasn't done anything dreadful lately?" I asked. "Not destroyed Dooley's battle of Waterloo again?" (Uncle Dooley was reenacting the battle of Waterloo with toy soldiers in an upstairs room. He took it very seriously.)

"He's done with Waterloo, more's the pity," Oona said.

"Done with it?"

"Wellington won. Napoleon has been sent to St. Helena. All over." She clapped her hands. "And now Dooley's lost. Doesn't know what to do with himself. I told him to repaint the soldiers and start another battle, but his heart has gone out of it."

As she was speaking, the door opened and Uncle Dooley came in. He was a tiny sprite of a man, in absolute contrast to his enormous wife. His eyes sparkled when he saw me.

"Here you are, Dooley. Something to cheer you up. Your favorite young lady."

Dooley beamed and came over to kiss my hand. "How lovely to see you, my dear." He turned to Oona. "She's looking awfully well, isn't she?"

"She always looks well. Picture of health," Oona said. "Darcy certainly picked a winner."

I felt my cheeks turning pink at this discussion about me.

"Where is the boy?" Dooley said. "Haven't seen him for a few days."

"He's gone, Uncle Dooley. I'm not sure where. You know what he's like."

"I wouldn't be surprised if he isn't a gun runner or a drug smuggler," Dooley said calmly.

"Of course he's not," Oona said. "He's a spy. You know that. That's why he can't tell us what he does."

They both laughed at this as if it was a great joke. Then Oona found a bell among the chaos and rang it. Instead of Treadwell the butler it was Queenie who appeared.

"You rang, Lady Whyte?" she asked. Then she saw me. "Whatcha, miss," she said.

Again I marveled that she could address Oona perfectly but had never managed to call me "my lady."

"We'll have coffee and some of that shortbread you made this morning, Queenie," Oona said.

"Wouldn't you rather have some of the plum cake?" Queenie asked. From the guarded look on her face I suspected another disaster.

"No, the shortbread, please. You know Sir Dooley is particularly fond of shortbread."

Queenie twisted her apron nervously. "It's just that it didn't quite turn out as I expected."

"But I tried a piece. It was delicious."

"That was before I tipped the rest into the washing-up water by mistake," she said. "I tried drying it out, but it don't taste the same really."

"Honestly, Queenie," Oona said with a surprisingly understanding smile. "Oh well. Plum cake it had better be."

As Queenie went out Oona gave me an exasperated grin. "She's getting so much better too. Whole days without an accident and she really does have a light touch with baking."

"So you wouldn't want me to take her off your hands, then?" I asked.

"Why? Were you planning to?"

"I have to go to London and then probably on to Italy," I said.

"But you have a new maid. You said she was a sweet little thing and so willing."

"Just not willing to leave her mother and come to what she calls heathen parts with me," I said with a rueful smile.

"Ah, so you want Queenie back. I knew it was too good to last," Oona said.

My brain was racing. Queenie was doing well here. Learning skills. Not making too many mistakes. And Oona and Dooley needed her.

"Dooley will be devastated, of course," Oona went on, glancing at her husband, who sat silently with a gloomy expression on his face. "No more bottoms to pinch. It keeps him perky, having the occasional bottom to pinch."

I stood up. "I'll go and have a word with Queenie," I said. "I'll leave it up to her."

I found her in the kitchen putting coffee cups on a tray. The kitchen was surprisingly neat and tidy. Newly baked bread rested on a rack. Something that smelled good was simmering on the stove.

"I hear you're doing really well here," I said. "Sir Dooley and Lady Whyte are pleased with you."

She gave a sheepish grin. "They are so nice to me. They appreciate what I do for them. And even Mr. Treadwell said I was getting to be a big help and he ain't normally the type what gives compliments."

"So you'd prefer to stay here, rather than come back to London with me."

She looked up, startled. "You're leaving? Going back home?"

"Only for a while. I have some things I have to do in London, then I may go and stay with Miss Belinda in Italy."

"Italy . . ." Her face became wistful. "I hear Italy's smashing. Lots of good food."

"So I said I'd leave it up to you, Queenie. If you want to stay here, I'm sure I can do without a maid. I just wanted to make sure you were happy here."

"Oh yes, miss. I like it here."

"Even if Sir Dooley pinches your bottom?" I lowered my voice.

She giggled. "There ain't no harm in him, miss. He just likes a bit of excitement from time to time, but he's harmless, ain't he?" Then she started to shake with laughter. "I mean, look at him. He's so small and skinny I could knock him flying with one punch if I wanted to."

The kettle boiled and she poured the hot water over the coffee grounds, without spilling any or burning herself. I made up my mind.

"Very well, then, Queenie. I'm going to leave you here at the moment. I'll be back in time to plan my wedding and we can talk then about your future."

She grinned. "Bob's yer uncle, miss," she said.

Chapter 3

Tuesday, April 9, 1935

On my way back to England. Rather sad to be leaving Ireland.

I caught the night ferry from Dublin to Holyhead. I couldn't help feeling a little guilty. Lord Kilhenny was clearly upset that I was deserting him.

"The rats are abandoning the sinking ship," he had commented.

"I'm sorry. I don't want to abandon you," I said, "but I have been summoned by Queen Mary, and one can't say no to a queen."

He grunted. "I suppose not."

"And in this case it's really important. She wants to talk to me about this line of succession thing. Presumably it won't be put to Parliament until she's spoken to me."

"Utter nonsense," he snapped. "I'd just ignore the whole thing and marry Darcy if it were me. Or you could become an Irish citizen and thumb your nose at the British monarchy."

"I can't really do that," I said awkwardly. "Anyway I'm just hoping it's only a matter of formality and we can plan the summer wedding as we had hoped."

"All right, then," he said. "You'd better get going if you want to catch tonight's ferry. I'll drive you to the station."

"Will you really? That's awfully kind of you," I said. Impulsively I leaned up to kiss his cheek and I saw him give an embarrassed smile. That was when I realized he had grown fond of me and I felt a glow of warmth knowing this.

"And don't worry. We'll all be back soon," I said.

"All?"

"Darcy and Alexandra and me," I said.

"That's not very likely. I think the princess has enjoyed playing at owning an Irish racing stable and has now gone on to new interests," he said. "We'll probably find that she's sold it to a sheik or another American—that is, if she ever gets home safely from that stupid round-the-world jaunt of hers."

"Don't be such an old sourpuss," I said. "She's very fond of you and of course she'll come back safely. You know Zou Zou. She lives a charmed life."

"We'll have to see, won't we?" he muttered.

"And in the meantime your job is to win the Grand National and let the world see that Kilhenny stables are back on the map."

He looked at me and smiled then. "You're a hopeless optimist, do you know that? But I can see why Darcy likes you. I'm going to enjoy having you around the place and bringing it back to life with grandchildren one day." Then he realized that he had shown emotion and said gruffly, "Go and get your bags, then, and I'll bring round the motorcar."

We didn't say much on the way to the station. I was trying to think of bright and encouraging things to cheer him up, but I couldn't come up with any. I could understand how easily he could sink into depression again in that big gloomy castle.

"So you'll come back after your little chat with the queen?" he asked as we pulled up outside Kildare Station.

That was when I remembered I hadn't mentioned Belinda. "Not right away," I said cautiously. "I might be going on to Italy for a little while. I have a school friend there who is not very well. She wrote to me and asked me to come and stay with her as she is all alone."

"An Italian, is she?"

"No, she's English."

"Then what in the name of goodness is she doing in Italy if she's not well? She should come home to England where there are good doctors."

"She has to stay put at the moment," I said. "The climate there is better for her."

"Oh, it's consumption, is it?"

"Something like that," I agreed, finding it hard to lie to my future father-in-law.

"Then make sure you don't catch it!" he said fiercely. He came around to open my door, carried my suitcase to the ticket booth, then gave me an unexpected hug. "Come home safely," he said.

I caught my train and then had a smooth crossing on the ferry, in contrast to the wild night that had brought me to Ireland. I realized how different that crossing had been. Then I had been in the depths of despair, terrified that Darcy wanted nothing more to do with me and my life was over. Now I had every hope for the future. As Lord Kilhenny had said, if the queen wouldn't allow me to renounce my claim to the throne then I'd move to Ireland. Simple as that.

I was brimming with confidence when I arrived back in London and the taxicab deposited me outside Rannoch House on Belgrave Square. I hoped my brother and sister-in-law wouldn't mind my spending a few days with them. It was raining hard as I went up the front steps, lugging my own suitcase, and rapped on the front door.

It was opened not by Hamilton, the butler, but instead I found myself looking at the face of my sister-in-law, Hilda, Duchess of Rannoch, usually known as Fig.

"Good God, Georgiana, what are you doing here?" she demanded in that voice that could cut glass. She looked down at my suitcase. "I hope you haven't come for long because we're planning to go back to Scotland."

"And a very good evening to you too, Fig," I said. "Thank you for the warm welcome and no, I haven't come for long."

"I suppose you'd better come in," she said and stood aside so that I could step into the front hall.

"You look like a drowned rat," she commented.

"It is raining rather hard and I didn't have a spare hand for an umbrella." I started to unbutton my raincoat.

"You don't have a maid with you?"

"Remember that you told me to get rid of Queenie? Well, I have."

"But I meant you should find a more suitable replacement. One does not travel without a maid. It reflects poorly on the family."

"As I've pointed out to you before, servants cost money and I have very little." I took my raincoat and hung it on the hall stand. "Shouldn't Hamilton be answering the front door? Don't tell me you've got rid of him? Doors should be answered by a butler, you know. Otherwise it reflects poorly on the family."

I saw a spasm of annoyance cross her face and tried not to grin. "Hamilton had to go home for a death in the family," she said. "He should be back in a few days. And we only brought a skeleton staff down from Scotland so we're muddling through. You'd better come into the drawing room. Did you dine on the train?"

"Yes, thank you, but I wouldn't say no to a cup of coffee."

She rang the bell and a maid was dispatched to bring coffee. "The house is all at sixes and sevens without Hamilton," she said. "I don't know what servants are coming to these days. You notice we don't even have a footman here. Jamie refused to leave his ailing mother. A servant, refusing to follow his masters. My mother would have a fit if she saw a maid serving at the dinner table."

The maid came in at this point with a tray of coffee and poured two cups. I thought she did it rather well.

"So what brings you back to London?" Fig asked. "I take it you have been in Ireland with that Darcy person."

"That Darcy person is the son of Lord Kilhenny, thus of the same social level as you," I said. "You too are the daughter of a baron, are you not? You only rose in the world when you married a duke."

Another flash of annoyance crossed her face. I decided that I was learning to stand up for myself rather well and decided to strike a crowning blow. "You asked why I am here. Queen Mary wants to have a chat with me about my wedding."

It was infuriating to Fig that I was related to the royal family and she wasn't, at least not by blood. It annoyed her even more that the queen seemed to be fond of me and was often inviting me for little chats. There was a frosty silence while I suspected she searched for something crushing to say.

"Where is Binky?" I asked.

"Went to bed early. Not feeling too perky. Actually he caught a cold as soon as he came back to this abysmal climate." She gave a dramatic sigh. "Oh, how one misses the Riviera. The flowers. The blue sea. The sunshine." She gave me a triumphant little smirk. "I suppose it rained a lot in Ireland? From what one hears it rains all the time."

"Pretty much the same as in Scotland," I said. "I should have thought you were used to rain by now, after all these years of living at Castle Rannoch."

"Just because one puts up with it doesn't mean one enjoys it," she said. "It's only when one sees how pleasant life could be elsewhere that one becomes a little discontent—especially with a husband who is coughing and sneezing all night."

I finished my coffee and assured her that I could carry my own suitcase up to my bedroom.

"Will you be going straight back to Ireland after your tête-à-tête with the queen?" she asked.

"No, actually I thought I might go and stay with a friend who is living in Italy," I said and was rewarded with an absolutely venomous glare.

IN THE MORNING I was greeted warmly by Binky, then received an equally warm greeting when I went up to the nursery to see my nephew and niece. Little Adelaide hung back shyly, having forgotten who I was but six year old Podge gave me a frank and accurate account of life on the Riviera with Fig's sister and brother-in-law, the cramped conditions, the spartan meals and how dreadfully boring his cousin Maude was. "And do you know, Auntie Georgie," he said, frowning, "they took me down to the beach every day, but there's no sand and the water was too cold to swim. It was a very boring beach."

I was still chuckling as I left them and went to Binky's study to write a letter to the queen. I apologized for not answering her sooner, telling her the letter had just been forwarded to me in Ireland. But I had come immediately to London and looked forward to visiting Buckingham Palace whenever might be convenient for her. I sealed the letter, walked through the rain to the postbox, came back and waited.

I didn't have to wait long. The next morning there was a telephone call. Fig answered it herself, in the absence of Hamilton, and came into the breakfast room looking distinctly put out.

"You're wanted on the telephone," she said. "It's the palace."

I jumped up. "Oh good." I gave her a bright smile as I hurried out of the room.

It was the queen's secretary on the line and he informed me that Her Majesty would be free that afternoon if I would like to come to tea. I accepted, naturally, and spent the rest of the morning trying to find something suitable to wear. The weather was so miserable that I didn't think even Her Majesty would be in a tea dress. I examined my meager wardrobe. I had never had the money to be fashionable and now my clothes seemed hopelessly dowdy and old-fashioned. I had taken my stout winter items with me to Ireland and they now looked a little the worse for wear. I did have my mother's cast-off silver fox coat, but it was raining cats and dogs and I didn't want to arrive looking like a drowned English setter. I settled on a gray jersey skirt, another pass-on from my mother, and added a peach cashmere cardigan, also from her. I should point out, for those who don't know, that my mother had been a famous actress before she married my father and had worked her way through a long line of rich men ever since. She had the most fabulous clothes, looked absolutely stunning, even now that she was over forty. However, she was several inches shorter than I and had a waist that men could still span with their hands (and I expect a good many of them had tried it!). So hand-me-downs were few and far between—not that I bumped into her often. She spent most of her time in Germany with the man she planned to marry, industrialist Max von Strohheim.

I sighed and tried on the skirt and cardigan over a cream chiffon blouse. Acceptable if not fashionable, I decided and paused, examining my five-foot-six frame in the mirror, wondering whether my mother might be persuaded to buy me a trousseau and what my wedding dress should look like. I had these sorts of fantasies quite often these days. It still seemed like something of a fantasy to me that a handsome, dashing man of the world like Darcy would want to marry a shy, slightly awkward and hopelessly naïve girl like me. But he had proposed. I proudly wore his late mother's engagement diamond on my ring finger and if the king and queen and Parliament said yes to the marriage today I could start planning a summer wedding. If Darcy came home in time from his latest assignment, that is!

Chapter 4

Thursday, April 11, 1935

Off to Buckingham Palace to have tea with the queen in a few minutes. How grand that sounds and how easy it is to write it! But golly, I'm always a bundle of nerves, even if she is a relative. Please don't let me knock over any statues or priceless Ming vases!

At three o'clock it was still raining hard and a fierce wind was driving the rain almost horizontally. I decided I simply couldn't arrive looking as if I'd been dragged from the nearest lake so I decided to throw caution to the winds and hail a taxicab.

"Where to, love?" he asked as I climbed into the backseat.

"Buckingham Palace, please," I said.

He chuckled, a deep throaty chuckle that turned into a cough the way it did with many Londoners who had lived with years of smoky fog. "Cor blimey. You going to have tea with the queen, are yer?"

"Actually I am," I said.

There was a silence, then he burst out laughing. "Go on, pull the other one! You nearly had me for a moment there."

"No, honestly," I said. "I am going to tea there."

"What—are you going to be presented with a medal or something?"

"No," I replied. "The king is my cousin."

"Blimey!" he said, turning to look at me as if he expected me to have grown a crown on my head. "Begging your pardon, Your Royal 'ighness. You don't expect a toff like you to be riding in a cab driven by the likes of me, do you? I thought your lot went around in Daimlers and Bentleys and coach and 'orses."

"Not all of us live that way," I said. "I'm rather a poor relation, I'm afraid. Even taxicabs are a luxury for me."

We drove around Hyde Park Corner and down Constitution Hill.

"So where do you want to be dropped off, Yer Highness?" he asked.

"Outside the front gates, please. I'm afraid they won't let you drive up to the doors and I'm going to get rather wet."

"What, one of their own family? We'll see about that," he said and turned into the front entrance, between those imposing gilded gates. Guards stood on either side, with rain streaming down their faces and running down their bearskins while they looked stoically straight ahead. Until we pulled up, that is.

"I've got a member of the royal family 'ere." The cabby leaned across. "And we don't want 'er getting wet when she comes to see the queen, do we?"

The guard bent to peer at me. "And you are, miss?" he asked.

"Lady Georgiana, the king's cousin, and of course I understand that you can't let a cabby drive into the courtyard."

"Who says we can't?" he said, giving me an unguardlike grin. "Go on, then, cabby, but make sure you come straight out again."

"Thank you!" I beamed at the guard. He stood back at attention, but allowed himself a hint of smugness in his expression.

So we swept into the central courtyard and a footman came out to open the door for me. He looked surprised at the cab.

"Lady Georgiana to see Her Majesty," I said.

He opened the door for me and I went to give the cabby a large tip. He pushed it back at me. "That's all right, love," he said, forgetting the "Royal Highness" this time. "I'll be able to boast about this in the pub all year."

So I was dry and feeling happy as I was escorted up the staircase to the queen's private sitting room. I was so relieved when we turned right for the private quarters and not left, which might have indicated one of the grander rooms—the Chinese Chippendale being my absolute nightmare, decorated as it was with lots of antique statues and vases. The footman knocked, opened a door and announced, "Lady Georgiana, Your Majesty."

The queen had been standing looking out of the window. The view was at the side of the palace, over the garden, which looked awfully bleak and desolate in this weather. She turned as I was announced. "So many days of rain recently," she said. "The king really misses his walks in the garden and one can't even see the daffodils from here. We'll have tea in a few minutes, Frederick."

"Very good, ma'am." He backed out.

She smiled and held out her hand to me. "Georgiana, at last," she said. "I was quite worried when I didn't hear from you."

I went over, curtsied and kissed her cheek, all without tripping, bumping noses or committing any other sort of faux pas. I really must be improving with age!

"I must apologize, ma'am, but nobody was in residence at Rannoch House. My brother and his family were in the south of France for the winter. They only returned a few days ago and forwarded the post to me. I came from Ireland right away." I should point out that my royal relatives expected to be addressed as ma'am and sir.

"I'm glad to know all is well then," she said. "Do sit down. You are looking well. I expect the Irish country air agrees with you."

I thought she was looking rather tired and drawn, but didn't say so as she led me across to a small brocade sofa and sat beside me.

"I trust you and His Majesty are both in good health?" I said.

She shook her head sadly. "I regret that His Majesty's health continues to decline," she said. "I believe it was the war that took so much out of him that he has never recovered. That and worry about David. He has said several times, 'That boy will be the death of me.'"

"I'm sorry to hear that, ma'am," I replied.

"His one aim seems to be to stay healthy enough for the upcoming jubilee," she said. "And he is determined to remain on the throne until David tires of that woman and marries someone suitable."

"Can you really see that happening, ma'am?" I asked. "When I last saw the Prince of Wales he appeared to be completely under her thumb."

Her Majesty sniffed. "The boy is weak. Always was. Strangely it is Bertie who appears to be the weak one, but he has a core of iron compared to his brother. If it weren't for his stammer he'd make a good king. And he already has heirs, unlike David."

"But he can never marry Mrs. Simpson, can he?" I asked. "She's married to someone else, for one thing, and as head of the church he could never marry a divorced woman."

She leaned slightly closer to me. "From what one hears, the American woman whose name I will not even pronounce seems to believe that when he is king he can rewrite the rules and pronounce her queen against all opposition."

"How silly," I said. "Parliament would never allow it."

"I wouldn't be surprised if she should think he can dismiss Parliament," the queen said with a sad smile. "And speaking of royal marriages . . ." She broke off as the door opened and a tea tray was wheeled in. It was laden as usual with all sorts of delicious foods—shortbreads and slices of rich fruitcake and lemon curd tarts and thin malt bread. I looked at the latter with a sigh of despair. Protocol demands that one eat only what Her Majesty eats and too often the queen selects just a slice of malt bread for herself. So I was overjoyed to hear her say as the dishes were placed on the low table before us, "Ah, shortbread. My favorite." She leaned forward to take a piece. "Do help yourself, Georgiana. And will you have Assam or Lapsang souchong?"

"Assam, please," I said, tentatively putting a piece of shortbread onto a Wedgwood plate.

A maid poured tea. "Will that be all for the moment, ma'am?" she asked. Then she curtsied and departed, leaving us alone.

"About my marriage," I dared to say. "We haven't heard anything more from the king's private secretary so I wondered if there was any problem with granting my request."

She looked up from her teacup, giving me the sort of haughtily severe look usually reserved for the Prince of Wales's friend. "Abandoning one's destiny and obligation is not a matter to be taken lightly," she said.

"I understand that, ma'am. And if I were closer to the throne of course I would think differently. But you have four healthy sons. You already have grandchildren and I'm sure they will produce many more. My own brother has two heirs. Before long I shall find myself fortieth or even fiftieth in the line of succession. So unless the Bolsheviks invade and behead the entire royal family or there is an even more virulent flu epidemic than the last one, I cannot foresee myself being called upon to ascend the throne."

A brief smile crossed her lips. "I do see your point," she said. "It should be a relatively simple matter, but for one thing. The British Parliament does not harbor kindly feelings toward the Republic of Ireland. Their former campaign of bombings and hostile acts has not endeared that nation to us, has it?"

"Darcy might have been born in Ireland. His father is an Irish peer and he is Catholic, but he is also a British subject, working, if I am not mistaken, for our government from time to time." I was amazed how passionately I was able to speak to her. No mumblings or stumblings. Thus emboldened, I decided to deliver the crowning blow, although that was probably an unwise choice of words. "And may I remind Your Majesty that my future husband saved your life and that of the king, taking a bullet in your defense when a communist agitator planned to assassinate you?"

She nodded. "Quite true." I could see she was looking almost amused. "Georgiana," she went on, "I have never seen you so eloquent or so forceful. Well done. I can see now how much this means to you. Of course I am aware that Mr. O'Mara chose to retain his British citizenship after the republic was established. In fact, the only stumbling block to your marriage seems to be his Catholic religion. I take it he is not prepared to renounce it?"

"He has said he would, as a last resort if all else failed. But I would not force him to do that. His religion means a great deal to him. And if you remember, Princess Marina was married at the abbey but also had a Greek Orthodox ceremony later. She was not forced to renounce her religion."

The queen nodded again. "Quite true. But for some reason our country does not harbor such hostile thoughts toward the orthodox religion. The Reformation and subsequent struggles have embedded a deep hatred of Rome into the British consciousness." She took a sip of tea while I held my breath and waited for what might come next. She put down the cup and saucer. "But in the end sanity will prevail, I am sure. To be honest with you I only wanted to hear from your own lips that this marriage was what you wanted. I would have preferred it if you had come to the palace yourself and asked the king and myself in person, rather than having your betrothed do it with a secretary on your behalf."

I had to smile. "I didn't know he planned to do that. He can be rather impulsive, and he was so relieved that his father had been exonerated and he was now free to marry."

"If we had said no, if we denied you this right, what would you do?" she asked.

"Move abroad. Defy the ban and marry there," I said.

She smiled now. "That's all I wanted to hear. Very well, Georgiana. You need worry no longer. I will make sure this goes through without a hitch and soon. When are you thinking of planning the ceremony?"

"In the summer, ma'am. Of course not too close to the jubilee celebrations."

"The jubilee celebrations will be over by the end of May," she said with a smile. "I see no conflict there. And you will be married in London or Ireland?"

"In London, I hope. Darcy was thinking of the church on Farm Street in Mayfair."

"Not Westminster Cathedral or the Brompton Oratory?"

I gave a sheepish grin. "I don't think I have enough friends and family to fill either of those."

"Your choice. It's your day, after all." She reached across and patted my hand. "Do you plan to convert to his religion?"

"I'm not sure at this moment. I do have to agree to raise our children as Catholics and I have no objection to doing that." I took a bite of shortbread and managed to chew and swallow it without coughing. I was making so many improvements. I was jolly proud of myself!

"So where do you go now?" the queen asked. "Back to Ireland?"

"No, ma'am. Darcy is away at the moment and frankly I find the castle rather gloomy with just Lord Kilhenny in residence. And I have a task I have to fulfill. A friend is currently living in Italy and not in the best of health. She has asked me to join her for a while."

Did I sense that the queen's ears pricked up? She turned to look at me. "In what part of Italy does she reside?"

"On Lake Maggiore. Near Stresa."

It was she who coughed on her shortbread. I wondered whether protocol would allow me to pat her on the back, but she took a sip of tea and recovered her composure. "A remarkable coincidence," she said.

"What is, ma'am?" I asked, trying not to sound too curious and carefully replacing my own teacup on the table so that whatever she told me next I did not react with surprise and slop tea into my saucer.

She turned toward me suddenly. "Do you know the Martinis?"

This was not what I had expected. "You make them with gin and vermouth, I think. I don't drink cocktails very often."

She shook her head. "No, I mean the family, not the drink," she said. "Old Italian family. The Counts of Marola and Martini?"

"I'm afraid I don't mix much with European aristocracy."

"But you know his wife," she went on. "You and she were school chums."

Oh no. Not another supposed dear friend I had either never heard of or long forgotten about? She had sprung these on me before when she wanted me to do something for her—usually something difficult or unpleasant.

"We were?"

"Well, maybe not bosom friends, as she must be a little older than you, but you were at the school in Switzerland at the same time. Waddell-Walker is the name."

"Oh yes. Camilla Waddell-Walker. I do remember her," I said. An image swam into my head of a bony, horsey-faced girl with a permanent supercilious sneer. Belinda called her Miss Cami-Knickers. She had been the prefect in my dorm during my first year at Les Oiseaux and she was always finding fault with Belinda and myself. Mostly Belinda, of course. I would have been a well-behaved young lady if Belinda hadn't tried to lead me astray. Camilla was constantly saying "It simply isn't done!" when we giggled or played pranks or behaved in any kind of unladylike way. Luckily she didn't know that Belinda sneaked out to meet ski instructors or to smoke behind the gardener's shed. I don't know what she would have said to those sorts of infringements!

The queen smiled. "Splendid. You do know her. As I was saying, she made a really good match and is now the Contessa di Martini.

Paolo's family is extremely wealthy and powerful in Italy, although I have heard that they are showing Fascist leanings, of which I do not approve. That horrible bald-headed man Mussolini." She shuddered. "I can't understand what these Continentals are thinking when they elect such unappealing leaders. Hitler—short, dark and that ridiculous hedgehog mustache—and Mussolini, bald and pudgy."

This was not getting us any closer to revealing why we were on this topic. She must have realized this because she said, "Now, where was I? Oh yes. The Martinis have a villa on Lake Maggiore. Near the town of Stresa. They are currently in residence and going to hold a house party next week."

Oh crikey, I thought. I bet she wants me to crash the house party and steal some antique for her. I should tell you that Her Majesty is passionate about antiques and will go to great lengths to obtain an object that completes her collection. Not that she would condone stealing, exactly, but if she found out that a particular jug that was missing from her Royal Worcester service might be found at a particular house or castle, she might be tempted to ask me to retrieve it for her. She had done so in the past.

She cleared her throat and went on. "My son the Prince of Wales is going to be a member of that house party. So is a certain American woman I will not name." She paused. "He is being rather obtuse and secretive about why he is going there. And it is all the more embarrassing as an official British delegation is being sent to an important conference there, at the same time. His father told him it would put them in an awkward situation if it were known that he was in the vicinity. They might feel obliged to include him in official functions, but he absolutely refused to change his plans. So this leaves me to wonder why this particular house party is so important to him, and a disturbing thought enters my mind. . . ."

She paused, toyed with a piece of shortbread on her plate, then looked up again. "We know the American woman has been looking into filing papers for divorce in the most discreet manner possible. We have been unable to find out whether she has actually succeeded in obtaining a divorce from Mr. Simpson. My fear is that she has done this and that she and my son plan to marry secretly at this villa."

"Golly!" I exclaimed. I'm afraid my list of expletives is somewhat limited. I hate still sounding like a schoolgirl, but this sort of thing just pops out in moments of crisis.

The queen then reached across and covered my hand with her own. Another completely uncharacteristic gesture. "As you can imagine, I am extremely worried. If my son presents this marriage as a fait accompli, could it then be dissolved? It would kill his father, I am sure of that. And would we then have a king married to a twice-divorced gold digger?"

"Oh, ma'am, surely not. He may be besotted with her at the moment, but he will do the right thing in the end. When he becomes king he will step up and do what the country expects of him."

She sighed. "One hopes so. But I am afraid, Georgiana. That's why I am so relieved to find out you will be nearby. You can be my eyes and ears on the spot. If there is a secret wedding ceremony the servants will know of it. Your friend the countess may even share the news with you."

My friend the countess probably wanted to see me again as little as I wanted to see her, but I couldn't say that. Instead I pointed out that I had not been invited and could not force my way into a house party.

"I shall write to the countess immediately," she said. "I shall remind her that you were school chums and tell her you will be in the vicinity and that you will naturally want to pay your respects to your cousin David, of whom you are so fond. I don't think she would dare to refuse a request from me, do you?" And she gave a little smile.

She picked up her cup and drained it. "I feel so much better now," she said.

I drank my own tea in silence. I wasn't quite sure what she

wanted me to do. If they were actually getting married, I could hardly rush in as they were saying, "Do you know any cause or just impediment why these two may not be joined together in holy matrimony?" and shout out, "He'll be the head of the Church of England and it forbids divorce and furthermore his mother forbids it!"

"What exactly do you want me to do, ma'am?" I asked.

"Just observe. Just let me know the truth. That's all I ask," she said. "I will, of course, be happy to pay for the travel expenses for you and your maid."

Ah. Slight problem here. "I'm afraid my maid will not be traveling with me," I said.

"Traveling without a maid?" She looked shocked.

"My current maid didn't want to leave her family in Ireland."

"A maid not willing to go where her mistress goes? What are servants coming to?" She shook her head, almost dislodging one perfect gray curl. "My maid would follow me to the ends of the earth if I asked her to. Can your family not lend you one?"

I didn't like to say that Fig would not lend me a hand if I was drowning. "I'm afraid not, ma'am. They have only brought down a minimum number of servants from Scotland."

"But you simply cannot travel without a maid across the Continent." She sounded quite upset now. "A young girl alone on a foreign train? There are any manner of rogues and thieves. And who would dress you?"

"I'm sure you have noticed that my wardrobe is quite limited, compared to most ladies of our standing," I said. "I shall take simple garments like these on the trip."

"But you will need evening frocks if you are invited to join the house party, which I hope you will be," she said. "I know. When I write to the countess I shall tell her of the mishap with your maid and hope that she might find you a local girl to assist you while you are in the area. There. That should take care of it." On the strength of this she poured herself a second cup of tea. "But I still don't like the idea of your traveling alone, Georgiana. You must take a first-class sleeping berth, naturally. And lock your door at all times. And let the porter in your car know you are alone and need to be watched over."

"Yes, ma'am," I said. "But please don't worry. I have traveled across the Continent before."

"I shall be happy when you are married and have a husband to take care of you, Georgiana," she said.

So shall I, I thought.

Chapter 5

Thursday, April 11

So it seems I shall be spying for the queen again. Crikey! How do I get myself into these things? The problem is that one just can't say no—at least I can't seem to say no.

I was deep in thought as I walked back to Rannoch House. The rain had eased up and I was too frugal to pay for a second cab fare. The queen had seemed genuinely worried about me as I took my leave of her.

"Could you not hire a maid for your trip?" she asked. "I hear there are agencies for such things these days. I do worry about your traveling alone, Georgiana. In my youth a young girl never went out without her chaperon. Do you have nobody in your circle of acquaintance who would want to accompany you?"

"Please don't concern yourself, ma'am," I said. "I shall be vigilant and really I should be quite safe in a first-class compartment to Italy."

But walking back I started to worry. I had traveled across the Continent before, but each time I had been accompanied. When I went to school in Switzerland one of the mistresses had escorted us from Victoria Station. When I went to Nice I had my maid with me and made friends with Madame Chanel and Vera Bate Lombardi on the train. And when I had to go to Romania for the royal wedding, the queen herself had provided a chaperon—the formidable Lady Middlesex. I wondered if she might take it upon herself to provide one again this time. All the more reason to make my journey as rapidly as possible.

And then I had a brilliant idea. My grandfather had been in poor health recently, his lungs suffering with the London smogs. I could take him with me. A few weeks on an Italian lake would be a marvelous tonic for him, and he could keep an eye on me on the journey. As quickly as this idea popped into my head I began to see the complications. My grandfather was a retired Cockney policeman. Could he share my first-class compartment? Would he want to? And when I arrived at Belinda's villa, would there be somewhere for him to stay? She had described it as small, after all. Then I brushed these doubts aside. It should be no trouble to find him a room in the village nearby. He'd be fed good food by one of Francesca's relatives and he'd be breathing good mountain air. And he would be near me, which was always a treat. I found myself smiling as I let myself into Rannoch House.

Fig's head poked out of the drawing room door as I was taking off my mack. I hadn't quite realized how much it was still raining and my reflection in the hall mirror was rather that of an orphan in the storm.

"Goodness, Georgiana, must you always arrive looking like a drowned rat?" she demanded. "I do hope you were looking slightly more civilized when you met the queen."

"Oh yes. I took a taxicab there," I said. "But the rain seemed to have eased up when I left the palace so I decided to walk."

"You'd better come in and warm up by the fire," she said. "We can't have you going down with pneumonia."

I thought this was rather touching for Fig until she added, "You'd upset our plans if we had to stay here longer, taking care of you. It's bad enough having Binky with a cold. I just hope that doesn't go to his chest."

I nodded. "His cough sounded nasty this morning. I don't think you should attempt to travel back to Scotland until he is fully healed."

"Ah, but you forget we have had central heating installed at the castle now. What a treat it will be not to freeze all the time."

"You'll still have to keep the windows open, remember," I said to her. "Family tradition and all that."

This time I did allow myself to grin as I went ahead of her into the drawing room and took a seat in one of the armchairs beside the fire. The remains of tea were still on the low table. It crossed my mind that such sloppiness would never be allowed when Hamilton was in charge.

"So what exactly did the queen want of you?" Fig asked as she took the other armchair. She had probably been dying to find out since I came home.

"Mainly to discuss my marriage."

"Have you actually been given permission to marry? That Darcy person is still a Catholic, isn't he? And Binky assured me that you are not allowed to marry a Catholic."

"I'm going to renounce my claim in the line of succession and never be queen," I said, smiling at her. "That's all it takes."

"Ah," she said. "So when will this wedding take place, do we know?"

"This summer, I hope. Darcy is away at the moment so we're not able to make any decisions."

"And does one take it that you'll want to be married from Castle Rannoch?" she asked, raising an eyebrow.

"Good Lord, no. Too far from anywhere. Although I do hope Binky will allow me to be married from this house, and you'll come down for the wedding."

"We'll have to see about that." She was clearly trying to come up with a reason why this would not be possible, so I added, "My dear friend the Princess Zamanska has already offered to arrange things at her place on Eaton Square, but I think it's only right that one marry from the family home, don't you?"

"Oh yes. Of course."

There was another silence. Fig stared into the fire, which now needed coal added to it. Clearly she was right when she said the servants were not up to snuff.

"Should I ring for someone to put coal on the fire?" I asked.

She sighed. "I presume one could learn to do it oneself." And she grabbed the tongs, lifted a piece of coal from the scuttle and placed it on the fire. "Really not so hard," she said. I didn't think it was likely to keep the fire going for long.

"So you'll be off soon, then?" she asked.

"Yes. I'll arrange for my ticket to Italy and be off in a few days," I said.

"Staying with a sick friend, you said?"

"Yes. Oh, and the queen wanted me to run a little errand for her while I'm there."

"Really, what kind of errand?"

"Oh, just something she wanted me to check up on when I'm in Italy."

Fig was glaring at me now. "Why is it she asks you of all people to perform little tasks for her? Why not someone else? Why not Binky?"

I could hardly say that my brother was sweet but clueless. Diplomacy won out. "I expect it's because I'm rather footloose at the moment and have nobody depending on me," I said.

This pleased her. "Ah yes. Of course. She wants to make sure you're given some sort of useful employment rather than mooning around in other people's houses."

While she was feeling pleased with herself I thought I might ask, "I don't suppose you have a maid to spare, do you? The queen was quite upset that I'd be traveling without a maid."

"A maid to spare?" she demanded, her voice now shrill. "My dear girl, have you seen the dire straits in which we are now living? I have had to put coal on a fire by myself!"

"Sorry," I said. "Silly of me. I'm sure I'll manage."

"There are domestic agencies," Fig said. "I'm sure they'd have a girl on the books who would love the chance to travel to Italy."

"Rather out of my budget, I'm afraid," I said.

"I don't know how you will staff a household when you marry. I gather the O'Mara fellow is as penniless as you are."

"We have the castle in Ireland where we are welcome," I said. "I expect we'll make do with a little flat in London."

"A little flat?" She looked horrified.

"Or, failing that, go to live with my grandfather," I said, knowing that always got a rise out of her.

"Your grandfather? The ex-policeman in Essex?"

"He's the only living grandfather I have, and he has told me I'd always be welcome with him."

"But Georgiana . . ." She was spluttering now. "A member of the royal family, living in Essex of all places. Think of the scandal. Think of the shame."

"But I won't be a member of the royal family when I marry," I said. "I'll be like any other Essex housewife. You can come and visit and I'll serve fish and chips from the corner shop." I looked at her face and added, in case she was about to have a stroke, "I am just joking, Fig. Just joking."

I did, however, think it wise not to add that I was planning to take him as my valet to Italy.

THE NEXT MORNING I went out after breakfast and caught the District Line out to Essex and my grandfather's neat little semidetached house in Hornchurch. The weather had brightened up, spring was in the air and I felt quite cheerful and hopeful as I walked up the hill from Upminster Bridge Station. It was always like a tonic to see my grandfather. If I ever had a proper home of my own I would invite him to live with us, I thought. I pictured him playing with my children—all remarkably good-looking with dark curly hair, naturally.

I already had a big smile on my face as I rang the doorbell. The smile vanished as it was opened by his neighbor, Mrs. Huggins. She was wearing a flowery pinny over a bright green jumper and her hair was tied up in a scarf with curlers poking out from it. Hardly the most welcoming sight. I took an involuntary step back.

"Oh, hello, Mrs. Huggins," I said. "Is my grandfather all right?"

"Right as rain, ducks," she said, giving me a broad grin. "Come on in and take a load off your feet. You'll cheer the old geezer up no end. Talks about you all the time, he does. Ever so proud."

As I stepped into the tiny front hall she yelled, "Albert! Get down 'ere and take a butcher's hook at what the wind just blew in."

I heard footsteps across the landing and my grandfather came down the stairs, cautiously, one step at a time. He was wearing his dressing gown and slippers, but his face lit up when he saw me.

"Lord love a duck," he said. "What a sight for sore eyes, eh, Hettie? We was just talking about you and wondering if you was still at that castle in Ireland. What an adventure, eh? We read all about it in the papers. Make us a cup of tea, Hettie, love, and we'll go through to the parlor."

The parlor was something new. Usually when I visited him we sat in his tiny kitchen and chatted. But today a fire was burning in the front room and it looked as if it had been newly polished and spruced up.

"So how are you?" I asked. "I see you're still in your nightclothes. I hope you haven't been ill again."

"Just a spot of the usual," he said. "Chest ain't too good, you know. But can't complain. I'll be seventy-five next birthday. Already passed my allotted threescore years and ten."

"Don't say that," I said. "You have to be around for a long time, to play with my children."

He gave a sort of tired smile. "We'll have to see about that, ducks. Ain't for me to decide, is it?"

"Let's not talk like that, Granddad. Anyway I'm here because I've come up with a super idea for you. How would you like to go to Italy? I'm going there in a few days and I think the Italian sunshine would do you a world of good. I could pay your fare and we'd be staying in a village on a lake. Good food and mountain air. What do you say?"

He was not looking as enthusiastic as I thought he would. "Dear, oh, deary me," he said. "I can't say I'm not tempted. Especially spending time with you, but . . ."

"Then let yourself be tempted. Come with me," I said. "I'm not traveling with my maid and I'd love a strong male to keep an eye on me."

"It's not as simple as that," he said. He was looking distinctly uncomfortable now. "You see, I'm sort of busy in the coming weeks. Got a lot on my plate, so to speak."

"Busy doing what?" I demanded, not pleased at being given the brush-off.

"Getting myself hitched," he blurted out.

"What?" I really didn't think I'd heard right.

He nodded. "That's right, ducks. Me and Mrs. Huggins. We're going to tie the knot."

"Granddad, no," I exclaimed. "You can't mean it."

He glanced toward the door and I realized I'd forgotten that she was in the house, probably listening in at this moment.

He lowered his voice. "It seemed like the easiest thing," he said. "I mean, she's over here a lot of the time, taking care of me when my old chest plays up. She's always making me food. And now her landlord wants to raise her rent so I thought, 'Why not? What's the harm in it?'"

What could I say—that I thought Mrs. Huggins was an awful old woman and I certainly didn't want a stepgrandmother who opened the door wearing curlers in her hair? It sounded so petty.

"Well, if you're sure that's what you want," I said. "If you really think she'll make you happy . . . ?"

He gave me a sheepish smile. "I have to confess it gets a bit lonely sometimes, after your grandma died. Just me and the wireless in the evenings. I could do with a bit of company. A friendly face. Someone to share a late-night cuppa with. And since she's a good woman and wouldn't think of moving in with me without doing it proper with a license and all, then I suppose marriage is what it has to be."

We both looked up as Mrs. Huggins came in, carrying a tray. She had rather a smug look on her face. "I suppose he's told you, then?"

"He has. I should congratulate you both. I hope you'll both be very happy." I was proud of myself for my restraint and good acting.

Mrs. Huggins nodded. "I hope you'll be able to come to the wedding, your ladyship," she said. "Add a touch of class, having you there."

"Of course I'll be there," I said. "It's not right away, is it? Only I'll be in Italy for the next few weeks."

"No, not right away, my love," Granddad said. "We thought we'd wait until June. More chance of good weather and we can have the reception in the back garden."

"That's good," I said. "I'll be back by then. And planning my own wedding, I hope. And you'd jolly well better come to that."

"You getting married too, fancy that." Mrs. Huggins put down the tray on the low table. "Where will it be held? Westminster Abbey, I shouldn't wonder."

"Not the abbey, I'm afraid," I said. "Because my husband-to-be is a Catholic. So it will have to be in a Catholic church."

"Marrying one of them Catholics?" Mrs. Huggins looked at my grandfather, shaking her head. "What do the king and queen think about that?"

"They are both grateful to my fiancé for saving their lives once," I said, determined not to share any of the complications of my upcoming nuptials.

"He's a good lad, your Darcy." Granddad was beaming at me. "Take good care of you, he will."

"Just like you'll take care of me, Albert." Mrs. Huggins laid her hand over his.

"That's right, love. Now how about pouring that cup of tea?"

Frankly I couldn't wait to drink my tea and be gone. I certainly didn't object to my grandfather marrying again. Actually I'd never met my grandmother. She must have died when I was in my teens, but in those days my mother's side of the family was kept well away from Castle Rannoch. But Mrs. Huggins did not fit my image of the warm grandmother and certainly not what I wanted for my grandfather. She was uncouth, crude and, I suspected, grasping. How could she possibly make him happy?

I stood up when I'd finished my cup of tea that was both too sweet and too strong. "I really have to be getting back to town," I said. "I have a lot to do before I go to Italy."

"Italy? Fancy that," Mrs. Huggins said, nodding to Granddad. "It's amazing how the upper classes get around, isn't it? She talks about it as easily as if she was going to Southend." And she gave a cackling laugh.

"She wanted me to go with her," Granddad said. "Thought it might be good for my chest."

Mrs. Huggins was still laughing. "You? In Italy with the toffs? Don't you go getting any ideas above your station, Albert Spinks. You're staying put, right here beside me."

As they both walked me to the door she asked, "Will you be taking that great-niece of mine with you?"

Oh golly, I'd forgotten for the moment that Queenie was related to her.

"No, actually she's staying with Darcy's relatives in Ireland. She's learning to be a cook."

"Well, blow me down," Mrs. Huggins said. "Learning to be a cook. Hear that, Albert? And she ain't burned down the kitchen yet?" She cackled again.

"No, actually she's proving to be quite good at it," I said.

"Wonders will never cease," Mrs. Huggins said. "So you've got yourself a new maid now, have you?"

"I have an Irish girl when I'm at the castle, but I'll be traveling alone," I replied.

"You want to get yourself one of them French maids," she said. "That's what the other toffs have, isn't it? Although maybe she wouldn't want to let Darcy loose in a house with a French maid, eh, Albert? Know what they say about them French? Hot-blooded, eh?" And she gave him a dig in the ribs.

Granddad was looking at me. "You go inside, Hettie. I'll walk her down to the corner," he said.

"Make sure you're back for the wedding," Mrs. Huggins said. "We'll have a good old blowout on the back lawn."

As soon as we were suitably away from the house Granddad took my arm. "You're not too happy about this, are you?"

"It's not what I want," I replied. "If you think she'll make you happy then I will try to be happy for you."

"I don't know, it seemed like a good idea," he said. "And when I heard they wanted to raise her rent or throw her out she was in such a state that I thought this might solve things all around."

"But you don't love her?"

He chuckled. "At my age love don't come into it, ducks. She's a decent old stick and she's a good cook. I don't think I can ask for much more."

I kissed his cheek. "I'll miss you. I wish you were coming with me to Italy."

He put his hands on my shoulders. "You'll be all right on your own? I don't like the thought of you traveling to foreign parts all by yourself."

"It's only one train journey. I'll be fine," I said.

He nodded. "And I look forward to coming to your wedding. It will be lucky I have to get a new suit for mine, won't it?"

He hugged me then and I hugged him back. I sensed him watching me as I walked down the hill. It was only when I was halfway down that I remembered something awful. When they married I'd actually be related to Queenie!

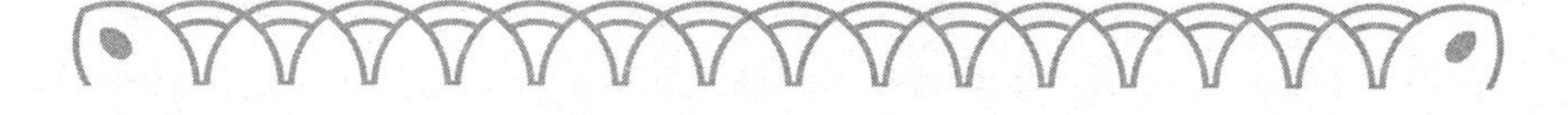

Chapter 6

Monday, April 15, 1935

On a train, heading to Italy, alone. Trying not to worry about this.

I left for Italy days later. I had considered writing to Belinda to tell her I was coming, but then I thought it might be a nice surprise for her to open her door and find me on her doorstep (better than Mrs. Huggins in her curlers, anyway!). I borrowed Fig's maid to clean and press my clothes. Fig was remarkably accommodating as I suspect she was anxious to get rid of me. I wrote to Darcy's father, letting him know where I'd be for the next few weeks, in case Darcy returned home. I went to Eaton Square to see if there was any news on Princess Zamanska, but there wasn't. Her haughty French maid said that there had been no news recently and pointed out that it took a good while to fly around the world. I was tempted to ask her if she'd like to come to Italy with me until her mistress returned, but then I thought of that face looking at my clothes with horror and decided against it.

So I set off alone, with one suitcase and one train case in a taxi to Victoria Station on a blustery afternoon in April. Now that

I was actually undertaking this journey I wasn't quite as confident. When I had traveled before at least I had Queenie to take care of my luggage. I supposed there would be porters everywhere, but it did seem a little daunting. The first part of the journey went smoothly enough. A porter found my compartment and loaded my cases onto the rack. The Golden Arrow pulled out of Victoria at 10:30. I was sharing my first-class compartment for this leg of the journey with a French couple who were far too chummy for British taste, gazing at each other, whispering and exchanging kisses. The other occupant was a Church of England vicar, who stared at them in horrified fascination. Luckily I had bought a copy of *The Lady* in the station and occupied myself by reading until we were passing through the Kent countryside, now awash in apple blossom. It took an hour and a half to reach Dover. I found a porter to carry my luggage onto the ferry across the Channel and the matching Fleche d'Or was waiting at the platform in Calais. Such a civilized way to travel. Before five we had pulled into the Gare du Nord.

From there I had to take a taxi to the Gare de Lyon, from which station I was to travel to Milan. So far so good, I thought. I was feeling rather pleased with myself as I went down the corridor to the dining car as the train left the city behind and night fell over the French countryside. I was a seasoned world traveler. A sophisticated woman at last. At the entrance to the dining car I ran into my first hitch.

"You have no reservation? I regret all the tables are occupied, madame," the maître d' said. "Perhaps you should return later?"

I hadn't realized one needed reservations.

"Could some food be delivered to my berth?" I asked.

He looked horrified. "But no, madame. This is a dining car, for dining. The sleeping car, it is for sleeping."

I was about to turn away when I saw a man waving to catch the attention of the maître d'.

"The young lady is welcome to share my table," he said.

He was rather an attractive man, with aristocratic bearing, blond hair and a neat little blond mustache. He rose to his feet. "If the Fräulein would care to join me it would be an honor. I dislike eating alone and enjoy good company."

"That is most kind of you, Count," the maître d' said. He turned to me. "May I escort you to the count's table?"

I could hardly say no at this stage; besides, I was jolly hungry. And he had a pleasant smile. And he was a count. "Thank you. Most kind of you," I said and followed the maître d' up the aisle.

The blond man gave a little Germanic nodding bow. "Rudolf von Rosskopf at your service, Fräulein. Or is it *gnädige Frau*?"

"Actually I'm Lady Georgiana, sister of the Duke of Rannoch."

Did I detect a sparkle of amusement in those blue eyes? "An English milady," he said, now reverting from the French we had been using. "How delightful. I took you for a countrywoman with your light hair and upright bearing. But you are English. Splendid. I like the English."

I smiled back as I took a seat opposite him. "Actually I'm only half English. The other half is Scottish and originally German."

"You have German ancestors too? You see, I knew this. A true Aryan. What were they called, these German ancestors?"

"Queen Victoria and Prince Albert," I said and was delighted to see his reaction.

"So? You are related to royalty. All the better." He snapped his fingers and a waiter appeared instantly at his side. "A bottle of your best champagne. A Dom Pérignon, perhaps?"

"Certainly, Count," the waiter said.

Rudolf von Rosskopf gave me a delighted smile as if he was a magician and had just produced a rabbit from a hat. "We shall have a jolly evening," he said. "Do you speak German?"

"A little, but your English is very good."

"I have many English friends," he said. "I like the English. We understand each other."

The champagne arrived and was poured. "So tell me." He leaned across the table to me. "What takes you to Milan? You go shopping for clothes? Almost as good as Paris, I understand."

"No, I'm going to visit a sick friend," I said.

"How very dutiful of you." He glanced down at my hand, looking for a ring, and saw my diamond. "Your young man, he doesn't mind you traveling alone across the Continent?"

"Of course not," I said. "He travels a great deal himself."

"I like modern women," he said. "So adventurous. So brave. So free."

I didn't think of myself as any of the above, but I smiled back as I sipped my champagne.

"Are you married?" I asked him.

"Me? I am footloose and fancy-free, as the Americans say. I enjoy the company of beautiful women. One day I suppose I must settle down and produce an heir or the title will die out, but for the moment I enjoy life tremendously." He drained his glass, then snapped his fingers for the waiter to refill. "Have you been to Berlin? It is the most exciting city in Europe. So civilized. So lively."

"No, I haven't been there yet, but my mother lives there at the moment. She seems to enjoy it."

"Your mother has good taste. You must come to visit soon and I can show you all the delights that Berlin has to offer."

"So what will you be doing in Milan?" I asked.

He shrugged. "Just visiting friends. I was in Paris and London on business and now I go to relax and enjoy good Italian food. I have to confess this one thing—Berlin is best in everything but food. In this aspect France and Italy surpass it. Ah . . ." He looked up as plates were placed in front of us. "You see what I mean?"

The first course was a rich seafood soup, with crab, shrimp and mussels floating in it. Actually it was hard to eat daintily and I concentrated on not dropping saffron-tinted liquid down my front. My table companion enjoyed it immensely, wiping his bowl clean with bread. Next came duck breast in an orange glaze, so tender that one could cut it with a spoon. Rudolf ordered a good claret to accompany it. And to finish, a meringue cake layered with fresh cream and chestnut puree. By the time the coffee was served, accompanied by tiny macaroons and chocolates, I was feeling quite mellow. We sat chatting while he smoked a thin cigar and sipped a cognac. I declined both, feeling already a little woozy. He told me about his childhood, his strict Prussian father who had sent him to military academy at the age of eight. How that father had been killed in the Great War. "Such a stupid war, a stupid waste," he said, shaking his head. "Supposed to achieve what? The destruction of millions of lives. None of the men wanted to fight—neither Germans nor English—but we were trapped into it by stubborn politicians. I only thank the good Lord that I was too young to be called up."

"Do you think there will ever be another war like that?" I asked. "Your Mr. Hitler seems to be militarizing the country."

He smiled. "There is no reason for Britain and Germany to go to war. Are we not the same people? Look at you—German grandparents and British. And you see what a delightful combination that makes."

I found myself blushing and was annoyed. "I should be going back to my berth," I said. I took out my purse to pay for my meal, but he chuckled, put his hand on mine and forced the purse back into my handbag. "Please put it away. The pleasure was all mine." The way he said the word "pleasure" and the way he looked into my eyes with a challenging stare made me feel uneasy. I stood up, cautiously, because I wasn't sure if my legs would hold me. They did. "I should be going," I said. "Thank you for a lovely meal. It was most kind of you."

He too rose to his feet. "Allow me to escort you to your sleeping quarters," he said, taking my elbow and steering me out of the dining car.

Oh golly. I'd heard about men like him, preying on innocent

women on trains. Even the queen had warned me. But I could hardly refuse him after he had treated me to a lovely dinner, and risk making a scene in a first-class dining car where probably half the diners knew him. I comforted myself that there was a concierge at the end of my car. I made a point of addressing him in his little cubby as we went past. "Good night, Pierre," I said.

"Good night, my lady. Your bed is made up and ready."

"This gentleman is kindly escorting me to my berth," I said.

We reached my destination and Rudolf opened the door for me. I wasn't sure what to do next. Was it really bad form to scream for help in the first-class section of trains? Was it even more bad form to give him a kick? I turned and gave Rudolf a radiant smile. "Thank you so much again, Count. You are very kind to take pity on a young lady traveling alone." And I held out my hand to him. He took the hand and brought it to his lips, his eyes never leaving my face for a moment.

"No, thank *you* for the delightful evening," he said. "And now I wish you pleasant dreams and hope we might meet again."

Then he clicked his heels, gave that jerky little bow and walked away. I was still quite shaky as I closed the door firmly behind me. I gave a sigh of relief as I collapsed onto the bed. Then I undressed with some difficulty as the train was swaying around quite a bit, made sure my door was locked, then climbed in between the cold sheets, curled up into a ball and tried to sleep. Suddenly I felt very alone and far from friends and longed for Darcy to be with me. "Soon," I whispered to myself. Soon I would no longer be sleeping alone.

I MUST HAVE drifted into sleep because I was awakened by the smallest of sounds. The click of a door latch. It can't be my door, I thought. I remember locking it. Then a strip of light began to show as the door was slid open and a dark silhouette appeared, filling the doorway. I sat up, now fully awake. Perhaps it was only the porter coming to check on me. But it was too big for the porter and I smelled the lingering scents of cigar smoke and a certain cologne.

"What are you doing here, Count von Rosskopf?" I demanded indignantly. He was sliding the door closed again.

He chuckled. "I should have thought that was obvious." He sat on the bed beside me.

"Absolutely not. And how did you get in? I locked the door."

He was still chuckling. "Do you not know how easy it is to bribe a train concierge, especially if one is a regular customer and generous with tips? I merely asked him to turn the other way while I borrowed the passkey."

"Then please leave again immediately or I will have to scream for help. Or have you bribed the concierge to be deaf as well?"

"You are quite delightful, do you know that?" He had inched closer to me now and reached out, stroking my cheek.

"Do you make a point of forcing your way into ladies' cabins?" I demanded, hoping that my Queen Victoria imitation might be enough to dissuade him.

"Oh yes," he said. "Often. It is such a fun sport, is it not? And among our class quite an accepted one. I could name plenty of names of those society women who have welcomed me to their beds. Names you would personally recognize, I assure you."

"Well, I'm not one of them," I said. "I don't know what gave you the idea that I might welcome a visit from you. I certainly did nothing to encourage you!"

"Oh, but you did, *mein Liebling*. When I kissed your hand and looked into your eyes you neither averted your gaze nor attempted to pull your hand away. You gazed back at me, which I took as a sign that my hand kiss was a pleasant experience and that you would like to take this to the next step. More kisses in many more places. Believe me, I'm awfully good at it, so I'm told. You would not regret the experience."

"But I just told you I'm engaged to be married," I said indignantly.

"What has that to do with it?" He laughed now. "I can assure you that your fiancé at this moment is opening the door to another lady's bedroom. It is an accepted sport. You have to face it."

"I certainly do not intend to face it. Now please leave immediately. And if my fiancé found out then it would be the worse for you."

He laughed again. "He'll challenge me to a duel? How delightful. I am also rather good at duels. I have wounded several men, because, you see, I am an honorable sort of fellow. I could shoot or stab to kill, but I don't. What's more, I am discreet. No one need ever know." His hand now left my shoulder where it had lingered and traced its way downward. I grabbed it and pushed him away.

"Can you not get it into your head that I am simply not interested? However famous you are as a lovemaker, I'm afraid I am going to reject your irresistible charms. Now please leave before I scream the place down."

To my relief he stood up. "Never let it be said that I forced myself onto a woman who did not want me. As I told you before, I am a man of honor. I shall leave you, Lady Georgiana, but I suspect you will regret this for the rest of your life. When you lie in the arms of your husband you will wonder what you might have missed."

He actually clicked his heels before he opened the door and disappeared down the hall.

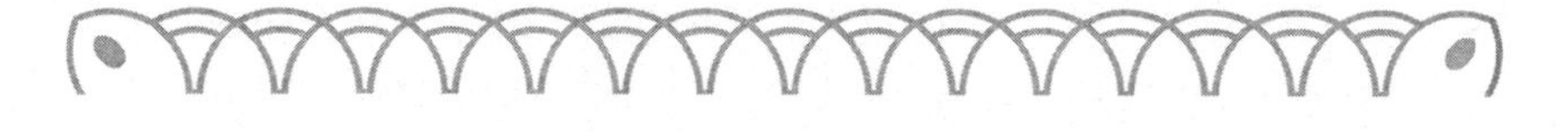

Chapter 7

Tuesday, April 16, 1935

On a train, heading for Italy. Narrowly averted rape! Golly.

I sat perfectly still for a long while. I was shaking and wished I had brought a flask of brandy with me. If he had not taken no for an answer, if he had forced himself on me, would I have been able to fight him off? And the fact that he took this kind of behavior for granted, and worse still, assumed that Darcy was behaving in a similar manner, was doubly unsettling. Surely Darcy wasn't, was he? But the nagging doubt lingered. I knew that Darcy had made love to a good many women before he met me. Might he not be tempted by a raven-haired beauty in the Argentine when he was far enough away from home that nobody would find out?

I lay down, staring at the ceiling swaying above me, but sleep would not come. When the first glimmer of light appeared through the blinds I opened them and saw we were passing through the mountains. There was snow beside the track. We crossed over rushing torrents. So we were either in Switzerland or already in Italy. I couldn't wait for the journey to end and to be safely in Belinda's little villa. I could imagine her laughing when I told her about the amorous count. She had also taken such behavior for granted and been free with her affections, and look where it had landed her—with a baby she neither wanted nor could take care of. I wondered if she'd made any plans yet for its future.

As I was thinking, the train plunged into a tunnel. After the upsetting events of the previous night I found my heart thumping as the carriage was only lit with an anemic emergency lamp. I sat staring at the door, alert and ready in case someone tried to enter. The tunnel seemed to go on forever and just when I couldn't stand it any longer we emerged to find the sun had risen over the mountains and was now shining on a more southern landscape. We were descending from the mountains. The farmhouses were painted in warm yellows and oranges, with tiled roofs and bright green shutters. A line of poplar trees ran beside a road, and there was new green in the fields. Then there were houses and streets, and shortly before seven we pulled into Milan's Central Station. I was grateful not to see Rudolf von Rosskopf as I found a porter to take my luggage from the train. As I looked around, wondering where I would find the train to my final destination, I realized that I was starving and instead found a place to change money and then had coffee and a roll at a station bar.

Soon I was heading northward to Stresa, in a less grand sort of train, and the track followed the shore of a lovely lake. Flowering shrubs were spilling over walls. Trees were in full blossom. The lake sparkled in the early sunshine. It looked quite delightful and my spirits rose. At last I'd be with Belinda and we were going to have a lovely time together.

We came to a halt at a small station. I read the sign, saw it was Stresa and put my head out of the window to hail a porter. There was no sign of one and I had to wrestle my own bags down a flight of steps, under the tracks and up again. I stood outside the station and saw that we were above the center of a small town. The lake, now ringed with mountains and dotted with small green islands, still sparkled, down below. I smiled as I took in the breathtaking scenery and smelled the scent of jasmine and mimosa in the air. I was going to have such a delightful time with Belinda . . . if I could just survive the few days of that house party. I looked around for a taxi but couldn't see one. I went back into the booking office and inquired in English, with much hand waving. The booking clerk clearly couldn't understand me, but a gentleman standing nearby came to my rescue.

"You come for meeting?" he asked. "Grand Hotel?"

"I'm afraid not," I said. "I come to see a friend."

"Ah." He nodded.

"What meeting is this?" I asked.

"Big meeting." He waved his arms expansively. "Important conference for Italy, England, France. Many important peoples coming to Stresa. Hotels full. That is good, eh?"

It appeared the taxis were all busy running around the important peoples. At last an ancient vehicle was found, with an equally ancient cabdriver. I showed him the address. He nodded and we set off, down to the lake and past several splendid hotels and villas. It seemed that Stresa was not the little out-of-the-way town I had pictured, but a sophisticated resort and the home of rich people. Belinda's village was a mile or so out of town. At first we drove with the lake to our left. On the other side of us was a high stone wall and then we came to imposing ironwork gates. "Villa Fiori." The taxi driver waved his hand, pointing at it. They were the only words he had spoken.

I tried to peer up the raked gravel drive as we drove past and got a brief glimpse of a lemon yellow palacelike structure. So this was Villa Fiori, where Miss Cami-Knickers was now the Countess of Martini. She hadn't done badly for herself, I thought. Immediately after the villa the road left the lakeshore and wound up the mountainside.

We came to a small village, not much more than a row of houses, clinging to the hillside, and in the middle a square built around a church. "San Fidele," said the taxi driver. Quite close to Villa Fiori, I thought. I wondered whether Belinda had run into her former nemesis. What a shock that would have been! The taxicab now turned off and bumped down a narrow cobbled lane, coming to a halt outside a small pink house that overlooked the lake. I got out and paid him what seemed like a ridiculously large sum, until I remembered that I was dealing with lire. When I converted, it turned out to be quite modest.

"*Va bene?* Is good?" he asked me. I nodded and he backed up the alleyway while I went up to the front door. It was by now nine thirty. Belinda had always liked to sleep in. I hoped she wouldn't be too angry at being awoken as I rapped on the front door. I waited. Nothing happened. I rapped again and called, "Belinda, it's me. Georgie."

Again nothing. The shutters were closed, there was a high hedge on either side and I had no way of getting around to the back of the house to see if she was enjoying that terrace with the orange tree.

"Belinda. Yoo-hoo!" I resorted to shouting, which would definitely have been frowned upon at home. I stood there in the street, not knowing what to do next. Either she was sleeping very soundly or she wasn't home. This was most annoying. After not sleeping all night my eyes were prickly and I wanted to sit and rest and eat a good breakfast. Where could she be, I wondered. I realized now my folly at not writing to let her know I was coming. What if she had gone to visit friends for a week or even longer? The baby surely wasn't due until the end of April at the earliest. Then I remembered Francesca, the local woman who took such good care of her. Francesca would know where she was. I tucked my luggage behind one of the potted shrubs that stood on each side of the front door and set off into the center of the village.

I walked back into the tiny square outside the church and saw a group of women standing together outside the baker's shop. I went up to them and asked if they knew Francesca. Well, to be more accurate I think I said, "Do you speak English? I'm looking for Francesca, Francesca who works for the English lady."

They frowned and looked puzzled. "Francesca?" I said again. *"Signorina inglese?"* And I pointed down the street toward Belinda's house. Recognition dawned.

"Ah. Francesca." Smiles now, but they were shaking their heads and saying lots of nos.

In the way of people who don't speak each other's language they were shouting, speaking slowly and waving their arms a lot, but I still couldn't understand why they couldn't tell me where Francesca was. Finally, one of them raised a finger to show a brilliant thought. "Giovanna!" she said.

"Ah, *sì*. Giovanna," the others echoed.

One of them took off, hurrying across the square. The others looked at me, nodding and smiling as if I'd be pleased with whatever or whoever Giovanna was. It seemed as if we waited a long time. The morning sun shone down on my too-thick overcoat and I wished I'd taken it off before I went searching. Pigeons flapped around and cooed from tiled rooftops. From down below came the sound of a bell tolling on a distant church. The delicious scent of baking bread wafted out from the bakery, reminding me how little I had eaten today. Then we heard running feet and the woman returned, this time with a small girl.

"Giovanna," said the woman, looking like a conjurer who has produced a rabbit from a hat.

The girl smiled shyly. *"Buongiorno,"* she said.

"Nipotina di Francesca," the women said in chorus. *"Parla inglese."*

"I learn Ingleesh in *scuola*," Giovanna said.

"Oh, wonderful," I said. "And you are Francesca's daughter?"

"She my grandmozzer," said the girl. "She not here. She go to my . . ." She frowned while she tried to come up with the word. "Sister of my mozzer. She have *bambino. Capisce?*"

I tried to put together what she was saying. The other women joined in, pantomiming a large pregnant belly and then rocking a baby. "Francesca has gone to see her daughter who is having a baby?"

The girl beamed at me. *"Sì,"* she said.

"But what happened to the English lady? Where has she gone?"

Again the little girl frowned. "Ingleesh lady go *clinica*." She paused. *"Clinica. Svizzera."*

Neither word meant anything to me. She repeated them. Light began to dawn. "She went to a clinic?"

Everyone nodded now, all of them quite aware of what had happened to the village's celebrity resident.

"Svizzera," they said in unison, pointing out across the lake.

"In Switzerland?" I asked.

The little girl nodded.

"Do you have the address of the clinic?" I asked. "Does anyone have the address?"

She shook her head. They all shook their heads.

"Did Francesca have the address? Could we telephone Francesca?" I was still gesturing and waving my arms a lot.

More head shaking.

I stood there while they stared at me, trying to decide what to do next. From what I understood Belinda had gone to a clinic in Switzerland. Francesca was away taking care of her daughter who was having a baby in another part of Italy and nobody knew the address where Belinda had gone.

"Does anyone have the key to the English lady's house?" I asked, miming entering a house with a key. I was sure Belinda wouldn't mind my staying there. But again I was met with blank looks. So what on earth did I do now? I didn't know how long post from England would take to reach Italy, where I was sure the system was not as efficient as ours. So it was possible the letter from the queen would not have reached Villa Fiori yet, even if she had written immediately. I simply couldn't present myself at the doorstep there, days before a house party. It simply wasn't done!

I could go back into Stresa and try to find a room, but I had just been told the hotels were full because of the big conference. And through these concerns for myself came the worry for Belinda. Her baby wasn't due for several weeks yet. So why had she gone into a clinic so early? Had there been some awful complication? If so she'd be alone and scared and I should try to find her first.

I looked around the women, who were still waiting expectantly. "Is there a hotel in the village?" I asked Giovanna. She shook her head.

"A room where I could stay for a few days until I find the English lady?"

She relayed this information to the crowd. There was much discussion, then they grabbed my arms and propelled me across the square, down a narrow alley street and in through the door of what looked and smelled like a rather disreputable bar. A loud conversation ensued with the bar owner, an old man with wisps of white hair and stubble who looked as disreputable as his establishment. I noticed the child was no longer with us and Italian was shouted at me with much gesturing. Then I was propelled again up a steep flight of stairs to a dismal little room over the front entrance. Okay, so if this was the only room in town I was definitely going back to Stresa. Surely there must be a small pension with rooms available there.

"Va bene?" they asked, waving arms at me.

I gave a weak smile. In truth I felt close to tears. As they descended the stairs, pleased at having accomplished this miracle, the old man sat on the bed and patted it with what looked a lot like a leer to me. "*Bene,*" he said. Oh golly. I had no way of communicating to them that I'd like someone to fetch my luggage. Not for the first time did I regret traveling without a maid. It had all seemed so simple in London. One took a train. One arrived. Journey complete. I hadn't bargained on complications like this. I decided to leave my bags where they were for now and get myself back into Stresa. There must be a better room than this available in the town.

I asked about a taxi. No taxi. Stresa? A bus? *Domani,* they said. Tomorrow. How did one get into Stresa? They looked astonished. It was only two kilometers, they told me, as if this walk was nothing at all. It would be nothing, but not with a heavy suitcase. So I trusted my bags to providence, hidden behind the shrub, took off my overcoat and set off down the hill, then along the road that skirted the lake. In truth it was a perfect day for walking. Ferry boats sailed across blue waters. Swallows darted, birds sang, jasmine and bougainvillea spilled over walls. I would have enjoyed it had I not been so tired, so warm and so frustrated.

As I passed the gates to Villa Fiori I peered up the driveway, but there was no sign of life. My feet began to lag and I realized I had only had a coffee and roll to sustain me after a sleepless night. I could not have been more relieved when the first houses came into sight and I walked into the town center. There were several small hotels in the streets behind the ferry terminal and I asked about a room. It appeared they were all full for the next couple of days, but then the conference would be over and they would have room for me. I gave up and collapsed at an outdoor café in the small town square. It was a pleasant little area, shaded by ancient sycamore trees, now just coming into full leaf. It wasn't yet time for lunch so I ordered a coffee and a rather sinful-looking pastry. As I was trying not to eat too greedily I heard a laugh that I recognized and I looked up to see the last person I expected to meet. A small dainty person with platinum blond curls poking out from beneath a scarlet pill-box hat. She was wearing scarlet linen trousers and a royal blue jacket. Nobody could have gotten away with this attire but my mother.

NORMALLY I WOULDN'T have been overjoyed to see her. She was the most self-centered person in the world and had paid no attention to her only daughter since she abandoned me at the age of two. But today she looked to me like an angel descending from heaven.

"Mummy!" I exclaimed, standing up so quickly that my chair almost fell over.

She stopped. Those famous large eyes opened in amazement. "Georgie! What on earth are you doing here?"

I remembered then my mother knew about Belinda's predicament. In fact, I had asked her if Belinda could stay at her villa, but received no reply. Luckily Belinda had inherited money and didn't need my mother's help after all. "I came to be with Belinda in her hour of need," I said.

"Oh, she came to this area after all, did she?" Mummy asked, pulling up a chair beside me.

"She came into some money," I said. "Which was lucky when you didn't reply to my letter. You did get it, didn't you?"

"Of course, darling, and I would have said yes in a heartbeat, but it was Max, you know. He didn't want to be associated with scandal and rumors. People might have whispered that the child was his."

I nodded. "Oh yes, of course. I see that now."

"But all is well if she's come into money and found her own place here, isn't it?" She snapped her fingers. A waiter appeared at a run. *"Cappuccino e biscotti,"* she said, turning back to me. "And you came to be with her. How sweet of you."

"That was the idea," I said, "but it seems she has already gone off to a clinic in Switzerland."

"Oh dear. The baby's not due yet, is it? Complications, I suppose."

"The problem is that I've no idea which clinic or where in Switzerland."

"It will probably be at the top of the lake, the Swiss end, around Locarno or Ascona," she said. "There are several good clinics there."

Locarno. That rang a bell.

"Is that where your villa is?" I asked.

"No, darling. We're on Lake Lugano. Not Locarno. Thirty miles away."

"So what are you doing here?"

"Max is attending a meeting and then we're going to stay with friends for a few days," she said. "We've been in Berlin for most of the winter and it's been so cold and dreary that I jumped at the chance of coming south and warming up. One does so miss the sunshine."

I realized she sounded just like Fig.

"Oh, I heard there was a big international meeting going on here," I said. "Is Max part of that?"

She looked amused. "Oh gosh, no. The international meeting is a high-level conference between England, France and Italy to discuss the Nazi threat. Max would certainly not be welcome." And she laughed.

"He's not a Nazi, is he?" I asked.

"Of course not, darling, but he knows how to play his cards right. One has to pretend to agree with these people if one wants to get lucrative arms contracts. Between you and me, Max is raking in the money these days."

"And you, how do you feel about living in a Germany run by that awful Hitler?"

"Darling, I stay well away from politics. And I have to tell you it's a very good life in Berlin. The best of everything and such jolly parties."

Her coffee and biscotti arrived. She dunked one and nibbled on it.

"This is rather nice, isn't it?" she said. "So go up the lake to Locarno and they'll find out which clinic for you. They are so civilized in Switzerland, which is why we have a villa there and not here. And of course, for the Swiss bank account." She grinned over her cappuccino.

I was trying to find a way to tell her about my current predicament without sounding pathetic when she looked up and put down her cup so forcefully that the coffee slopped onto the table. "What's he doing here?" she asked in a shocked voice.

I turned to follow her gaze. A group of tourists had just come into the square—a coach party, maybe, or from a ferry that had just arrived. Suddenly there was noise and activity all around us.

"Who?" I asked, peering through the crowd.

She got to her feet, clearly agitated. "The last person in the world I wanted to see."

She darted between the umbrellas and tables, then vanished down the nearest alleyway.

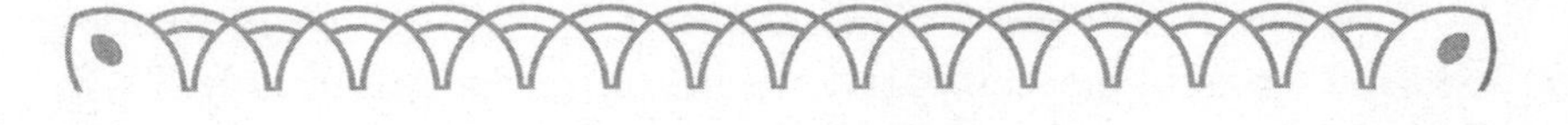

Chapter 8

Tuesday, April 16

All alone and nowhere to go. Not sure what to do next. And now my mother has run off before I could ask if I could stay with her. Chin up, Georgie. You can handle this.

I finished my coffee and pastry, and waited for her return, but she didn't come back. The waiter presented the bill.

"The signora is gone?" he asked, looking at the hardly touched coffee.

"It appears so," I replied. I drank her coffee and ate her biscotti since I would now be paying for them. I was intrigued to know who might have upset her like that. A reporter, maybe? But usually she craved publicity and adored being followed by reporters. Perhaps all that had changed since she became engaged to Max. Perhaps he was the possessive type and didn't approve of her picture appearing in newspapers and magazines. A detective, then? But again, she had been the model of propriety recently. The newly arrived travelers had now all gone and the square was quiet again. And as usual my mother had vanished before she could be of any help to her daughter. So typical of her! I supposed I could find out quite easily which hotel in Stresa she was staying at. It would be one of those grand palaces on the lakeshore, obviously, but I could hardly ask to stay in her suite. And at least I now had some idea how to find Belinda. I paid my bill and asked a couple of English ladies, sitting at a nearby table, how one traveled to the Swiss part of the lake. Was it better to take a train or a boat?

"Oh, goodness me," one of them said. "One can reach Locarno by train but it's most inconvenient and quite alarming. One has to change in Domodossola and then take the little train through the mountains. We did it once, didn't we, Dolly? And we swore never again."

The other woman nodded agreement. "No, the ferry is the only way to travel. So much more pleasant, even if it does take a long time."

"How long is it?"

They looked at each other, conferring. "About three hours, wouldn't you say, Dolly?"

I had no idea the lake was so big. But then I reminded myself it was called Lago Maggiore (the major lake). So I walked across to the ferry terminal and found a boat would sail at eleven. It was indeed a lovely trip all the way up the lake, calling at small towns nestled beneath green mountain slopes. Occasionally one caught glimpses of high snow-clad peaks beyond. I would almost allow myself to relax and enjoy the view, until the worry crept in again. What if I didn't find her? I certainly couldn't go back to that awful room above the bar. I supposed as a very last resort I could locate Mummy and appeal to her, but I hated to do that.

There was no way to tell when we had moved from Italy into Switzerland, but I did notice some more modern-looking buildings on hillsides. We sailed through a narrow opening at the head of the lake and there was the town of Locarno, another attractive town clinging to a mountainside at the edge of the lake. I found a taxi, this time a new and clean Mercedes, and asked about the clinics in the area.

"For the TB?" my driver asked.

"No, to have a baby," I said.

"Ah." He looked at me, trying to tell if the visit was for myself.

"My friend is there," I said rapidly. "I heard she had gone into a clinic but I don't know which one."

"She have money?" he asked.

I didn't understand what he was getting at, but then I realized he wanted to know what type of facility she could afford. "Yes, she has money," I said.

"Ah," he said, smiling, "then it must be . . ."

I almost wept at having a driver who spoke English and wanted to be helpful. He drove me up through the town to a white modern building overlooking the lake.

"You wish me to wait?" he asked.

I thought of the extra cost. But there was a long steep hill back down to the town. Then I reasoned the queen was going to pay for my ticket and Belinda had also offered to pay, so for once I wasn't going to be destitute. "Yes, please," I said. "If it looks as if I'll be here long I'll come out and tell you."

He nodded and produced a newspaper to read. I pushed open glass doors and entered a marble foyer. There was one glass table against the wall but no decoration except for a large and very realistic crucifix. Not a flower or a picture in sight. "Sterile" was the word that sprang to mind. And devoid of life. I stood there, looking around, wondering what to do next, when there came a soft footfall and a young woman in a nun's habit with a crisply starched white wimple approached me.

I asked if Miss Warburton-Stoke was a patient and told her that I had come out from England to be with her. I was worried she'd say she'd never heard of Belinda or that she had checked in under an assumed name, but she gave me a knowing look. "The English lady? Yes. This way, please."

She took me up a broad flight of stairs and along a white tiled hallway, then opened a door at the end. It was a bright room with a good view of the lake but again very hospital-like. No flowers, no soft chair, just a neatly made white bed, a small white chest beside it and white curtains at the window. The bed was empty, but I spotted the back of a head that I recognized. She was sitting in a rocking chair on the terrace outside, her knees covered in a blanket, reading a magazine. The sister ushered me through the open French door.

"You have visitor, signorina," she said.

Belinda turned around, a look of amazement and delight on her face. "Georgie! I can't believe it! How did you find me?"

"It wasn't easy," I said.

She rose to her feet and I saw that she was still very pregnant. It felt strange as I hugged her and the bump got in the way.

"I'm so sorry I didn't come before. I didn't get your letter until last week," I said. "It came to Rannoch House and there was nobody there, so it just lay on the mat. But I came as soon as I read it." I helped her back into the chair and pulled up another chair for myself. "And I went to your little house, but Francesca is away and nobody knew anything. If I hadn't bumped into my mother, I don't know how I'd have begun to find you."

"Your mother's here? Oh, of course. The famous villa."

"I met her in Stresa," I said. "Max was attending some kind of meeting, I gather. But how are you? I was so worried when I heard you'd already gone into the clinic. The baby isn't due for several more weeks, is it?"

"Three, to be precise," she said. "I can't wait to get it over with. It's so uncomfortable, Georgie. Although I gather the next stage is even more unpleasant. God, I wish it were over and I could go back to being normal again."

"So what are you doing here if you have three more weeks?" I asked. "Isn't it frightfully expensive?"

"It is, rather, but worth every penny at the moment. I've had an awful shock, Georgie." She leaned closer to me and looked around before she went on. "I thought I'd chosen a hideaway for myself where nobody would know me. And then one day I was out for a walk when a motorcar went past with the top down and you'll never guess who was in it."

"Would it have been the dreaded Camilla Waddell-Walker?"

"How on earth did you know?" She stared at me in amazement.

"Because I have been instructed to pay a call on her. She lives at Villa Fiori. Practically your neighbor."

"I just found that out," she said.

"I can understand that you wouldn't want to bump into her in your present condition," I said. "Rather embarrassing."

"But that's not the worst of it." Belinda's voice sounded quite desperate. She leaned toward me and grabbed my hand. "It was the man behind the wheel of that motorcar. Her husband."

"She's married to an Italian count, isn't she? A Martini? Which I confused with the drink when the queen mentioned him." I was trying to lighten the conversation, but she didn't even smile.

"Paolo di Marola and Martini," she said. She looked at me, waiting for the penny to drop. "You remember Paolo, don't you?"

My jaw dropped a little. "Your Paolo? The handsome Italian racing driver you once had a fling with?"

She nodded. "That's the one."

"Oh crikey," I said. "But I thought he was engaged to a devout Italian virgin."

"He was. Apparently she broke it off when she learned about his lifestyle. And his carryings-on with unsuitable females like me."

"So he married Miss Cami-Knickers instead?" I asked. "But I thought he made such a big thing of his family needing a devout Catholic bride for him."

She gave me a withering glance. "Unfortunately Miss Cami-Knickers comes from an old English Catholic family. You know, one of the few who kept the faith through the Reformation? Hence quite suitable as a bride. And coming from a rich family didn't hurt either. All those palaces cost a lot to keep up."

I looked at her with understanding. "Oh, Belinda, how awful for you. Of course you wouldn't want him to see you."

She shook her head fiercely. "I wouldn't want either of them. Can you imagine how she would crow over this? 'I always knew she'd come to a bad end,' she'd say. And Paolo. I simply couldn't bear to have Paolo see me like this. Between ourselves, I always thought he really loved me and would have married me if things had been different." She stopped as her voice cracked. Belinda had always seemed to me so strong, so confident, so worldly that it was a shock to see her so vulnerable suddenly. "So I fled," she added. "Closed up the house and checked in here early."

"What's it like? It seems rather . . . uh . . ." I paused for the right word. "Quiet?" I suggested.

"Quiet? It's bloody awful. Like living in a morgue. The sisters appear and disappear without saying a word. Some of them are openly critical about my lack of a husband and obvious sin. The meals are about as plain as you can get and lights-out is rigorously enforced at nine o'clock. No radio. No music. Utterly dismal."

"Surely there are other clinics you could go to if you hate it here," I said.

She shook her head again. "This one is supposed to be the best for delivering babies, and they also arrange for adoptions to devout Catholic families, which is the best I can hope for right now. I'm not sure how I'll feel once I have the baby, but I simply can't keep it."

She gave me a blank look of despair.

"I wish Darcy and I were already married, then I could adopt it for you and you could come to visit," I said.

"Wouldn't that have been lovely." She reached out again and took my hand. "You've always been so good to me, Georgie. You came all this way. But how infuriating that you arrive just when I have to stay hidden. And we could have had fun together before the baby." Her grip on my hand tightened. "Can you still stay? I'd really like someone to be here when it actually happens. I'm a teeny bit scared, you know."

"I can stay if I've somewhere to sleep," I said. "Do you have the key to your house with you? I don't mind staying there."

"Francesca is away. You'd have nobody to do the work."

"I'll survive," I said. "I can prepare simple meals and sweep floors."

"Surely your maid can do that. Did you leave her in Stresa?"

"In Ireland," I said. "Queenie is now an assistant cook and my new maid wouldn't leave her mother. So I'm maidless."

"How annoying for you," she said.

"I'm supposed to attend a house party at Villa Fiori in a few days and the queen has asked our friend the countess to find me a maid while I'm there."

"You're supposed to attend? Who on earth invited you? And why did you say yes?"

"It was the queen, actually. One does not say no to the queen."

She looked amazed. "What on earth does the queen want you to go there for?"

I leaned closer to her. "Actually, between ourselves, to act as her spy. The Prince of Wales is attending the house party and so is Mrs. Simpson. The queen is frightened she has now obtained her divorce and they will marry in secret."

"Golly!" Even Belinda used words like that when startled sufficiently. "What are you supposed to do, rush in and say, 'I forbid the wedding'?"

"I can't see myself doing that. I could cable Buckingham Palace. Parliament could annul the marriage, I suppose."

"Darling, I think it's already been consummated." Belinda gave a wry smile.

I smiled back. "It is good to see you," I said. "I've missed you."

"Haven't you had Darcy to keep you company? Much more exciting than little *moi*."

"We were at his father's castle together for a while, but then he went off again somewhere mysterious. You know what he's like. I have no idea where he's gone or when he'll be back. Maybe when we're married he'll finally tell me."

"So the wedding is all arranged, is it?" She took my left hand and examined the ring. "Very nice."

"It was his mother's. And it's not exactly arranged yet. We're hoping this summer, but it still has to be cleared by the king and Parliament. The line of succession not marrying a Catholic, you know."

"How silly," she said. "I'd go ahead and marry him anyway and then there wouldn't be much they could do about it."

"I know we could always do that, but I'd rather do it properly. It would create less tension with the family. The queen seems to think there will be no problem." I squeezed her hand. "If we have a summer wedding you'll be able to come, won't you? Will you be my chief bridesmaid? Or matron of honor or whatever it is?"

"Of course," she said. "Let's hope by then I've managed to find a good home for little Humphrey or Matilda."

"You're not really going to call the baby one of those, are you?"

"I'm not going to call it anything. Better not to get attached. It's the only way, Georgie. Of course I'd want it to go to a good home . . ."

"You make it sound like a puppy, Belinda," I scolded.

She grinned. "I'm afraid I'm not cut out to be maternal. Unlike you, who will have hundreds of kids and play games with them and everything."

"I hope so." I savored the picture that came into my head. "But to more practical matters, I've a taxi waiting. And the only steamer going back to Stresa today leaves at three."

"Do you have to go back?" she asked. "Why don't you stay here?"

"I've left my bags hidden behind a bush outside your house, so I should go and do something about them."

"You don't really want to stay at my house, do you?" she asked. "Of course you are welcome to stay there, but it's awfully far away. It would be nicer for me if you got a room near the clinic. Maybe they even have guest rooms here. I'll ask, shall I?"

I stood up. "I've an idea. Why don't you come back to your house with me? Now that I am here I can look after you and you don't need to go out and show yourself."

"And what do I do when you have to leave? You will be deserting me for Miss Cami-Knickers and Villa Fiori," she pointed out. "And who knows how long you'll be staying there?"

"Oh yes. That's true," I said. "I really wish I hadn't agreed to it, but it's so hard to say no to the queen. She just takes it for granted that one will do what she asks." I gave her a bright smile. "But house parties are usually only for a few days, aren't they? Then maybe I can rescue you and take care of you in your little house."

"Yes. That would be nice." She managed a smile too—a sort of wistful, sad smile that was so unlike Belinda. She had always been the bubbly one, optimistic, full of ideas. I hated to see her like this. I put a hand on her shoulder. "It will all be over soon and then it will just seem like a bad dream and you'll be back to your old life."

She stared out past me. "I wonder if I will ever go back to my old life after this."

Chapter 9

Tuesday, April 16
Spending the night at Belinda's little house in San Fidele

I'm so glad I've found Belinda and at least I know where I'll be staying (not in a nun's cell at the convent, thank heavens!).

Belinda rang for one of the sisters when I had hugged her and was ready to leave.

"Are there guest rooms at the clinic if my friend wishes to stay?" she asked.

The sister stared at me with a cold and haughty stare, her face as white as the wimple that surrounded it. "Guest rooms? This is not a hotel, miss, it is a clinic," she replied in a crisp Germanic voice.

"But she has come out from England to visit me," Belinda said. "I would be happy if she could stay nearby."

The sister frowned. "She could perhaps have one of the sisters' cells until she finds somewhere more suitable. Sister Maria Theresa is visiting the motherhouse at the moment."

I gave Belinda a horrified look. The thought of a cell in the convent, surrounded by those terrifying nuns, was a little too much, even for someone like me who was used to the austerity of Castle Rannoch.

"Oh, I wouldn't want to inconvenience you," Belinda said hastily.

"I'm sure the taxi driver will know of something nearby," I said. "I'll go and retrieve my bags and I'll have to stay the night in your house. Then I'll come back to you in the morning."

She gave me a bright hopeful smile and found me the key. I watched her standing on her terrace, waving, as I came out of the front entrance. The taxi driver did indeed know of a restaurant nearby that also rented out rooms. We stopped there and I was shown a simple but pretty room with a window overlooking the lake. So much nicer than the room-from-hell with the leering old man. I gave a sigh of relief. A modest price was agreed and then we drove rapidly to catch the afternoon ferry.

It was dark by the time I returned to Belinda's little house, retrieved my bags from behind the bush and installed myself in her bedroom. It was a pretty little place with tall windows that opened onto the terrace and the lake beyond, marble floors and a giant bathtub in which I had a good soaking. Then, feeling refreshed, I cooked myself some pasta I found in the pantry, added some tomato paste and Parmesan cheese to it and ate it, watching the lights twinkling across the lake. I did not return to the lecherous landlord. I decided I had never committed to taking the room, I knew no Italian to tell him my intentions and I was rather afraid he might demonstrate *his* intentions if he got me alone again.

I slept well that night and awoke to the sun streaming in through my window. I walked into the village and bought fresh bread, still warm from the oven, local cheeses and ham. Then I enjoyed a jolly good breakfast on the terrace. I left my big suitcase at Belinda's and packed a bag with essentials to take to Switzerland. I certainly wasn't going to lug that heavy bag all the way into Stresa! It was a good morning for walking, the air still chilly and a mist hanging over distant mountains. There was activity at Villa Fiori this time, which I took to be a good thing. It must mean that the owners were in residence and the staff were preparing for the house party. Gardeners were at work and I could see the beds beyond the gate being weeded and planted with new flowers. As I passed I thought one of the gardeners looked up and stared at me. Knowing the Italian habit of appreciating pretty women I continued on my way with a big smile on my face.

I caught the ferry back to Locarno and took a taxi up to the restaurant where I'd be spending the next few days. I installed myself in my new room, then walked over to the clinic, where Belinda and I spent the day chatting on the terrace, catching up on news. I regretted that I had no London gossip for her and my life in Ireland sounded incredibly dull, but she seemed eager for any news from home.

"You're so lucky to have Darcy," she said. "And to know that if anything happens, you know, he will marry you. But then, I thought that rat would marry me. He certainly hinted at it . . . 'our wonderful future together,' that's what he said. Wasn't that supposed to be a proposal?"

I nodded in sympathy.

"But I'm sure Darcy takes good care that accidents won't happen," she went on.

"Belinda, accidents are not going to happen because we haven't actually . . ." I stammered at saying the words.

Her eyes opened extra wide. "You mean you still haven't? And you've lived under the same roof for months? What's wrong with you?"

"Nothing's wrong with either of us," I said, my cheeks flaming with embarrassment. "And recently it's mainly been Darcy's idea. Since we became engaged and he went to confession, he's treated me with kid gloves on. Catholics seem to be funny that way."

She smiled. "Darcy of all people. Who would have thought he could remain chaste for more than a week?"

And there was that seed of worry again. Would he remain chaste when he was far away? I knew I should trust him absolutely, but everyone else seemed to take bed-hopping for granted. I pushed such thoughts to the back of my mind and entertained Belinda with stories about the awful Fig, Darcy's father and his romance with the princess.

I repeated this routine for the next three days, each day checking the local newspaper for any mention of the Prince of Wales and the house party. Unfortunately, the weather changed and we were confined to her sterile room, sitting on her bed or on the hard chairs while wind and rain battered on the window. By the third day I was finding it a strain to think of bright and cheerful things to talk about and was actually wishing the house party might soon start. So on Sunday morning I was pleased to see the headline I wanted: *English Prince Comes to Stresa*. And a picture of the Prince of Wales with Mrs. Simpson at his side standing by his motorcar beside the lake. I read on. *The prince will be attending a private party and was not part of the English delegation that has just departed.*

It was time to become the queen's spy. I caught the ferry back to Stresa, much to Belinda's disappointment. I saw her waving to me from her terrace as the taxi took me down the hill and felt a pang of guilt about leaving her. Only for a few days, I reminded myself. Bells were ringing for Sunday church services as the ferry cruised down the lake toward Italy, their sweet chimes echoing back from the steep hillsides. It was a serene and picturesque scene and I tried not to let my apprehension about what I was facing overwhelm me. It was only a house party, I told myself. Nothing I couldn't handle for a few days.

I took a taxi up to Belinda's house and packed what I hoped was suitable clothing into my suitcase. Then the taxi drove me down to Villa Fiori. We came to a stop outside the gates while the driver gave me an inquiring look. "We go in?" he asked in Italian even I could understand. I hesitated. If I arrived in a taxi it would seem that I was intending to join the house party. I knew the queen was going to suggest I join the party, but what if her letter hadn't arrived?

"I'd better get out here," I said and had the driver unload my suitcase. I paid him and he drove off, leaving me standing outside those imposing wrought-iron gates, listening to the gentle lap of the lake water. The wind ruffled my hair and I tried to smooth it down while I took in the scene before me. Beyond the gates the gardens sloped up the hillside, beautifully manicured formal lawns and flower beds giving way higher up the hill to terraces, trees and parkland. The yellow gravel driveway was lined by palm trees and ended in a forecourt in which a fountain was playing. The villa itself was what one expects an Italian palace to look like—pale lemon yellow with white shutters on either side of arched windows. There were statues decorating the roof and at the front a sweeping flight of steps led up to a marble balustrade. All very grand! I swallowed hard and took a deep breath before I dared to push open those gates.

Gardeners were still working as I walked up the drive, trying to look as if my suitcase was lighter than it really felt. One of the gardeners had removed his shirt and was bending to plant a border around a fountain. When he stood up again I couldn't help noticing that his physique was . . . well, admirable. I couldn't see his face because he was wearing a broad-brimmed hat, but I sensed him watching me as I continued up the drive. Again I allowed myself a smirk. So Italian men found me attractive. Then I reprimanded myself. I was about to become a married woman. Surely I shouldn't be noticing the chest muscles of gardeners?

As I approached the villa I spotted a group of people, sitting on a terrace beneath an arbor of wisteria. I felt suddenly shy and awkward. Why had I not asked the driver to take me to the villa? I must look pathetic, staggering up the drive carrying my own suitcase and dressed in my unfashionable tweed suit. And what if the letter still hadn't arrived and here I was with my suitcase? Had the queen actually suggested that I join the house party, or merely that I should be welcomed for a drink if I showed up? Why on earth hadn't I left the suitcase at Belinda's house and pretended I had just dropped by to pay my respects? Then, when they suggested I should stay, I could have acted as if I was surprised and they would have sent someone to pick up my belongings. But now I was committed. I couldn't retreat without being noticed. It was only a matter of time before one of them looked up and . . .

I was startled by a great scream. "Georgie!"

I was even more startled to see that the scream came from my mother. She had risen to her feet and was running toward me, her arms open. "Georgie, my darling!" she exclaimed in that voice that had filled London theaters. "What a lovely, lovely surprise. I had no idea you were coming to join us. Why didn't somebody tell me?"

She flung her arms around me, something she was not in the habit of doing. Then she turned back to the others. "Which of you arranged to bring my daughter to me? Was it you, Max, who suggested it? You knew I was pining for her, didn't you?"

I had prudently put down the suitcase before she attacked me. Now she took my hand and dragged me forward. "Everybody, this is my darling child, Georgie, whom I haven't seen for ages and ages. And I had no idea she was coming to join us." She gazed at me adoringly. "And now you're here. It seems like a miracle."

I noticed she had failed to mention that she had bumped into me a few days ago and at that time there had been no talk of inviting me to join her. Nor had she seemed overjoyed to see me. As I smiled back at her I wondered what she was up to.

Several other members of the party had also risen to their feet as she led me up steps to the arbor. Among them I recognized Miss Cami-Knickers herself. She looked older, perfectly groomed, incredibly chic as she stepped down from the terrace and approached me.

"Georgiana. How delightful to see you again after all this time.

I was so pleased to receive a note from the queen herself suggesting that you join our party."

I shook the hand that was offered. "I do hope this has not inconvenienced you in any way, Camilla," I said. "When I told Her Majesty that I'd be staying nearby I really had no idea she'd invite me to be part of your house party. But she was insistent that I pay my respects to my cousin, the Prince of Wales."

"But not at all," Camilla laughed. I remembered she had always had a horsey sort of laugh. Her horsey looks had definitely been improved with impeccable grooming and expensive clothes, but the laugh was unchanged. "Actually we're horribly short on women at the party, so you are a godsend at evening up the numbers. Come and meet my husband and the other guests."

I followed her up to the terrace, where several men were now standing to greet me. One of them I recognized immediately as Paolo, Belinda's former love. I saw from his face that he also remembered me, but I also saw the warning sign flash in his eyes. "Pretend you don't know me," could not have been more clear if he had shouted the words.

"My husband, Paolo, Count of Marola and Martini," she said proudly.

"My dear Lady Georgiana, you are most welcome, especially since my wife tells me you and she were old friends from your school days." He took my hand and kissed it.

"How do you do, Count?" I said, inclining my head formally. "But please let us dispense with formality. Why don't you call me Georgie?"

"Georgie. How charming." He smiled. I had forgotten how incredibly handsome he was. I could see why Belinda had been quite smitten at the time.

Camilla took my arm and moved me on. "And of course you already know Herr von Strohheim?"

My mother's beau, Max, clicked his heels and said, "Georgie. I am pleased to see you again," in his stilted, staccato English. At least it was better than when he first met my mother and spoke only occasional monosyllables.

"Max, how are you?" I said, shaking his hand. He too looked handsome in a blond and Germanic way and I was reminded of my encounter on the train with . . .

"And this is Count Rudolf von Rosskopf," Camilla said, and I found myself face-to-face with my would-be seducer.

He too took my hand and drew it to his lips. "We meet again, Lady Georgiana," he said. "What a delightful surprise. And I had no idea that we would run into each other again so soon. It must be fate, drawing us together." He looked rather pleased with himself and his eyes flirted with me.

"Behave yourself, Rudi," my mother snapped. "This is my young daughter, you know."

"Not too young," Rudi said. "Ripe and ready for adventure, I think."

"Now, Rudi, you are to do what Claire says and behave yourself," Camilla said, slapping his hand, which still held mine. "Or I shall send you packing." She put a hand on my shoulder. "Come, Georgiana, let me show you to your room and you can freshen up before you join us."

I went to retrieve my suitcase, but she waved this aside. "One of the servants will bring it for you. Is that all your luggage or is the rest to follow?"

"That's all," I said.

"My, but you travel light." She shot me a surprised look as she led me across the raked gravel forecourt and up onto the marble terrace that ran around the house, then pushed open one of the French doors at the side of the house. As soon as we were out of earshot I turned to her. "I really must apologize for this, Camilla. Being foisted on you like this. When I mentioned to the queen that I was coming to this part of the world I had no idea that she'd suddenly take matters into her own hands and think that I needed company and needed to be with my cousin."

"Not at all," Camilla said. "Pleased to have you join us. I meant what I said about not enough women. And several frightfully boring men. My husband's uncle, who is not my favorite person, and a couple of German officers. Equally stuffy and correct. You'll be a ray of sunshine, as your mother and Rudi have already demonstrated."

"Yes," I said, still wondering why my mother had put on such an extravagant performance of maternal feeling. For whose benefit, I wondered. Was she trying to convince Max what a good mother she had been?

"Has the Prince of Wales already arrived?" I asked.

"He has. He came last night with his—uh—companion," she said, giving me a knowing look. "But they are out on the lake on a friend's yacht. You'll see them at dinner." Camilla stood aside and invited me to enter through the French door. I stepped into a room that would have made Buckingham Palace look dowdy. I had been in some grand rooms in my time, but this was one of the grandest. The ceiling was high and painted in gold and blue. The furniture was gilt, upholstered in pale blue silk brocade. There was a similar patterned silk wallpaper on walls that were lined with old masters—scenes of Venice by Tintoretto, and then various religious subjects by painters I should have known. There were Persian rugs on a white marble floor and huge displays of flowers on low tables. Camilla wove her way past groups of furniture and floral displays as if she didn't even notice them, and we moved from the room into a long hallway.

I think I gasped. It was like a miniature Versailles, lined with mirrors and stretching the whole length of the house.

"How magnificent," I exclaimed.

"Yes, it is rather grand," she said. "But nothing to compare with the palazzo in Rome. I must say it took me a while to get used to this sort of over-the-top decorating. It's like perpetually living in a museum. Our house in England is quite large but also quite plain. I expect yours is too."

"Compared to this, absolutely." We exchanged a grin of understanding. I realized then that she might be welcoming me as an ally.

"We've come a long way since Les Oiseaux, haven't we?" she said.

"You certainly have," I said. "I still don't have a home of my own. I feel like the poor relation when I stay with my brother."

"How beastly," she said, just before I added, "But I am engaged to be married, if all goes well."

"Goes well?" She raised an eyebrow as she led me along this hallway to a broad flight of marble stairs.

"We have to get official permission from the king and Parliament," I said. "I'm marrying a Catholic."

"Are you? Gosh, what an annoying complication. Do you think they'll say yes?"

"The queen seems to think so. If they don't, we'll go and live somewhere else," I said. "It's not as if the king doesn't have plenty of sons and will soon have plenty of grandchildren."

"How true. So have you snapped up a dashing European prince?"

"A dashing Irishman."

"Interesting. So will you live in Ireland?"

"I'm not sure. The family does have a castle, but Darcy is away a lot. Maybe just a flat in London most of the time."

"Darcy?" she asked, looking genuinely interested now. "Darcy O'Mara?"

"Yes, do you know him?"

"My dear, our mothers were related. We'll be cousins of some sort. I'm surprised he is going to settle down. I always thought of him as the ultimate man-about-town. Another Rudi." She gave me an approving smile. "Well done. You've tamed a tiger."

"I hope so," I said, but the words echoed in my head. Another Rudi. Golly, I hope not. And it did cross my mind that her husband,

Paolo, had certainly been no saint before his marriage. Had he given her cause for worry since?

She led me up a curved marble staircase, then along an upper hall, also hung with mirrors and family portraits, many of them apparently of cardinals and a couple of popes. Then she opened a door at the far end.

"I've put you in here. Nice and quiet and relatively simple." I followed her into a room I would never have described as relatively simple! But it certainly was lovely, with windows on two sides, looking out over formal gardens, high trimmed box hedges, a fountain, banks of azaleas. It had a white canopy bed, piled high with silk quilts, an armchair in front of a marble fireplace, a dear little gilded writing desk in the window and an enormous carved wardrobe that took up most of the inside wall. I couldn't help thinking that my poor suitcase of clothing would look completely lost in a piece of furniture that size, also that it would have been perfect for games of sardines.

"It's lovely," I said. "Thank you."

"You'll be relieved to get out of those travel-worn clothes," she said, eyeing my suit. "Have you just arrived from London?"

I wasn't going to give away that Belinda lived close by. "Just from the Swiss part of the lake," I said. "My friend is in a clinic there."

"Oh dear. TB, I suppose. Everyone comes to Switzerland for TB."

I made a sort of grunt of agreement. Let them think TB rather than the truth.

"It's kind of you to come and visit her. I take it she's no longer contagious?" She gave me a nervous glance as if I might be a carrier of the plague.

"Oh no. She's not contagious," I said. "Just very bored."

"Anyone I know?" she asked.

"I don't think so," I said hurriedly. "And of course she doesn't want it known that she's recovering in a clinic."

"Naturally. Quite understandable." She looked up as there was a tap on the door. "Ah, here is Raimondo with your bags."

A burly young man in elaborate footman's livery brought in my suitcase, placed it on the floor, bowed, muttered, "Contessa," and went again.

"Now, about a maid," Camilla said. "You didn't bring one."

"No, I'm afraid my new Irish maid had complete hysterics when she found out she had to go abroad, so I had to leave her behind."

"Her Majesty asked me to find a local girl for you, but actually I'm going to share my maid, Gerda. She's incredibly efficient and can handle two of us with ease." She glanced toward the door in case someone might be listening. "Between ourselves, she is almost frighteningly efficient. She's Austrian but has worked for several distinguished families in London so her English is good. I haven't had her long. I was so lucky to find her. My former maid, Monique, who was terribly sweet, met with a horrible accident recently. She was French, you know, and a trifle absentminded. Never could quite get used to the idea that traffic was on the wrong side of the road and she stepped out in front of a bus one day. So upsetting. But fortunately a friend recommended Gerda. Her mistress had just died suddenly, so it suited both of us." She had been walking around the room as she spoke, straightening a hand mirror on the dressing table, pulling back the net curtain . . . She seemed ill at ease.

"You know I really don't have to stay if my being here is one complication too many, Camilla," I found myself saying.

She turned then and came over to me, putting a tentative hand on my arm. "No, Georgie. I'm actually really glad you're here. Just like old times, eh?" And she put on a bright smile.

Chapter 10

SUNDAY, APRIL 21, 1935
VILLA FIORI, LAKE MAGGIORE, ITALY

Well, I've arrived at a frightfully impressive villa. More like a palace, actually. Not only is the Prince of Wales here but my mother too! And such an effusive greeting! What on earth can she want?

As soon as I was left alone in the room I took off my jacket, laid it on the bed, admired the view to the mountains from the side window, then went over to the French doors that opened onto a little balcony with an ironwork chair and table. Jasmine and wisteria had climbed up to the balcony and spilled over it, sending out a heady scent. I took in the formal gardens with their topiary hedges. I glimpsed a swimming pool and behind it grounds that rose in a series of formal terraces, decorated with statues before woodlands took over the top of the estate. Quite delightful. I decided I might enjoy myself here after all. There was that gardener with his shirt off. I saw him look up as if he sensed my presence and ducked inside the room just as a voice behind me said imperiously, "You wish me to unpack your clothes, Lady Georgiana? I am Gerda Stretzl, the contessa's maid."

The words were spoken in almost perfect English but with the clipped pronunciation of a German speaker, and the *w* of "wish" turned into a *v*. The person who stood behind me was tall and erect with fine cheekbones and light blond hair pulled back into a chignon. She was wearing the customary black lady's maid's outfit, which robbed her pale complexion of all color and made her look a bit like a walking skeleton. Her face showed no expression as she stood there.

"Ah, Gerda," I said, thinking that the name really suited her. "It's very kind of you to take on this extra work, especially when your mistress is so busy."

"The contessa requested that I do this and my job is to obey," she said.

"I won't need a lot of help," I said. "I have traveled quite light because I had to leave my own maid at home."

"Yes, I see," she said, picking up the jacket from where I had left it on the bed. "This is in serious need of good cleaning and pressing. Please let me assist you out of the skirt and into something more suitable."

Oh crikey. I had a feeling that the contents of my suitcase would not qualify for more suitable in her eyes. This was confirmed as she took out a skirt, a summer dress, the one long evening gown I had brought with me. They hung looking forlorn in that great wardrobe. I was going to make a joke about being able to conceal a regiment in there in the good old days but decided she would have no sense of humor.

"I think you have not had the benefit of a good maid for some time now," she said. "Or this gown would have been packed with tissue paper and thus not creased like this."

"You're right," I said, not wanting to admit that I packed the suitcase myself, also that I hadn't had a maid who knew what she was doing for years now. I had had to choose the one evening dress that Queenie hadn't ruined by ironing the velvet the wrong way, burning a hole in it or otherwise wrecking. Gerda made small noises of disgust as she continued to empty the suitcase.

"Has your ladyship brought her jewel case with her?" she asked.

"Just a few items to wear in the evenings," I said. "I was really only planning to come to Italy to visit a sick friend, not find myself part of a fashionable house party." This, of course, was a lie, but I didn't want to admit that these items of clothing represented the best of what I owned.

Within seconds she had eased me out of my skirt and into my dressing gown. "I think the flower-pattern tea dress will be suitable for the afternoon," she said. "I will go and press it right away."

When she'd gone I examined the contents of my wardrobe and chest of drawers, everything put away in exact little piles. Golly, I thought, this is what a real lady's maid is like. Maybe one day I'll be able to afford one like Gerda. I wondered if I'd take Queenie back when I married and gave a little shudder. It would be nice not having to dread Queenie ruining or losing something every time I travel. I'd given up Kathleen as a hopeless case. If she wasn't prepared to leave Ireland I saw no future for her as my maid. I sat at my dressing table and took a brush to my hair.

"Oh, my lady, allow me," said a voice behind me and there was Gerda again, holding up a dress that looked like new. "Let me assist you into this and then I'll do your hair for you."

I stepped into the dress and she did up the buttons with lightning speed, then she sat me at my dressing table and styled my hair.

"It's quite curly, isn't it?" she said. "I always use a little of a special pomade to smooth out the waves. I'll fetch some from the contessa's room. She won't mind."

And I sat there, being transformed into a sleek-looking woman. Then she applied a hint of rouge to my cheeks and lips.

"There," she said. "That's better, isn't it?"

"Much," I said. "Gerda, you are a genius."

She looked quite pleased at this. I believe I almost saw a smile. "You are most kind, my lady. I merely do my job."

"How do you like living in Italy?" I asked her. "I hear you are from Austria and have been living in London for quite a while."

"That is correct," she said. "I am not sure that I will like Italy as much as London, but the contessa is most agreeable. And I was fortunate to find this situation so quickly after the tragic death of my mistress."

"Oh dear. I'm sorry," I said. "You were fond of her?"

"It is not a maid's job to be fond of an employer, but she treated me with respect and it was certainly an interesting household. Her husband was a cabinet minister. I probably should not mention which one. It was a great shock to me as well as him when she killed herself. I still blame myself and feel responsible."

"How could you be responsible if someone decides to take their own life?" I asked.

"I should have checked on her sooner," she said and a spasm of pain crossed her face. "She asked me to run her bath. I did it just the way she liked it with lavender oil. I helped her to undress, and to climb into the tub. Then I said she should call me when she was finished. I went back into her bedroom and busied myself sewing on a button. Then it occurred to me that she had been in the bath for a long while and the water must be getting cold. I opened the bathroom door and found the water bright red. She had slit her wrists."

"How horrible for you," I said.

"If only I had checked on her sooner, I might have prevented it," she said.

"Don't blame yourself, Gerda," I said. "If someone is determined to end their life, they will do so. Had she been depressed?"

"She had not been herself," Gerda said. "Of course I was not privy to the details of her personal life, but something was troubling her, and her husband was always too busy to notice."

"Well, at least you have landed in a good situation here," I said. "This lovely villa and a house in Rome."

"Yes," she said. "I have secured the perfect position for my needs. I am most grateful."

As she spoke she was removing items from my wardrobe. Then picked up the shoes I had been wearing. "I shall attempt to improve these and be back in time to dress you for dinner, my lady. Will that be all now?"

"Yes, thank you, Gerda."

She bobbed a little curtsy and left, closing the door quietly behind her. Golly, I thought. I'm not sure I'd want a maid like that. Camilla had been right. There was something rather terrifying about her.

I went down to join the party under the arbor, hoping that tea was now being served because I was definitely feeling peckish. I had eaten a pastry at the ferry plaza, but I hadn't really had a decent meal since I arrived in Italy. There was now a crystal jug of fresh lemonade on the table but no sign of food other than a dish of olives. Clearly tea was not part of the daily regime at Villa Fiori. I tried not to look disappointed as I sat in the chair Max had pulled up for me.

"You're looking very nice, darling," my mother said. "That dress really suits you."

I smiled, but inside I was still dying of curiosity about what had brought about this change. Usually she told me my hair was a disaster, my clothes frumpy and I needed makeup. I had taken a couple of sips of lemonade when my mother stood up. "I know, darling, why don't you and I take a turn about the grounds. They are quite lovely, you know."

She held out her hand to me. I stood up, taking her hand. Max started to stand up too. "That is a good idea. We need exercise before dinner."

"Not you, darling." She turned to give him her dazzling smile. "Georgie and I have lots of catching up to do. This is girl time. You men must take your exercise somewhere else."

She slipped her arm through mine and led me down the steps. We passed the lines of perfectly manicured topiaries, past the fountain with doves sitting on the marble rim. To one side of us was a sparkling swimming pool. Beyond it was a small octagonal building of white marble, again adorned with classical statues. Mummy hadn't said a word so far, but her arm was still tightly entwined in mine. She led me upward, toward the terraces, and we walked along a pathway with a high wall, covered in blooming vines on one side and the view down to the lake on the other. About halfway along there was a recessed arbor, semicircular, with a small fountain built into the wall and a marble bench running around the edge. Mummy glanced back over her shoulder. "Thank God," she said.

"For what?"

"That nobody is following us." Her hand squeezed my arm. "I am so glad you're here, darling. I can't tell you how glad."

"You've never seemed exactly delighted to see me before. Including the other day in the square in Stresa. In fact, you ran off in the middle of a conversation—and you left me to pay your bill."

"That's because I saw somebody, darling. Someone I did not wish to encounter again." She drew me down to the marble bench beside her. Water bubbled from a stone lion's mouth set into the wall behind us. Bees buzzed among the wisteria flowers.

"I need your help, Georgie," she said in a low voice.

"Are you in some kind of trouble?"

"It could be utterly devastating, darling. I simply don't know what to do. You have to help me. Promise you'll help me."

"Of course I'll do what I can," I said, thoroughly alarmed now. The look on her face was quite desperate. "Tell me what's wrong."

"It's that man, Rudi. The one who kissed your hand. He was the one I fled from when I spied him in Stresa. I nearly died when we arrived at the house party and I found that he had also been invited."

"He's been pursuing you? You're normally the one who can handle any man with ease."

"Not this time, darling. And of course I know how to keep any man at arm's length when I want to. No, it's much worse than that." She brushed back a strand of hair that the wind had blown across her face and composed herself again before she said, "Rudi is quite an attractive man, as you have noticed. I met him in Berlin. Max was away on business as he often is and Rudi and I had—well, a harmless little fling. At least I thought it was a harmless little fling until he turned up with photographs he had taken. He had a hidden camera, you see. And some kind of timing apparatus that could take the pictures while he was . . . otherwise engaged. So he came to see me one day and he showed me the pictures. Darling, they were shocking. Even I was shocked, and as you know, that takes a lot."

I nodded.

"And he said he would send them to Max if I didn't pay him a lot of money."

"Blackmail?" I asked.

She nodded. "I had no idea he could stoop so low. I thought he was a gentleman. And obviously I couldn't come up with that amount of money without Max noticing. What's more, I don't believe one should give in to blackmail. But if Max saw those pictures . . ." She shook her head as if trying to get rid of the vision of them. "Darling, you know what Max is like. Strict Lutheran upbringing. Very prudish. That's why he's insisting on our marrying, because he is riddled with guilt about our sinful relationship. But he thinks he's been the only man in my life for some time now and if he found out about Rudi well, that would be the end of everything. He'd break off with me and with him would go all the lovely money I do so enjoy."

"So you really do want to marry him, do you?" I asked. "He makes you happy? You can picture spending the rest of your life with him?"

I felt her hesitate before she put on a bright smile. "Of course he makes me happy. He is wonderful in bed. Conversation is, well, limited, and Berlin is fun, but it's not England, is it?"

"You have plenty of money of your own, don't you? You could live well without him if you decided to."

"I am not without cash," she said. "And I do have the little villa in Nice and I could always go back to the stage if I felt like it, so it wouldn't be the end of the world, but I like being with Max. I enjoy the kind of power he has. And yes, to answer your question, I do want to marry him." She covered my hand with her own. "And think of your future, darling. It's unlikely that Max and I would have children. You'll be the heir to millions. He might be persuaded to spring for a big wedding for you and Darcy. To buy you a property, perhaps?"

"Now who is blackmailing?" I asked, but I smiled. "So exactly what was it that you wanted me to do? Talk Rudi out of his wicked ways?"

"Oh no, darling. I want you to steal the photographs for me."

"Crikey!" I exclaimed. "How do you expect me to do that?"

"Because he has them here with him. He told me so. He even threatened to reveal them at an opportune moment. He's trying to force my hand. He's grown impatient and waited long enough, he said. It's pay up now or suffer the consequences."

"Odious man," I said. "He tried to seduce me on the train, you know."

"As you say, odious man. So we have to stop him, don't we, Georgie? You've done some clever undercover work, haven't you? You've solved murders, and recovered jewels. This should be a piece of cake for you."

"A piece of cake?" The words came out louder than I had intended. "Do you know where he is keeping the photographs?"

"I have no idea," she said. "His bedroom is in the main corridor where we are all staying, but that might be too obvious, might it not? Oh, and he does seem to go over to that little marble pavilion from time to time. I've no idea why, unless he meets one of the maids there."

A picture of Gerda came unbidden into my head. Certainly not her, I thought.

"But of course he could have hidden them anywhere in a house like this. Inside one of the thousands of books in the library. Inside one of the many vases and urns, behind a painting . . . It would have to be somewhere clever because he must know that I'd be looking for them."

I stared at her. She was looking at me as if she was now completely confident in my abilities. "Mummy, I've just arrived as a guest in a strange villa where I know nobody. I can hardly start turning their house upside down, can I? Why don't you confide in Camilla? She could get the servants to help."

"Confide in Camilla? Are you mad? For one thing I hardly know her. We're only here because Max is chummy with Paolo's uncle who is also a guest at this shindig." She leaned closer again. "She is about the most straightlaced and unapproachable woman I've ever come across. I mean, look at her. If she wasn't married to a delectable Italian count she'd be the village spinster. Oh no, darling. Camilla would never understand in a million years. She'd never help." Her hand was still patting mine. "That's why I'm relying on you. You are my only hope. The tenuous tie to our future happiness is entirely in your hands."

You can tell she was an actress, can't you? Normal people don't say things like that even in moments of stress. If it hadn't been so serious I would have giggled.

Now she grabbed my hands fiercely. "You will help me, won't you? You won't let your poor mother die of shame and despair."

What could I say? "I'll do what I can," I said.

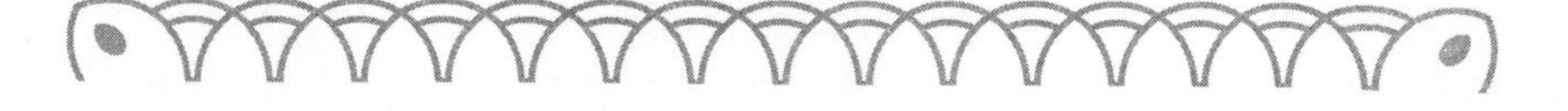

Chapter 11

At Villa Fiori
Still Sunday, April 21

It wasn't the first decision in my life that I regretted almost as soon as I uttered the words.

"Good. Well, that's settled, then. Such a load off my mind. You have no idea." Mummy stood up, brushed off her skirt and held out a hand to pull me to my feet. "We should be getting back to the others," she said. "Max will wonder where we have been." Then she froze, putting her finger to her lips. "Someone's close by," she said. "I thought I heard a movement behind that hedge." Her face had gone very white again.

I stepped out of our arbor and looked around. "It's only one of the gardeners, sweeping the leaves from the path," I said.

"They certainly keep enough staff here, don't they? These grounds look immaculate. And the house—Max was most impressed. He's thinking of building us a villa like this outside Berlin when we marry."

She seemed quite cheerful now. I moved closer to her as we made our way along the raked gravel of the path and then down the steps to the main lawns.

"You'll have to help me if you want me to do this, Mummy," I said. "Have Max arrange to take Rudi out on the lake or something so that I can search his bedroom."

"That should be easy enough to arrange, I suppose," she said. "Yes, that might be a good idea. Then there would be no chance of his showing up unexpectedly. Although of course the most sensible thing to do, if Max was out on the lake alone with him, would be to push him overboard. I wonder if he can swim."

"Mummy!" I exclaimed.

"Well, it would take care of things nicely, wouldn't it?" she said. "A little boating accident? Who would dispute that?"

I gave a nervous little titter. "I can't see upright and noble Max agreeing to push your former lover over the side of a boat," I said. "Besides, Rudi looks quite strong and fit to me. There might be a struggle and Max would be the one to go overboard."

"Oh dear, you're right." She shook her head so that those dainty blond curls danced. "How annoying. There must be a way to silence the man without having to give him money. But in the meantime, you do your best to find the wretched photographs, and if all goes . . ."

She broke off as we saw Max coming toward us. "Ah, there you are," he said. "Did you have a good stroll? I was testing the swimming pool, but it is too cold, I think."

"Much too cold," Mummy said. "If you crave water, I suggest we all go out on the lake tomorrow. Why don't we ask Camilla to arrange a picnic to one of the islands? I'm dying to explore Isola Bella, aren't you?"

"Tomorrow?" A worried look crossed his face.

"What else would we be doing tomorrow?" she asked. "We are here to enjoy ourselves, after all."

"You are right." He nodded. "There is no reason we should not take a picnic on the lake. No reason at all."

I thought it was a rather strange thing to say.

When we returned to the terrace we found it was now deserted. No sign of Rudi, nor Camilla. Even the lemonade had been cleared away.

"Everyone has gone inside," Mummy said. "I suppose it is getting chilly. There is quite a breeze from the lake now and one forgets it's only April."

"What time do they dine here?" I asked. "Should we be changing for dinner soon?"

"No rush, darling. They eat quite late. At least they did last night when we arrived. After eight, anyway."

My heart sank. Another three hours before I would have food. I just prayed my stomach didn't growl. I followed Mummy and Max into the villa.

"I think I'll go up and get a cardigan," I said. "It's becoming quite chilly and the maid insisted that I put on a summer frock."

"The maid insisted?" Mummy raised an eyebrow. "Darling, you have to learn to control servants. Maids can only suggest."

I shook my head. "Not this one. She's quite formidable. She belongs to Camilla, actually. I'm glad she's not mine."

"Oh yes, Camilla's maid. I've encountered her. What a dragon. Yours is hopeless, I seem to remember," Mummy said.

"True, but I think I'd choose hopeless over formidable," I said as I left them heading to one of the sitting rooms and went up the stairs alone.

I sat at my dressing table brushing my windswept hair while I tried to calm my racing thoughts. It was hard to digest what my mother had just told me, even harder to realize that I had actually promised to help her!

As I came out of my room I heard voices coming from the half-open door of the next room along the hall.

"You will think carefully about my little proposal, won't you?" said a male voice softly.

"Don't rush me. One day you'll go too far."

He chuckled. "But I enjoy going too far, as you very well know."

I crept past and made my way hurriedly down the stairs, not wanting anyone to think I was eavesdropping. I heard the sound of my mother's voice and found her with Max now in a sitting room whose tall windows looked onto the lake. The view was spectacular with the snow-capped peaks in the distance lit by slanting afternoon sunlight as a steamer cut through the choppy water.

Paolo stood up as I came in. "Ah, there you are. Too cold to stay outside, don't you think? Come and meet my mother and uncle, Georgiana."

I saw then that two more people were sitting in high-backed chairs on either side of an ornate marble fireplace in which a fire now glowed. Paolo led me over to them. "Mother, may I present Lady Georgiana Rannoch?" he said formally. "She is a cousin to the Prince of Wales."

I looked into the haughtiest face I had ever seen (and I've seen haughty faces in my time). The face was long and thin with a hooked nose. Her eyebrows seemed to be perpetually raised in a surprised look. And her lips were pursed. They did not unpurse when she saw me. Instead she held out one bony hand. I wasn't sure whether I was to shake it or kiss it. I also wasn't sure how to address her. I opted for the safe English "How do you do?" and shook her hand. "I'm afraid I don't speak Italian."

"My mother speaks a little English," Paolo said. "And of course very good French."

"You speak French, naturally?" she asked me in French, raising a lorgnette to examine me more closely.

"Naturally," I replied in French. "I was at school in Switzerland with your daughter-in-law. We had to converse in French most of the time."

"Your accent is just as bad as hers," the old woman said, glancing across at Camilla, who was now sitting on the window seat. "I think the English are incapable of learning foreign languages. We Italians, on the other hand, have great facility."

"Maybe because we are an island and haven't been invaded for a thousand years," I replied. "We have less need to learn them."

I saw the eyebrows jerk a little higher.

"I hope your behavior is more correct than that of His Highness," she said, reverting to passable English. "He brings a married woman with him. I do not approve. But he is a prince. He ranks higher so I must say nothing."

I couldn't think of a suitable answer to this, but it did seem to indicate that Mrs. Simpson was still considered a married woman. That must mean there had been no mention of a swift and secret wedding between her and the Prince of Wales. I think I felt a small sigh of relief.

I turned back to Paolo. "And this is your uncle?"

"Yes," he said. "My uncle Count Cosimo di Marola. Uncle Cosimo is right-hand man to King Victor Emmanuel and adviser to our beloved leader, Il Duce—Mussolini. A very important man these days, so be nice to him."

Uncle Cosimo's face was very different from that of Paolo's mother. He had those handsome good looks one sees in older Italian men, strong chin, iron gray hair, much like the Caesars on Roman coins. He examined me with bright, alert eyes, studying me appraisingly the way only an Italian man does. Then he nodded. "I like. She can sit beside me."

"Uncle, behave yourself," Paolo said. "She is related to English royalty, remember."

"I do not wish to ravish her," Uncle Cosimo said. "I only wish to enjoy admiring her fresh youthful face and body."

Paolo's mother snorted in disgust.

"You're embarrassing her, Uncle Cosimo," Camilla said primly. "Come and sit over here with me, Georgie."

I accepted, gratefully. There was no way I wished to find myself between the lecherous uncle and the disapproving mother. I felt a stab of pity for Camilla and wondered if these two were always part of their lives. As I crossed the room I glanced into the farthest corner and almost tripped over a low table. Someone was sitting there—someone dressed all in black with a skull-like face, staring out with unseeing eyes while his lips mumbled. I wasn't sure whether I was seeing a ghost for a second.

I grabbed Camilla's arm. "Who is that?" I whispered.

"That? Oh, that's Father Francesco. He's our priest," she said. "Strange for a Protestant to understand but the Martini family has its own resident priest to say masses for us. We even have a chapel at one end of the villa. I should give you a tour."

"I'd like that," I said.

"You can hold the fort, Paolo," she said, turning to her husband. "I'm going to show Georgie the lay of the land."

"What must I hold? Which fort? Which land?" he asked, frowning.

"Honestly, you're hopeless," she said. "I merely meant that I'll give her a tour of the villa."

"Is it my fault if your English language has so many ridiculous expressions? In Italian we say what we mean and mean what we say."

Camilla just laughed and led me from the room. We went through other sitting rooms, each decorated with antique furniture, classical sculpture, fine paintings, Persian rugs. Then the long gallery, followed by a dining room with a table long enough to seat fifty. A magnificent chandelier hung over it and tall silver candlesticks were placed along it at intervals. After that came a ballroom, looking mysterious in half darkness with the heavy drapes drawn over the windows. Then she led me into a library of leather-bound volumes, complete with gallery above and a spiral staircase to reach it, a music room with piano and harp, Paolo's study and at the far end of the hallway she paused, looking back at me expectantly. "And this is the jewel in our crown, so to speak."

Camilla turned into a narrow side passage, went down three stone steps and pushed open a heavy studded door. We stepped into a tiny chapel with an ornate gilded baroque altar, the walls adorned with fine religious art. The scent of incense hung heavy in the air and a shaft of sunlight sent a pattern of colors across the floor from the stained glass window. It felt as if I'd stepped into another century or even another world.

"This feels very old," I said, my voice echoing from the vaulted ceiling. "How old is your villa here?"

"Only a hundred years," she said, "but Paolo's family had the chapel brought up here and reassembled from a former palace in Turin."

I was actually glad when she ushered me out again. "We have mass every morning at eight and you're always welcome to join us," she said brightly. "You might want to get used to our strange Catholic ways."

I nodded, thinking there would be no way I'd want to find myself in that overwhelming little chapel. As one raised in the Church of Scotland it felt quite unlike my idea of religion. And the thought crossed my mind that maybe Darcy felt at home in churches like this and I'd have to get used to the Catholic way.

"You have so many beautiful things," I said, trying to change the subject.

"Yes, so many," she said. "I wonder if I shall ever feel comfortable here. Actually I'm glad when we entertain because this place doesn't feel so like a mausoleum. Paolo and I rattle around in it and the servants are so well trained that they flit invisibly. It's unnerving, to tell you the truth."

I wondered how long they had been married and whether there were any children yet? There was certainly no sign or mention of them and one didn't quite know how to bring up the subject.

"So it's usually just the two of you here?" I asked.

"Except for Paolo's mother. She's always with us when we are in Italy."

"Do your own parents ever come out to visit?"

She shook her head. "My parents echo the words of that famous quote 'Abroad is utterly bloody,'" she said, laughing. "Daddy was sent to France in the Great War and that has colored his opinion of anywhere outside England. They are terribly county, you know. Horses and dogs and happy at home."

I nodded. "But you like it here?"

"In small doses," she said. "One certainly misses things about England. The corner sweet shop. The hunts. Nursery tea with crumpets."

She gave me a sad sort of smile.

"I suppose that's the price for marrying an Italian count," I said. "Everyone must have thought you'd made a really good match."

"It does have its benefits," she said. "And Paolo is really very sweet. It would be different if . . ." She broke off as one of the invisible servants materialized in the hallway in front of us. He was an ancient and most distinguished-looking butler. In fact, if I'd met him alone, I would have thought that he might have been another uncle, not a servant. He spoke to her in low tones and she nodded. *"Sì. Va bene,"* she said.

He disappeared again and she smiled at me. "That is Umberto. He's been with the family for forty years. He wanted to know whether he should serve aperitifs in the lake room now or wait for the remaining guests. I told him there was no need to wait. When the others return I'm sure they'll want to bathe and rest and I expect you could do with a drink."

I could do with food, but I couldn't say that. We returned to the group and found Paolo deep in conversation in Italian with his uncle while Mummy and Max sat by the window, looking bored. They cheered up when a silver tray was produced and we were handed glasses of Campari. I sat sipping mine, watching the view from the window and thinking about things. I thought of Camilla, who didn't seem very happy, and thought how unfair it was that

Belinda might have been mistress of this house, had it not been for religion. Then Mummy laughed, and I turned to look at her and remembered . . . in one of those over-the-top ornate rooms Rudi had hidden the incriminating photographs. How on earth could I ever be expected to locate them? Camilla had mentioned the invisible and efficient servants. They'd be bound to notice my every move and report it to her. Oh golly. Why did I ever let myself be talked into things like this? Was it because it was so seldom that my mother wanted or needed me or showed any interest in me? And who doesn't want to be needed by their mother?

"Drink up, Georgie," Paolo said and indicated that the butler should top up my glass. I nodded my thanks but really I wasn't enjoying the flavor that much and I worried about alcohol on an empty stomach.

Voices echoing from the marble hallway announced the arrival of newcomers. I braced myself to face Mrs. Simpson. I always found her quite terrifying although I was learning to stick up for myself a little more these days. But it was not the royal couple who came into the room but three men. One of them was Rudi. He was laughing and looked extremely pleased with himself. The other two looked the epitome of German military officers, both in uniform decorated with a lot of braid and medals. The older one, a great bull of a man with large jowls and a monocle in one eye, walked with the air of one who is used to being obeyed. The younger man, slim, light haired, walked two paces behind, but also managed to convey that air of arrogance.

"The wanderers return," Paolo said in English, standing to greet them. "Just in time for an evening drink."

"Gut!" The older one nodded. "We have great thirst after a long walk. We went halfway up that mountain. We have a fine view of the lake." His English was rather like Max's—staccato syllables with a pause between each. He broke off when he noticed me. "*Ach.* We have a new visitor, I see."

"Yes, this is Lady Georgiana, cousin of the Prince of Wales," Paolo said. "She was staying in the area so naturally we invited her to join the party. Georgie, this is General Spitz-Blitzen from Germany."

The big man clicked his heels and jerked his head in an abrupt bow. "Lady Georgiana," he said.

"General." I nodded back. "I'm pleased to meet you."

"And this is my adjutant, Lieutenant Klinker."

The young man repeated the heel click and head jerk.

"Klinker unfortunately has no English," the general said.

Klinker stared at me through pale blue eyes that I found rather unnerving. Rather like staring at a fish. I was reminded of Prince Siegfried whom I'd once been slated to marry. He had a similar fishy look and a similar expression that indicated he found the world distasteful.

"And where have you been, Rudi?" Camilla asked as the latter helped himself to a glass of vermouth.

"Oh, here and there," he said. "Afternoon stroll along the lake, you know. Admiring the view and reciting poetry." I noticed that he shot my mother an amused look and I wondered if he had possibly managed to follow us through the grounds and eavesdrop on our conversation. In which case my chances of finding the photographs were nil.

"You should have climbed the hill with us. So energetic. So healthful," the general said.

"The Germans place too much emphasis on physical culture, I think," Paolo's mother said. "Always in training. Training for what, I ask myself?"

"What is the Latin expression?" the general said. "*Corpore sano* . . . Healthy body, healthy mind? Think what your Roman ancestors accomplished. They were the fittest people ever and they ruled the world."

"Until they were overcome by barbarians from the north," Paolo's mother said through her pursed lips.

There was an embarrassed silence.

"Another drink?" Camilla asked.

I looked around the assembled company, so mismatched, so little in common. Who had thought it might be a good idea to assemble them for a house party and what had made the Prince of Wales want to join a group of people so different from his usual fun-loving set?

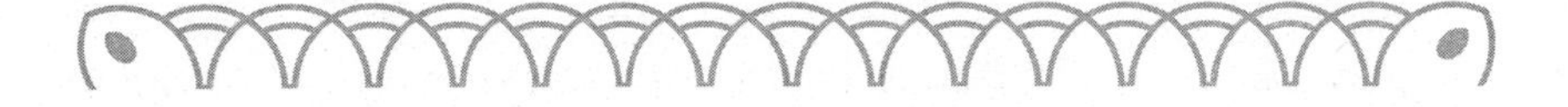

Chapter 12

April 21
Villa Fiori

I wish I had never agreed to come here. Now it's even worse than I thought. How am I ever going to find those photographs?

The royal couple had not returned by the time Camilla suggested we go up to change for dinner.

When I went up to my bedroom I found Gerda was waiting for me. On the bed lay a black dress I had never seen before.

"That's not mine," I pointed out.

"I know this," she said. "It belongs to my mistress. I try to make better your velvet dress, but I think it is not possible. Somebody has tried to iron it the wrong way and left marks." She shook her head in disgust. "I do not think this dress is suitable to wear to a dinner party with distinguished guests. The other ladies will be fashionable. And so I borrow a dress from the contessa for you."

"Oh, but I couldn't, really," I stammered. "My own dress isn't too bad if I wear my fur stole with it."

"The contessa will not mind if you wear her dress. She has many such gowns. The American lady also buys her frocks in Paris. And the other English lady does too. You should not look inferior to them. You are above them in rank."

She wasn't the sort one could argue with. I was swiftly undressed. She made little disapproving noises at the quality of my underwear. "It is lucky that this dress requires no brassiere," she said. "Does your family not give you money for clothes?"

I suppose I should have told her that it wasn't her place to speak to me like that. But she was such an impressive sort of person that I found myself saying, "Unfortunately my branch of the family is quite poor. I have received no allowance since I came out."

"Then you must make a good match like the contessa has done," she said. "You must ask the count to introduce you to his friends."

"I am engaged to be married, you know," I said. "My fiancé is to inherit a castle in Ireland, and one day I will inherit a large property in England. So I'm not worried. It's just I'm somewhat short of funds right now."

"I will see if the contessa has gowns she no longer wears," Gerda said. "It is a pity that the other English lady is so much smaller than you. She has much money and beautiful clothes."

I realized then that she did not know that the other English lady was my mother. Good, I thought. Let's keep it that way.

As she talked she eased me into the black dress. It was long, tight and quite slinky. It didn't go at all with Camilla's personality, which I felt was definitely county set, like her parents. She would have been more comfortable in jodhpurs and boots. I couldn't picture her in a backless dress like this one. I couldn't picture myself in it either, until I glanced in the wardrobe mirror and I actually looked rather good. I suppose my one asset was my height and boyish figure. Even Gerda nodded approvingly. "Yes," she said. "That will do, I think. Now we make the hair. Sit please."

I sat at the dressing table. She brushed my hair, forced it into waves and added a black feather into a diamanté clip she had apparently brought with her. Something else she had borrowed from the contessa, I thought. Golly, I hope those aren't real diamonds. And then, even more disturbing . . . I hope Camilla doesn't look at me in the middle of dinner and say, "Who said you could wear my diamond clip and my dress?" in front of everybody.

Gerda was now applying dabs of rouge to my cheeks, brushing my lips with lipstick and drawing a line over my fair eyebrows. "There," she said. "That is better. Now your jewel case, please?"

I indicated it on the chest of drawers. She opened it and made another small grunt of despair. "You did not bring diamonds with you, I see."

I didn't like to admit that the only diamonds I possessed were in the family tiara I had inherited and I wasn't allowed to wear that until I married. "I only bring the minimum of jewels when I travel without a maid," I said.

"Diamonds or emeralds are the only stones that complement a black dress," she said. "I see you only have rubies."

"Or pearls," I pointed out.

She sniffed. "Pearls are never worn in the evening. Then it must be the rubies, I suppose." She sighed as she removed them from my jewel case and draped them around my neck. "That will have to do. You have no perfume?"

"Also left at home," I said. "Just some eau de cologne for the journey."

"One cannot wear eau de cologne at the dinner table," she said firmly. "Tomorrow I will see what perfumes my contessa has tired of."

Golly, I was to be the poor relation. Pitied and donated to. This had to stop right now. "Please, Gerda, I'm sure you mean well," I said, "but I'm only here for a few days and I really came to be with a sick friend."

"The contessa would not want a fellow Englishwoman to look inferior to Continental people, I am sure," she said. "She is proud of her heritage. We must all be proud of our heritage. Especially Aryan people like you and me when we are among non-Aryans."

She removed the towel that had been covering my shoulders, took a clothes brush from the dressing table and whisked it a few times. "Yes," she said. "You are now ready. You may go down to join the others. But please take care on the stairs. This skirt is quite narrow."

I was being dismissed. I found myself thinking back to Queenie with great fondness. True, she was hopeless as a maid. It was true she had ironed my velvet the wrong way, burned a hole in another of my dresses, unraveled my knitted skirt and generally destroyed most of my clothing. But if having an efficient maid meant feeling as if I was being lectured by Nanny in the nursery, then I'd choose Queenie any day.

As I came out of my bedroom the door next to mine opened and to my horror I saw Rudi emerge, looking devastatingly handsome in tails.

"How fortuitous," he said. "We are neighbors. Tonight we shall lie next to each other like two peas in a pod. How delectable. So convenient."

I wanted to say we were not going to be lying next to each other, but I didn't think I could do it without blushing. And a thought did go through my mind that someone more skilled than me could arrange a romantic tryst with Rudi and get him to confess where he had hidden the photographs. I was not about to try it. I was also trying to remember whether there was a lock on my bedroom door. Oh dear. I hoped so.

As we came to the better-lit part of the corridor he examined me and exclaimed, "You look very nice. Quite the sophisticated lady. Now I shall no longer believe you to be the innocent schoolgirl. I think you have been hiding your true nature from me, Lady Georgiana."

"I have no reason to hide anything from you, Count Rudolf," I said.

For a moment his eyes held mine, questioning. Then he laughed, a gay, carefree laugh. "You really are quite delightful. So no more of this girlish pretense, my lady. I am sure you would enjoy a romantic encounter just as much as I would. And I assure you I am very good at it. There are ladies here who would testify to the fact."

"I told you that I am engaged to be married," I said, channeling my great-grandmother to the best of my ability.

He was still laughing. "What has that to do with anything? All the better when a woman is married. Then she has nothing to worry about."

"Apart from her husband finding out," I said.

"Some men are less open-minded than others, this is true." We had reached the top of the stairs. He took my elbow and helped me down, step by step. Since I couldn't shake him off without risking falling down the staircase I had to endure his closeness. And I was thinking about what he had just said and the snatch of conversation I had overheard coming from his room earlier that day. Surely there were no women here other than my mother, Paolo's mother and Camilla. And my mother had been in the garden with me. That meant that the woman's voice I had heard in Rudi's room had to have been Camilla's. Camilla and Rudi . . . So my mother had been wrong about Camilla being straightlaced.

I broke off these thoughts as the sound of laughter came from the long gallery to our right. Rudi had not released my elbow and I couldn't think of an efficient way to shake him off. As we entered, the laughter ceased as suddenly as if somebody had flipped a switch. To my horror I saw that all eyes had turned to me. And among those staring was Mrs. Simpson.

"Good heavens, Georgiana," she said. "I almost didn't recognize you. You've certainly grown up in a hurry. Has Count Rudolf been teaching you a thing or two?"

"Count Rudolf has done nothing more than escort me down the stairs in a very tight skirt," I said. I was trying to gauge whether Gerda had actually asked her mistress's permission to lend me the dress. "How nice to see you again, Mrs. Simpson. And you too, sir." I nodded to the Prince of Wales.

"Good to see you too, young Georgie," he said. "And looking absolutely spiffing too. Quite the elegant lady these days. But what are you doing in this neck of the woods? I was quite surprised when Mother wrote that you'd be joining us."

"I was quite surprised too, sir," I said, returning his smile. "I had tea with your mother and happened to mention that I'd be coming here to visit a friend who is currently in a clinic nearby, and of course she thought it would be lovely for me to join you. I didn't have much say in the matter."

"One doesn't, with the queen," Mrs. Simpson said. "She certainly likes to get her way. She didn't instruct you to push me off a cliff, did she?"

The others laughed a trifle nervously. I couldn't think of a suitable answer to this and was glad when the prince replied. "If she'd only get to know you, I'm sure she'd like you, Wallis. She's just being stubborn."

"But are you not still married to Mr. Simpson?" Paolo's mother asked.

There was an intake of breath and a moment's silence before she said stiffly, "We are officially separated these days until a divorce can be amicably arranged. He has no wish to continue the marriage any more than I do. He's gone home to America and here I am, footloose and fancy-free." And she turned to give the prince an adoring glance.

I heaved a sigh of relief. They weren't legally divorced yet. There would be no sneaking off to hold a secret ceremony. This thought was followed by one of annoyance that the queen had put me through this for no good reason. I wondered how soon I could make my excuses and go back to Belinda. Then I remembered Mummy. Bugger. (Yes, I know I should not even think words like that, but it did seem the most apt sentiment.) The moment she had entered my mind we heard footsteps tapping on the marble and Mummy herself came down the stairs, her arm slipped through Max's. They looked a very handsome couple, he in his white tie and tails, she in red silk evening pajamas and a bright red feather in her hair. In her other hand she trailed a white mink stole.

"Well, well, if it isn't the actress herself," Mrs. Simpson said. "How are you, Claire, honey? Looking good for your age."

"And you look good for yours, Wallis," Mummy replied, her comment delivered with undertones as only a great actress can. "I have never been better. I have found the man of my dreams and we are going to get married. What could be more perfect?"

"I congratulate you," Mrs. Simpson said. "Have you learned to speak German yet?"

"I'm taking lessons. And Max's English is making great strides."

"A stride? This is a walk, no?" the German general asked.

And we were into another discussion on the silliness of the English language. I was relieved when the dinner gong sounded and we followed the prince and Mrs. Simpson into the dining room. I was even more relieved to find I was seated beside my cousin and the silent German officer Klinker. Rudi was on the other side of the table between Mrs. Simpson and the priest. I thought that was a just punishment for his sins. I glanced down the table and realized that there were thirteen of us. Surely that was a bad omen. I should never have come.

The dinner passed easily enough, course after course with a never-ending stream of antipasti—prosciutto, tiny mussels and clams, stuffed baby tomatoes, spicy sausage. Then followed mushroom risotto, veal in cream sauce, a rich sponge cake, fruit and then a cheese board to die for. Each course was accompanied by the correct wine and I began to feel a little woozy by the end of the meal.

The wooziness grew worse when we went through after the meal and were served after-dinner limoncello and chocolates. Mrs. Simpson complained that they had had a long day in the fresh air and she was ready to turn in, so I took my cue from her and excused myself as well. I gave a sigh of relief when Rudi did not attempt to follow me. I let myself into my room and my heart jumped as a figure stepped out to greet me. It was Gerda, who had been waiting, apparently in the dark.

"The evening was satisfactory, I hope?" she said as she took off my rubies and removed the pins from my hair.

"Very satisfactory, thank you. The dress was much admired. Please thank the contessa for me for allowing me to wear it."

From her silence I got the feeling that she had not asked the contessa and that Camilla might be feeling seriously miffed. She continued to undress me with terrifying efficiency, immediately putting my shoes on the top shelf of the wardrobe and hanging up the dress. "You may wish to wear it again," she said.

Then she helped me into my nightdress and turned back the bed. "Will that be all, my lady? May I bring you up some hot milk to help you sleep?"

"No, thank you. I'm sure I shall sleep very well. It's lovely to be taken care of so well," I said.

"It is my job. For this I am trained," she said. "I take it you would like a cup of tea in the morning, as this seems to be the custom of English ladies."

"Yes, please. I do like morning tea."

"At what hour shall I bring this?"

"When is breakfast usually served?" I asked.

"Around nine o'clock," she said. "Should I bring your tea at eight?"

"Thank you."

"Then I bid you a pleasant good night." She gave a little bow and let herself out, leaving me feeling breathless. I crossed the room and turned the key in the lock. At least I'd not have to worry about any nighttime visits from Count Rudi!

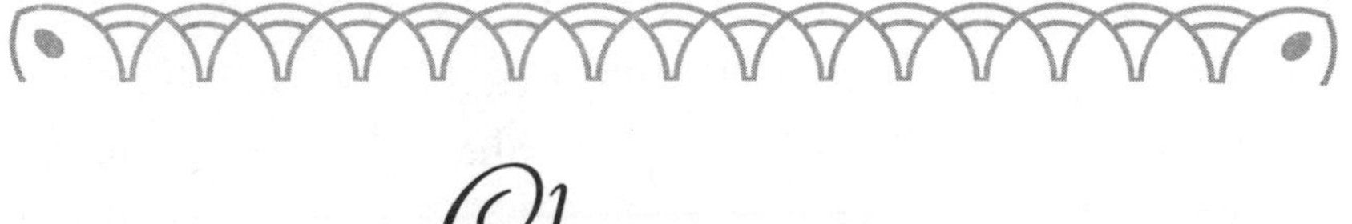

Chapter 13

The night of April 21
My room at Villa Fiori

Trying to sleep but I am so wound up. If I could just slip away and escape back to Belinda I would do so. But I promised my mother . . . damn.

I wandered around the room for a while, reluctant to turn the light out, feeling uneasy and unsettled. I went over to the French windows and opened them, having been used to sleeping with the windows open even in a howling gale from a childhood at Castle Rannoch. Then I stepped out onto my little balcony. The scent of jasmine was heady in the night air. The gardens below were bathed in darkness. It was like being in the middle of nowhere. I stood there, suddenly overwhelmed by a feeling of loneliness. What was I doing here when I could have been chatting with Belinda, or even keeping Lord Kilhenny company in Ireland? Anywhere rather than this. It was clear now that the queen had jumped to conclusions and that the prince and Mrs. Simpson were not planning a secret wedding here.

So there was no good reason for me to stay. Except that Mummy had foisted her latest problem onto me. It was her own fault, I thought angrily. If she had a tryst with another man when she should have been faithful to Max, then she should suffer the consequences. I should just pack up and leave in the morning and go back to the friendly little room near the clinic.

But of course I knew that I couldn't leave Mummy in the lurch. I would try to help her. It was that Rannoch sense of duty that had been rammed down my throat from the day I could toddle. Although how I was ever going to find those photographs in a place like this was mind-boggling.

"Damn and blast," I muttered. I should point out that I swear only when alone, again as a result of my upbringing and having my mouth washed out with soap by Nanny for once saying "bloody."

A night breeze blew up and I pulled my robe more firmly around me. I glanced across to make sure that Rudi was not watching me from his balcony. I was relieved to see that there was too big a gap between us to make a leap across possible. At least that was one thing I didn't have to worry about and I could leave my window open.

I gave one last look across the gardens. If only Darcy had been here it would have been a romantic scene. Why did he have to be so far away?

"I want to go home," I whispered to myself, but the problem was that I no longer knew where home was. One day I'd have a home with Darcy and I would be safe and loved. I'd just have to be patient a little longer.

I went inside, pulled the French doors half closed, climbed into bed and turned out the bedside lamp. I still felt queasy from the big, rich meal and just prayed that sleep would come. Outside my window I heard the sigh of the breeze, the rustle of wind in tall trees, the distant hoot of an owl. From down the hallway I heard voices, the sound of doors closing. I lay there, tense, waiting to hear if someone was trying my door to see if it was unlocked, but the sounds had died away to complete silence.

"You'll be all right," I told myself. "There are other people sleeping on this corridor."

I MUST HAVE drifted off to sleep because I awoke to the smallest of sounds. I sat up, instantly alert. My gaze went to the door. A narrow strip of light showed beneath it and no shadow seemed to be blocking that light. Then I heard the sound again—the slightest of squeaks of a rusty hinge as one of the French doors was opened. It was still completely dark. Had it just been a trick of the wind that had opened that door?

Surely there was no way that Rudi could have made it across the big gap between our rooms. The walls were smooth stone. All the same I was going to be ready for him. I considered finding something to use as a weapon—the jug from the washbasin? The statue in the niche above my bed? Then I decided that much as I'd like the satisfaction of bringing either of them down on his head it was too risky. He was an odious man but that statue was marble. I couldn't risk killing him. So I slipped silently out of bed and retreated toward the door. My hand closed around the key, ready to turn it, scream and flee if necessary. If someone had come into my room, at least he would have as hard a time finding me as I was having seeing him.

I stood there for what seemed an age, hearing and seeing nothing. I was imagining things, I told myself. The wind had blown open the French door. I should go back to bed. I had just made up my mind to leave the security of the door handle when I heard the floorboards creak. Then I thought I heard somebody whisper, "Georgie." Suddenly I felt more angry than afraid. I was not going to be intimidated by a lecherous blackmailer like Count Rudolf. My hand left the doorknob and slid across the wall, trying to locate the light switch. I found it and took a deep breath. Then I flipped the switch, while saying in my most Queen Victoria–like voice, "How dare you come into my room! You'd better go back the way you came instantly or I shall open this door and waken the entire household. And have you thrown out like the despicable person you are!"

I stood blinking in the light from the bulb high in the ceiling above. Nobody was standing near the French windows. Then I looked over to my bed on the opposite wall and let out a little gasp. He was actually sitting on my bed, presumably thinking that was where he'd find me.

"Caught like a rat in a trap!" I said. "Now you'll be sorry."

As I turned the key in the lock he stood up. "Wait, Georgie," he whispered. "It's me. Darcy."

I froze, staring at him as if I were seeing a ghost. Darcy was standing there, dressed in a black fisherman's jersey and black trousers, his dark curls windswept.

"What on earth are you doing here?" I blurted out as I went over to him. He put a finger to his lips, warning me to keep my voice down.

"How about 'It's lovely to see you, my darling?'" he whispered.

"Of course it's lovely to see you," I whispered back. "But why creep in like this? I thought you were the odious Count Rudolf. You're lucky I didn't clobber you with that statue. I was thinking of doing so."

"Rudolf? Has he been creeping into your room?"

"This is my first night here, but he certainly hinted earlier that it was convenient that our rooms were next to each other . . . so that we would be lying next to each other, as he put it."

"I'll kill him," Darcy muttered.

"Don't worry, I locked my door. And I was prepared to scream the place down."

"So I heard." He grinned.

We were now standing facing each other beside my bed. My greatest desire was to throw myself into his arms, but my heart was still racing from my fright and I was still angry that he had put me through this. "Why didn't you tell me you were coming in a more conventional manner? You could have written, or even sent a telegram, or do you make a habit of creeping into ladies' boudoirs at night?"

"Only when I have to," he replied. "You see, I can't let anybody know I'm here. I've been spying on the place. I was completely taken aback when I saw you arriving today. I had no idea you'd be involved in this. What are you doing here?"

"Not my idea, I assure you. I came out to be with Belinda. Her baby is due quite soon. Then the queen asked me to spy on the Prince of Wales. She had got it into her head that he was planning a secret marriage to Mrs. Simpson so she had me invited to this house party. But more to the point, what are you doing here?"

Darcy crossed the room silently and closed the French doors.

"More serious stuff than that, I'm afraid," he said when he came back to me. "I considered staying hidden and not letting you know that I was here, but then I decided that you could be most helpful to me, someone actually in the house, in a position to overhear conversations."

I sat on the bed and he sat down beside me. "What's going on, Darcy?" I whispered.

"That's what I've been sent to find out," he said. "You might know that there has been an important international meeting in Stresa. Top-level men from England, France and Italy discussing what to do about the Nazi threat to Europe."

"I did hear something about it," I said.

He nodded. "It seemed too much of a coincidence that several high-ranking Germans just happened to be at a house party with Count di Marola, who is Mussolini's top adviser, and with the Prince of Wales, immediately following that meeting."

"They might all be friends of Paolo and Camilla."

"Might, but they are not. I presume the Germans must have met in Berlin society, but no indication that they have met the Italians or the Prince of Wales before. So why now? That's what I've been sent to find out."

"But how are you supposed to do that if you are not part of the house party yourself?" I asked.

"I've been keeping an eye on them as closely as I dare," he said.

I stared at him and suddenly my face lit up. "You were the gardener who was watching me."

He nodded. "Quite right. I nearly dropped my rake when I spotted you."

"And I thought how good you looked without your shirt on. And I had to remind myself that I'm almost a married woman."

"I'll remember that any future gardener needs to be over sixty," he said dryly.

"How on earth do you get away with pretending to be an Italian gardener? Your Italian isn't that good, is it?"

"Simple, my darling. I told the other gardeners that I have been lent from Countess Camilla's house in England as she wanted the gardens to have a more English feel to them. People like gardeners seem to accept what they are told if it seems plausible. Of course, the only fly in the ointment has been that I've actually had to do some work."

"And developed muscles. As I've noticed," I said, smiling at him. "But why go to such lengths? Why not write to Camilla and ask to be invited? She is some sort of relative of yours, I gather."

"For that very reason," he said. "She knows who I am. People would be suspicious of why I was here. It might change their plans."

"What kind of plans?"

"That's what I'm here to find out."

I was still trying to control my racing thoughts. My brain didn't function well in the middle of the night, after several glasses of strong wine and with the man I loved only a few inches away from me. "High-ranking Germans?" I said. "Is Count Rudolf a high-ranking German?"

"Let's just say he moves in Hitler's inner circle," Darcy said, "and he's the sort of person who knows what's going on in Berlin. He most certainly picks up gossip to report back to the Nazis. They are quite ruthless, you know. People cross them and people disappear."

"So Rudi is Hitler's little spy? Yes, I can see that," I said. I was about to blurt out that he was also a blackmailer, but I changed my mind at the last second. I didn't think that Darcy had a high opinion of my mother. And even though I didn't think too highly of her myself, filial loyalty made me keep quiet now. I moved on instead. "But don't tell me that boring German general is a high-ranking official!"

"Top military strategist to Herr Hitler, so we're told."

I frowned. "Military strategist? But they were disarmed after the Great War. Surely they can't be planning any sort of military action now."

"They are busy rearming themselves at an alarming rate," he said. "In fact, your mother's beau, Max von Strohheim . . ."

"He's not a Nazi, is he?"

"Maybe not one of them, but he's getting awfully rich while his factories turn out tanks and guns."

I looked at him in horror. "Are you sure? I thought his factories made machinery and motorbikes and things."

"Oh yes, they do. But we suspect those legitimate enterprises are cover for the weapons."

"Crikey," I exclaimed before I remembered that I had forbidden myself to say that word any longer. "I wonder if my mother knows? And Granddad—it would kill him if his daughter married a Nazi sympathizer. He still hates the Germans because my uncle, his only son, was killed on the Somme."

"Von Strohheim may be more opportunist than sympathizer," Darcy said. "But he's clearly important enough to Germany to be invited here."

"I don't understand," I said. "You said England just had a meeting with Italy to discuss ways to combat the Nazi threat. So Italy should be on our side. They don't like the Germans."

"You forget that Mussolini is a fellow Fascist. Hitler looks up to him—admires him."

I thought about this. "Darcy, you keep saying 'Hitler this and Hitler that.' But he seems like such a funny little man to me. Surely he can't really be dangerous."

"Oh, I don't think you should underestimate him," Darcy said. "He understands the German people. He knows how their pride was crushed with the defeat in 1918. He knows how they've suffered under reparations, how they've lost their life savings under devaluation. They want to believe in somebody. If he promises he's going to make Germany great again, they'll follow him."

"So you think this is a serious meeting between Hitler's top chap and Mussolini's man?"

"I do."

A thought just occurred to me. "But the Prince of Wales? Where does he come into this?"

Darcy shook his head. "We have no idea. We were as curious as you are when we learned that he was coming here. This isn't his usual type of hedonistic party with beautiful people. He doesn't seem to be a close friend of any of the participants. So this is where you can be really helpful to me. I can only overhear snatches of conversation out in the grounds or near open windows. You can overhear whole conversations. Nobody sees you as a threat. You can wander into rooms by mistake, claim to be looking for a missing book in the library."

I went to say "crikey" again but swallowed it back. "You want me to be a real spy," was what I managed to say.

"Something like that." He took my hand. "I don't think you'll be in any kind of danger, or I wouldn't ask you to do this. And I'll be close by. I'm bunking with the other grounds staff in the cottages at the back of the property. You can actually get a glimpse of my roof from your balcony—which was how I knew which room you were staying in, by the way. I spotted you when you came out earlier, and then again, rather more flimsily attired. You should be more careful when you come out in your night attire, my lady. You never know who might see you." His hand brushed mine, the gentlest of touches, but it sent shivers up my spine.

I looked up at him and our eyes met. "I've missed you," he said. "God, you look desirable tonight." He sighed, his finger still casually stroking the back of my hand. "But I should probably be getting back. You need your sleep and so do I, although I can't say the local gardeners work particularly hard. They seem to lean on their shovels and smoke for most of the day. But we do have to be up at six."

Now that he was actually here, beside me, and I could feel his warm breath on my cheek, I was reluctant to let him go. "So how can I get in touch with you if I need you?" I asked. "I can't just casually stroll over to the gardeners' cottages."

"Why don't you leave a towel or something over the chair on the balcony?" he said. "That way I'll know."

Something had just struck me. "How did you get up here in the first place?"

"Climbed the wisteria. Good sturdy plant that."

"Goodness, Darcy, be careful, please," I said, then I added, "Oh no, I've just thought of something. If you can climb up the wisteria to my balcony that means that other people could too, including horrible Rudolf."

He nodded. "You should probably keep your French doors shut—yes, before you say it I know you've been brought up to sleep with the windows open, but in this case . . ."

"You're right," I said. "But if I close the French doors, how can you get in?"

"I'll tap, gently," he said. "I'll only be coming if you've summoned me."

I put my hand up to touch his face. "I feel so much better knowing that you're close by," I said. "I can tell Rudolf that if he tries anything I'll summon my beloved to challenge him to a duel."

"Don't do that," he said hurriedly. "From what I've heard he really has been challenged to many duels in Berlin and Paris, and usually wins. He's a good swordsman, and a good shot."

"Oh, that's right. I remember now that he told me he enjoyed fighting duels. What are you good at that he's not?" I asked.

"Conkers," he said. "I was the village champion in Kilhenny."

"Conkers at dawn, then." I started to laugh.

Without warning he took my face in his hands and kissed me. The kiss was full of the hunger and longing of being apart. We fell back together onto my pillow. I could feel his heart thudding against mine. Desire was singing in my head. Nothing mattered anymore. I knew that all I wanted was Darcy to make love to me. But at the same time that small voice of Rannoch duty started to whisper in my head that we were passing the point of no return and . . .

Darcy raised his lips from mine. "We should stop right now, or I don't think we'll be able to," he said breathlessly. "This is neither the time nor the place. Sorry, I got a bit carried away."

"You weren't the only one," I laughed uneasily.

"I noticed." He was eyeing me with amusement. "I'm beginning to think that we might need a chaperon for you when I'm away."

"There's only ever been one man for me, Darcy," I said. "I can't wait until we're married."

"Neither can I," he said. "Oh, I see now. This was blackmail, was it?"

I sat up, staring at him in dismay. Had he an inkling of what Rudolf had been doing? How had he found out? "Blackmail?" The word came out as a squeak. "What do you mean?"

"The reason you came here. You do something for the queen and she makes sure you are given permission to marry. Tit for tat."

"I suppose that did cross my mind," I agreed.

He slid off the bed and stood up. "I must go. Take care of yourself."

I nodded, still reluctant to let him go. "You take care of yourself too. If the German Fascists are ruthless then I'm sure the Italians are too. You never know who else might be working here undercover."

"True," he said. "But don't worry. I'm always careful."

I crossed the room with him and he opened a French door. As he was about to leave I put a warning hand to halt him, and peered out first. No lights were burning. As far as I could see in the light of a waxing moon the other balconies were empty. I nodded to Darcy. He gave me a peck on the cheek, then swung himself over the railing with ease. I heard leaves flutter to the ground as he climbed down the creeper. Then I detected a soft footfall on the gravel beneath. I gave a little sigh and retreated into my bedroom.

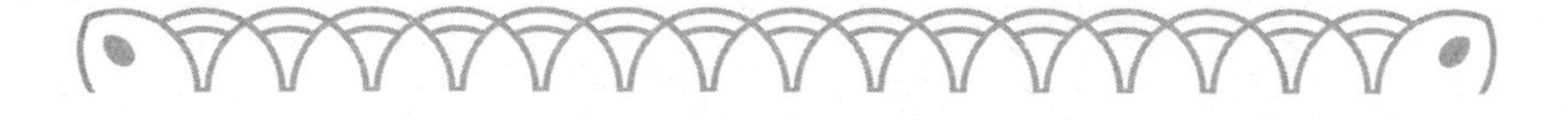

Chapter 14

Monday, April 22, 1935

Now that I know Darcy is nearby I feel so much better about everything!

The next thing I knew I heard the doorknob being jiggled. I jumped up, instantly awake and ready to fend off the amorous Rudi, only to find it was broad daylight. There was now a light tap at my door. I went over and turned the key. Gerda stood there looking disapproving.

"I am sorry to disturb you like this, Lady Georgiana," she said. "But I was not expecting to find the door locked. I bring your morning tea." She placed the tray on the bedside table, went over to the French doors and drew back the curtains. "It will be a fine day, I think. A little mist but warm later." She went over to my wardrobe and opened it. "The skirt and blouse are suitable for this morning, I think," she said, bringing out two hangers. "It is a pity you did not bring trousers with you. Smart ladies wear them these days, even on occasions like this, you know. So useful if you go out in the boat."

"I'm afraid I possess no smart trousers," I said. "Only tweeds suitable for tramping through heather on shoots."

She made a little noise of disapproval. "The skirt, then. I leave you to enjoy your tea. Ring for me when you wish to dress and I will assist you."

Of course there was no way I was going to summon her back to put on my blouse and skirt. I drank my tea, which was very weak by English standards, then I went down the hall to have a bath. Fortunately, I didn't encounter Rudi or anybody else when I was in my dressing gown; in fact, the rest of the household seemed to be still asleep. I dressed, brushed my hair and went downstairs. The dining room stood deserted. Breakfast had not been laid and I wondered where it might be served. It also occurred to me that this gave me a good chance to do a little snooping on my mother's behalf. If I was seen by the staff I could tell them I was looking for breakfast.

I moved swiftly through the dining room, but the only hiding places were behind statues in niches. I realized then that Rudi could not risk hiding the photographs where the servants would routinely dust and clean. The hiding place had to be clever and not likely to be disturbed. I moved through to the elegant salon and poked around inside vases, behind paintings on the walls and under side tables. Nothing.

I wandered through to the library. What a daunting room that was. He could have hidden the photographs between the pages in any of those hundreds of books. But then he'd have to remember which one, so there had to be some rhyme or reason to it. On the end of a row, maybe, or his favorite color, or a title that meant something to him. I stared at the book titles. They were either in Italian or Latin. I managed to translate Dante's *Divine Comedy*. Perhaps Rudi would have chosen something simple like that, I thought, and took it down from the shelf. The pages smelled old and musty and there was nothing tucked inside the book. I returned it and continued to browse, but gave up after a while. I couldn't take out every single book. This needed more thought and, what's more, I was decidedly hungry.

It seemed to me most likely that he would hide anything important in his own bedroom, and if I could lock my door, presumably he could lock his. If Mummy could only lure him out onto the lake today, I might have a better chance. I came out into the hallway, listened for sounds of other people being awake and heard the clinking of cutlery. I followed those sounds to the lake view room and saw that a table had been laid with coffee and various types of rolls. It seemed as if we might not be getting a hot breakfast.

I had just buttered a crispy roll and added apricot jam when I heard the sound of feet approaching and Paolo appeared, escorting his mother.

"We just come from mass," he said to me.

"You did not wish to attend?" his mother asked with her usual critical frown.

"I'm not Catholic," I said.

"But I am told you will marry a Catholic," she said. "It is good to understand our habits. Are you already under instruction?"

"Instruction?" I asked.

"But naturally. Instruction in the faith is necessary before marriage. Our priest can instruct you while you are here."

The thought of being anywhere alone with that scary priest was not appealing and I couldn't see Darcy getting up for morning mass every day either. "I am not sure I'm going to convert," I said and saw her look of horror.

"You will not take your husband's religion?"

"I'm really not sure," I said hastily.

Paolo seated his mother and poured her a cup of coffee, thus avoiding further interrogation. When his uncle Cosimo joined us and started a conversation in Italian with the dowager countess, Paolo came to sit with me in the bay window.

"So how is our friend Belinda these days?" he asked, glancing over to see if the others were listening. "I think about her often. Such a fun-loving girl, wasn't she?"

I nodded. "Yes. Fun-loving."

"She must be married by now, I suppose? Some chap will have snapped her up."

"No, she's still single. Hasn't found the right man yet."

"A pity." He stared out past me to the lake, which was still shrouded in mist. "That she was not suitable for my family, I mean. I liked her a lot. I think we could have had a happy life. Religion can be so annoying, don't you think?"

"I hope it won't be for me and my fiancé," I said.

"Don't misunderstand what I say," he said hastily because his mother and uncle had now fallen silent. "Camilla is a good person. A devout person. But one could never call her fun."

I thought of the conversation I had overheard in Rudi's bedroom. Paolo didn't seem like the sort of person who would easily forgive a straying wife. I was in midthought about this when Camilla herself entered. She was wearing navy linen trousers and a striped nautical top with a white jacket over it. Her face looked quite tense but broke into a smile when she saw me.

"Oh, Georgie. You're already up. Lovely. Have you had something to eat? Should I ask Cook to boil an egg for you?"

Much as I would have loved an egg I told her that I was quite happy with the rolls.

"It took me a while to get used to Continental habits," she said. "How are you, *mio caro*?" She put a hand on Paolo's shoulder. "I'm sorry I didn't make it to mass today. I must have overslept."

Again I shot a look at her. Was there a reason for her oversleeping? She did look quite pale and tired. Then I wondered if there might be another reason—perhaps there was a baby on the way. I wasn't sure how long they had been married, but producing the heir seems to be the most important thing for great families.

She poured herself a cup of coffee and came over to join us by the window. "I hope this mist will clear," she said. "Some of our guests were suggesting we take a picnic to one of the islands today."

"Good idea," Paolo said. "We'll have to wait and see. No sense in making the trip if there is no view."

"Absolutely not." She turned to me. "You haven't been to Isola Bella yet, have you, Georgie?" I shook my head. "The gardens are so beautiful, and the view back to the shore—stunning."

I realized I'd have to find an excuse not to join them at the picnic, but I couldn't claim illness now or she might put it off until I was well. So I gave an excited sort of smile and went back to my roll. One by one our fellow guests appeared. Camilla made the announcement that a picnic on the island had been suggested.

It wasn't met with much enthusiasm in some quarters. "Honey, we were on a boat most of yesterday," Mrs. Simpson said. "I don't think I'm keen on another watery day."

"Oh, but you haven't seen Isola Bella," I said, coming to Camilla's aid. "I'm told it's spectacular."

"I think I'd rather go shopping." Mrs. Simpson turned to the prince. "Is there a town or something around here where one can buy things? Shoes and gloves, I mean. I do adore Italian leather."

"The closest big town would be Milan," Camilla said.

"Wallis, I'm not motoring all the way back to Milan so you can buy more shoes," my cousin said. "You must have a thousand pairs anyway."

"But shopping makes me happy, David." She reached out her hand to pat his leg.

"I thought I made you happy," he said.

"You do, my darling. But so does shopping."

I thought I detected a derisive snort from the dowager countess.

"We'll stop over in Milan on the way home," the Prince of Wales promised.

"Didn't your father want you to rush back for . . . whatever it was this time?" Mrs. Simpson said with annoyance in her voice.

"I do have duties to perform, you know. My father is not a well man. I have to take my share of the family firm's responsibilities." He gave a nervous chuckle.

"I do not think this will be a good day for boating on the lake." The general peered out into the mist. "This fog is thick. Dangerous, I believe."

"It should lift later," Camilla said. "It usually does. But I'll hold off on telling Cook about the picnic until we're absolutely sure we're going."

"Why don't you ladies go?" Max said. "It seems to be your idea."

"Oh wonderful, you want to send us off into the fog alone," Mummy replied tartly. "Now that's chivalry for you."

This made everyone laugh and broke any tension there might have been. We went our separate ways after breakfast, but I couldn't attempt to do any snooping with guests wandering in and out of rooms and reading newspapers in odd corners. I just had to hope that the mist would lift and they would go. By eleven it was still cold and misty and I despaired of anything happening that day. Then miraculously, around noon the last strands of mist dissipated and the sun shone from a brilliant blue sky.

"You see, we can go after all," Mummy said, standing up to look out at the lake. "I knew it would work out."

"I'll go and tell Cook," Camilla said. "And, Paolo, you should tell Marco that we will want both the launches. We can't all pack into one."

"If you're sure about this," he said.

"Why wouldn't I be sure? It's a perfect chance to show our guests the beauties of the area." She sounded rather huffy as she went off.

Hampers were carried down to the dock. I waited until the advance party had already set off down the drive, then I cornered Camilla. "I hope you don't mind if I don't join you," I said. "I've just come down with one of my headaches, and the only thing to do is to lie in a dark room until it passes."

She was instantly solicitous. "Oh, you poor thing. I get migraines too sometimes. So beastly, aren't they? What can we get you?"

"Nothing, thank you." I tried to sound weak and suffering. "Please don't worry about me. Look after your guests. I'll be fine if I can just rest alone."

"If you're sure. I don't mind staying back to keep you company. I've been to the island hundreds of times."

"Oh no. Please go," I said. "There's really nothing anyone can do and I hate to spoil your day. I will be fine if I can just rest for a while, I promise."

"Very well." She nodded and went to find the others.

I watched from the window as they were helped, one by one, onto the sleek teak launches and off they went. A feeling of euphoria came over me. I was free to get on with my task. And the first thing I wanted to try was to get into Rudi's room. I had just gone upstairs and was standing in the hallway outside his door when Gerda appeared behind me in that unnerving way of hers.

"Lady Georgiana?" she demanded.

I spun around, trying not to look guilty. "Oh, Gerda. I didn't go with the others because I am not feeling well," I said. "I'm just on my way to lie down."

"So the contessa told me. I came to see if you would like some broth, maybe? Or an egg?"

I realized that I'd better eat or I'd get nothing until dinner. "Thank you. I should have something nourishing," I said as I opened my own door. "Maybe I could manage broth and an egg."

"I will fetch immediately." She set off briskly down the hall. I went into my room, closed the drapes and lay on the bed, trying to look like the Lady of the Camellias. She returned with a small bowl of clear soup, a boiled egg and thinly sliced bread. As soon as she had gone I gobbled them up. Not exactly enough food for a healthy young woman, but it would have to do.

She came for my dishes a little later and nodded approval that I had eaten everything. "Soon you will be better, I am sure," she said.

"I hope so. Now I'll sleep while it's nice and quiet and I'm not likely to be disturbed." I hoped she took the gentle hint.

I waited until she had gone, then I tiptoed to Rudi's door. The handle didn't turn. Ah, so he had locked it and taken the key with him. Then it occurred to me that my key might just fit. I removed it from my door and tried it. But no luck. The darned thing didn't budge. Why had I never acquired the skill of opening a lock with a hairpin, such as one reads about in books? Actually this lock was so old and imposing that I didn't think a mere hairpin would ever do the trick. I walked away, reluctantly. I thought it was all too possible that Rudi was indeed keeping incriminating evidence in his own room.

But I had to go on searching. I waited a little longer to see if Gerda was going to reappear, then I crept down the stairs, looking out for servants. With any luck they were having an afternoon siesta in their own rooms while their masters were away. I tiptoed into the library and tried the map drawers, even climbed the ladder to the gallery, but after a good hour of searching I came up empty-handed.

I wasn't sure what to do next. Then I remembered the little marble temple in the grounds. Mummy had said that Rudi liked to spend time out there. How conveniently far from the villa. I let myself out through the French doors onto the terrace and stood for a while, staring up at the balconies above. I observed the sturdy wisteria up which Darcy had climbed. Rudi's balcony had no sort of creeper. Thank heavens for that, I thought. At least I didn't have to worry that he could climb down from his balcony and then up to mine. But also I had no way of getting into his room, even if the shutters weren't closed, which they were. Then I pretended to stroll aimlessly, admiring flowers, just in case I was being observed, but all the time heading in the direction of the little octagonal building.

It lay conveniently behind a high topiary box hedge, on one side of the swimming pool. Its door faced the pool and as far as I could tell was not visible from the main villa. What's more, it was not locked. The knob turned easily in my hand and I stepped inside. In contrast to the opulence of the villa this was a place of uttermost simplicity. It consisted of one octagonal room, lit by thin arched windows. The walls were white marble; so was the floor. It felt unpleasantly cold and a little damp. I looked around me. The only furniture was a large round table in the center of the room, covered in a bright woven cloth, several upright chairs dotted around the room and a thin chest against one wall on which rested a tray with a full decanter and glasses. On the center table was an ashtray, a box of matches and a pack of playing cards. So somebody must come out here from time to time. I couldn't think what sort of appeal a place like this might have. There was no bed or sofa, so no use as a site for a tryst. Then I realized that it smelled of tobacco so I presumed this was where male visitors came when they wanted to smoke in peace.

I looked beneath the tablecloth. I explored every drawer of the small chest, but they only contained an extra ashtray and another pack of playing cards. I even looked under the chair cushions. But again I found no incriminating evidence hidden there. I had just decided that Rudi would not have hidden photographs in a room with so few hiding places and I was wasting my time, when I heard voices. Male voices. A deep man's laugh. I peeked out of the window and saw a group of men coming around the box hedge. At first I thought they would be gardeners and I would be safe where I was, but then, as they came into full view, to my horror I recognized them. Leading the way were Paolo's uncle with the two German officers, and behind them Rudi, Max and the Prince of Wales. What's more, they were heading straight for the little temple.

Chapter 15

Monday, April 22
In a small marble temple at Villa Fiori

Help! When I agreed to be Darcy's spy I never thought it would entail anything like this!

I had no time to wonder what they were doing back from their boat ride so soon. In fact, I had no time to think rationally. If I'd been closer to the door I might have opened it to greet them, bluffing it out with something breezy like, "Oh hello, you're back, I see. Had a good day? I thought this place might be good to take a rest, but it's rather dreary, isn't it?"

But they were going to reach the door before I could and I simply couldn't face being caught looking embarrassed like this by a group of men, including Max and my cousin. Also I'd have to explain to Camilla why a girl with a bad headache had chosen to go to a cold and damp marble room that smelled of cigar smoke. I looked around like a trapped animal. No curtains at the thin arched windows. No wardrobe. Nowhere to hide. At the last second I saw that the tablecloth reached almost to the floor. I dived under it as the door opened.

"Ach, gut," said General Spitz-Blitzen, entering first. "This room was a good idea. Far from the ears of servants, *nicht?*"

"And it was also dashed clever to claim you wanted to see how fast the boat could go because you were thinking of buying one, Max," the Prince of Wales said. "You knew damned well the women wouldn't want to get their hair windblown."

"And they will be hours exploring those gardens on the island," Rudi added.

"Please, we should not speak English," the general said. "My aide, Klinker, does not understand it."

"Well, my German isn't too hot," the prince said.

"Do you gentlemen speak Italian?" Paolo's uncle asked.

It was obvious that they didn't.

"Don't worry. I will translate for Klinker," Rudi said. "I think we can all manage in English besides him."

"Good show," the prince said. "That makes it easier. Now, since we are supposed to be here smoking, we'd better light up cigars. Then someone can bally well tell me what this is all about."

"Take a seat, gentlemen," Rudi said.

Then to my horror they pulled up chairs to sit around the table. It wasn't the biggest of tables and it had one central pillar instead of legs. I pressed myself up against this. Legs and feet appeared on all sides. I saw the highly polished black boots of the general and Klinker, Rudi's Italian suede, the prince's Church's shoes. Max was wearing sensible walking shoes while Paolo's uncle's were clearly Italian and too pointed to be practical. The general immediately stretched out his legs and the tip of his toe hit my thigh.

"Verzeihung," he muttered, apologizing.

I just prayed that they wouldn't all decide to stretch out their legs at once. If I would have felt stupid at being found in the little pavilion, imagine how utterly ridiculous I'd feel being caught hiding under a table. They'd think I was an imbecile!

"Cigarette or cigar, General?" Rudi asked. I heard boxes being opened, a match being struck.

"Hang on, I have my lighter," the prince said. Then, "Damn. I dropped the bloody thing."

I saw a gold cigarette lighter drop to the floor and then bounce toward me, under the table. Any second now someone would bend to retrieve it and I'd be discovered. I grabbed the lighter and quickly put it out toward the edge of the tablecloth.

"Let me retrieve it for you, sir," Rudi's voice said and his elegant hand came down. It swept close to me, almost brushing my ankle. I squeezed myself tighter to the table leg. The hand passed and closed over the lighter.

"Here you are, sir."

"Thanks awfully," said the prince. "Let me light your cigar, General."

For a moment there was silence as cigars were lit and the herby smell of smoke crept down toward me.

"I see that Count Paolo is not with us," Max said. "Is he not privy to why we are here?"

"He is not," Paolo's uncle replied. "He stay behind on the island to look after the ladies. I ask him to favor me and invite my friends. He may suspect, but he is a good boy. He can be trusted."

"I hope so," the general said. "This is too important to take risks."

"So which of you invited me here, on false pretenses?" the Prince of Wales asked. "I can tell you Wallis was quite annoyed when she found that none of our friends would be attending this little shindig."

"I am sorry for the deceit, Your Royal Highness," the general said. "But I assure you it was completely necessary. Count Cosimo will explain."

I heard the Italian clear his throat. "You will know that an important conference just concluded in Stresa?" he said haltingly. "England, France, Italy. Their diplomats met to discuss how to deal with the Nazi threat."

"Yes, my father wanted me to go and open the bally thing," the Prince of Wales said. "Quite put out when I refused, but frankly I didn't see what I could contribute."

"Naturally. Your Highness sensed that this meeting was completely wrong. That was because it was; it was a meeting of the wrong people." This time it was the general's voice. "Why would England and Italy want to form an alliance with France, your old enemy? And England has historic ties with Germany. Is not your own family German, Your Highness? Have not the kings of England been German for two hundred years?"

"That's true enough," the Prince of Wales said, "but there is still plenty of bad feeling about the Great War, you know. We lost a whole generation of young men."

"We too," Max's voice said. "It was a foolish war, a war that neither side wanted or should have started. Over the shooting of an archduke we wipe out millions."

"That was the excuse," the Prince of Wales pointed out. "I'm afraid it was the ambition of my father's cousin the Kaiser that was behind it."

"You are right, Your Highness," the general said. "Over the ambition and pride of a Kaiser a great nation is brought to its knees."

"And I can tell you that my country has no wish to form an alliance with France. Our beloved leader, Il Duce, Signor Mussolini, is a great admirer of Herr Hitler," Paolo's uncle said. "A great admirer of what he is doing in Germany now."

In the background I heard the murmur of Rudi translating for Klinker.

"I understand that you also admire our leader, Herr Hitler, Your Highness," the general said.

"From what I've seen, I'd say the chap knows what he's doing," my cousin said. "He's certainly putting Germany back on the map. Wallis thinks he's brilliant."

"The lady is correct," the general said. "He is a brilliant man. He talks and millions follow. He will make Germany great again, you will see."

"Is that why you asked me here?" the prince said cautiously. "To get me to agree that Hitler is a good thing for Germany?"

"More than that, Highness," Paolo's uncle said. "Much more than that. Mussolini realizes that the true alliance should be between our country and Germany and yours. We are having the conference that really matters, here and now."

Crikey, I thought, holding my breath. Until this moment I had thought that being detected under the table would just be a matter of embarrassment for me. Now I began to think that I might be in real danger. What was happening here might influence the future of our world. These men couldn't risk my telling anyone what I was overhearing now. David wouldn't let anything happen to me, I told myself. But those others—they might want to silence me when my cousin wasn't around. A quick push down the staircase, or even poison in my drink.

The prince cleared his throat. I thought he sounded nervous when he said, "You brought me here to forge a secret alliance with Italy and Germany?"

"Precisely," the general said.

The prince gave an embarrassed little chuckle. "I think you overestimate my power, gentlemen. You have the ear of Mussolini, Count. And you advise Hitler on military matters, General. I have no power at all. I go around and open hospitals and visit factories and tell people they are doing a jolly good job. On special occasions I ride with my parents in a coach through London and people cheer. I am a puppet at best."

"But we hear your father is in poor health," Count Cosimo said. "He may not live much longer and you will be king."

"Yes, but even when I'm king I answer to Parliament."

"But you meet the prime minister regularly. You advise, don't you?" the general said. "And you are an intelligent man. You can see that the best chance for the future of our three nations is to work together. Our common enemy is communism. In Italy the communists are still powerful, are they not, Count Cosimo?"

"They are indeed," Paolo's uncle agreed.

"And in Germany too. You do not have a communist threat in England?"

"We've had a few rabble-rousers, agitators stirring up the working class," the prince agreed.

"Russia is clever. Do not underestimate her," the general said. "Russian agents work in each of our countries to bring down the government and put communism in its place. This is why we must stand together. We can dominate Europe between us. Keep Russia at bay. We will agree not to fight each other. We will stop more blood from being spilled."

The prince cleared his throat again. "I might be able to see the benefit in this, but I have to tell you that Parliament is not likely to listen to my opinion."

"But the British people, they love you, I think," the general continued. "If you get them on your side, they will tell their government what they want."

There was a long silence, then the prince said, "Max, you've been very silent. What do you say?"

"I own factories," Max said. "I make motorcars and machinery and money. It is not my business to run a country. But I tell you that communism will be bad for all of us. The people in Russia live in poverty. They have no motorcars. No luxury. We do not want this. We must fight it together."

"I don't think there is a serious communist threat in England," the prince said with conviction.

"The czar did not think that he was in danger in Russia and look what happened to him," General Spitz-Blitzen said.

Another long pause. "So did Hitler and Mussolini send you here to meet with me?" the prince asked.

"No, they do not know we meet," Paolo's uncle said. "But they will be pleased when they hear what we have done today. Yes, they will be most pleased, of this I am sure."

"What exactly do you want me to do?" the prince asked.

"Make your father see that it will be good for England to have Hitler and Mussolini as friends," the general said. "Tell him that Britain may need strong allies. Together we will stop the spread of communism, *nicht?* We can count on you to tell him this, can we not?"

"I can tell him," the prince said. "Whether he will listen is another matter."

The room was getting smokier by the minute. I could feel my eyes stinging and my nose tickling, but I didn't dare move the hand that anchored me to the table leg. Don't sneeze, I told myself. Whatever you do, don't sneeze.

Of course the moment I thought that, the tickle in my nose became worse. I eased my hand away from where it had been wrapped around the table leg and I pressed it to my nose.

Just when I thought I couldn't hold my breath any longer and a great sneeze would come bursting forth, Max said, "We should not be away too long, in case the women return."

"But we have been having a chin-wag and quiet smoke," the Prince of Wales said.

"We did not wag the chins, I think," the general said. "Oh, English expression. Of course."

"So what happens next?" David asked.

"Nothing. We pretend this meeting has never happened. But

when the moment comes we shall know we can count on you, Your Highness."

"Which moment is this?" the prince asked.

"The moment when alliances must be made, to defend Europe. To stop outside threats."

"I see. You think it will come to that?"

"Yes, I think it will," said the German voice. I wasn't sure this time whether it was the general or Max.

I heard the sound of chairs scraping as they were pushed back on the bare marble. The table rocked as the men stood up.

"We should not leave together, I think," the old Italian said. "I think you take a stroll in the grounds, maybe. Me, I go back to the villa. You join me, General?"

"If you wish."

"Come on, Klinker," Rudi said. "We'll take the stroll."

That left Max and the prince. I lifted the tablecloth cautiously a few inches. As they approached the door the prince said in a low voice, "Why exactly was Count Rudolf here? He didn't say a word except to translate for Klinker."

Max chuckled. "You do not know the way things work in Germany. Hitler trusts nobody. You may be sure that Rudolf is here to keep an eye on the general and report back."

"He's a spy for Hitler?"

"Probably," Max said. "Why else would he be here when he could be on the Riviera or in Paris having his usual good time?"

And their voices died away as they walked down the gravel path.

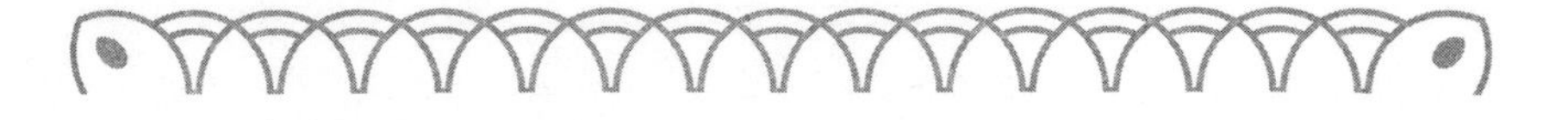

Chapter 16

Monday, April 22
At Villa Fiori with things becoming more complicated by the minute!

I waited a long moment, just in case they had forgotten something and came back for it, then I extricated myself from my yoga position under the table and stretched out my limbs. The air in the room was still hazy with smoke. I would have found it hard to breathe even in the purest of air. What I had overheard had completely shaken me. And the fact that the Prince of Wales seemed to be a willing participant unnerved me even more. Surely an alliance with Hitler's Germany could never be a good thing, could it? From what we had heard his Brownshirts behaved like bullies and thugs. And Mussolini? He was a dictator, after all, and all dictators I knew about had come to bad ends.

I was dying to tell Darcy what I had learned and decided to risk my own stroll about the gardens in case I could find him alone. I hadn't realized how big the grounds were. There were so many different sections, separated by stands of trees or high hedges. I saw two gardeners working in the kitchen garden, but they were both stocky Italian men. However, I decided they might know where Darcy was working. I went up to them and with lots of arm waving I asked where the English gardener was working.

At first they stared at me as if I was a madwoman, then they understood and nodded. "Ah. *L'inglese.*" Then they shrugged as if it was no concern of theirs where he might be. Then one of them curled a lip in contempt and muttered something. The other agreed. As I left them I thought I understood what they had said: He works too much, or too hard. They didn't like him because he showed them up. I had to smile, the first smile I had permitted myself all day.

I continued on, away from the formal lawns, to where the ground rose in a parkland of tall trees and flowering rhododendron bushes. Suddenly a cold wind swept through the trees, sending branches rustling and rattling. I looked around me, feeling alert and alone. Had I been followed? I forced myself not to break into a run as I made my way back to the more cultivated part of the gardens. When I came out onto the lawns I stood and gave a sigh of relief. Silly, I said to myself. Nobody knew I'd been under the table and had overheard. I was quite safe.

Perhaps Darcy was not working at this moment but in his cottage. I turned toward the far side of the grounds and came upon the row of stone cottages with red-tiled roofs, each cottage no bigger than our horses' stable. However opulent the villa was, the hired hands certainly didn't live in luxury. Poor Darcy, I thought, then I realized that he probably didn't mind. He enjoyed adventure. I stood looking at the front doors, wondering which one housed Darcy. The green-painted front doors were all closed. So were most of the shutters. I could hardly go and knock on doors, could I? If word got back to the villa that I'd been hobnobbing with the gardeners people might get quite the wrong impression. For the same reason I couldn't ask one of the other gardeners.

"Rats," I muttered. Why did life always have to be so complicated?

I'd just have to put my signal on the balcony tonight and wait to tell Darcy then.

As I made my way back to the villa I heard the scrape of a rake on gravel and came around a topiary hedge to find Darcy working there.

"Darcy," I whispered as I went up to him. "I have to talk to you. I've just found out something amazing. You won't believe . . ."

He was still wearing the big hat that shaded his whole face and a loose blue smock. He looked up and said, *"Scusi, signorina?"* then went back to raking.

"There's nobody around," I said softly. "And I have to tell you. I've just come from a meeting and you won't believe . . ."

"Ah, there you are, Lady Georgiana," said a voice. I almost jumped out of my skin as Rudi came around the topiary. "Your maid was concerned. She did not realize you had gone out when you felt so unwell. I came to find you."

"I needed fresh air," I said. "The room felt stuffy and at home I take a walk on the moors when I have a headache."

"Not a wise time to take a walk, I am afraid," he said.

I looked up at him, shocked and wondering what he was hinting at. Then he added, "Any minute now it will rain and you will be soaked."

I looked up at the sky then and saw a bank of black clouds building out over the lake. The wind was now blowing more fiercely.

"Allow me to escort you back to the villa, Lady Georgiana," he said, offering his arm.

I could hardly refuse, could I?

"Thank you, Count Rudolf," I said and tried not to glance at Darcy as I was led away.

Had he heard me trying to talk to Darcy? Did he suspect? Then I told myself, What was there to suspect? I was talking to one of the gardeners. Ladies have been attracted to outdoor staff before, after all. I had read that banned book, *Lady Chatterley's Lover*. Belinda had got her hands on a copy when we were at school and we had read it under the covers. I remembered we had had a narrow escape when Camilla was our dorm monitor and had made a surprise late-night check on us. Luckily Belinda was quicker thinking than I and had said that I thought I had a flea in my bed. Camilla certainly had no desire to hunt for fleas and beat a hasty retreat. I found myself smiling now at the memory. Oh, Belinda, I thought. I wish I was with you now.

I hadn't been noticing where Rudi was leading me until I saw that we were in the arbor where I had first met the company the afternoon before. So I was completely taken by surprise when he suddenly grabbed me and was kissing me. I tried to fight him off, but he was really strong, his arms wrapped around me like a boa constrictor. I wondered whether Darcy was still close by and whether he would come to my aid, but no help materialized as Rudi pinned me against one of the marble pillars and was pressing his body against mine.

Finally I wrenched my mouth free. "Let go of me this instant," I said.

He was laughing. "You fight like a little tiger," he said. "I shall enjoy the conquest all the more. For trust me, I shall conquer. You, my dear, will be in my arms and in my bed before this week is over."

"Absolutely not," I said. "And if I report this conversation to our hostess she will have you thrown out of the villa."

He was still chuckling. "I think not," he said. "Our hostess and I are old friends. But keep fighting, my darling. I do so enjoy the chase."

I was so tempted to scream. Darcy would hear and would come to my rescue. But then his true identity would be revealed and he might even find himself in danger. I wasn't sure what might have happened next, but we heard voices close by. Ladies' voices, sounding alarmed. Rudi broke away from me and we emerged from the bower in time to see Camilla, my mother and Mrs. Simpson actually running up the path, holding on to their hats. Paolo was bringing up the rear.

"Ah, there you are, you naughty boy," my mother called in that voice of hers that could project to the top gallery in a theater. "We were waiting on the island for you to come back!"

"You men abandoned us. Such lack of chivalry," Mrs. Simpson said, looking extremely miffed. "And then we saw the storm come up and we couldn't see any sign of your boat."

"We were worried," Camilla said. "The water was getting rough. We thought something had happened to your boat. We thought that Max had tried to see how fast it would go and it had flipped over. But no. When we came into the dock, there was your boat, already tied up, and we realized you had come home ahead of us."

"Obviously not caring whether we drowned in the storm or froze to death," Mrs. Simpson added.

"A thousand apologies, dear ladies," Rudi said, "but do not blame me. I was not in charge. It was your husband's uncle who looked at the sky and said we had better make for home before the storm broke. He said your boatman would surely have seen the change in weather and informed you that you had to leave. We were surprised when we did not find you here. But no matter now. We must all make for shelter before . . ."

He had no chance to finish the sentence as there was an ominous rumble of thunder and the heavens opened. We ran for the house—Mrs. Simpson and my mother outsprinting everyone—but were quite drenched by the time we stepped into the marble foyer. Servants appeared, looking anxious and muttering excuses, as if our soaking was their fault. Camilla gave an order and they scurried off.

"I think we all need a hot bath," she said. "We only have three bathrooms, I am afraid, so I will allow my guests to go first. One of you can use my bathroom. My maid will take care of you."

"Oh no, Contessa," I said, reverting to formality, as befitted the occasion, "I was only in the garden for a few minutes. I have not been chilled like you ladies. I will be quite content to rub myself dry with a towel."

"You are very gracious, Georgiana, and I accept," she said. "I have to confess to being frozen to the marrow. I've instructed Cook to heat broth for us all, and the butler will send up brandy."

I hurried up to my room before I could risk another encounter with Rudi in the hallway. I went over to the French doors and looked out. The rain was coming down in a solid sheet and the grounds were deserted. A flash of lightning made me step away from the window. It was immediately followed by a great crack of thunder and hailstones bounced off my balcony. If this continued I couldn't expect Darcy to risk climbing up the creeper to me tonight. How and when was I ever going to get in touch with him?

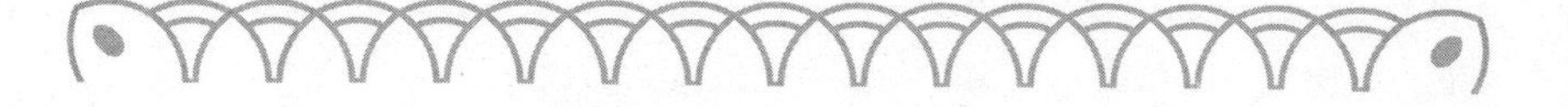

Chapter 17

Still Monday, April 22
At Villa Fiori

Plots and espionage and attempted seduction: at least nobody can say I lead a dull life! But I'm worried that Rudi might find a way into my room and nobody would hear my cries with the racket this storm is making.

I dried off, dressed in a jumper and skirt and drank my broth without Gerda putting in an appearance. No doubt she was taking care of Camilla, for which I was glad. I didn't think she would approve of wearing morning clothes in the afternoon, but all I wanted at this moment was to be warm. As I came downstairs I glanced down the hall of mirrors and saw Rudi, sitting alone and writing a letter. Might he be writing another blackmail note? The thought crossed my mind that if I positioned myself correctly I could read what he was writing in the mirror. Accordingly I wandered through the salon, apparently aimlessly, until I came to a place where I could actually see the piece of paper reflected in the mirror. Then I realized that not only was he writing in German, but in German script, which was quite impossible to decipher.

At least it wasn't a threatening letter to my mother, I thought. She certainly couldn't read German script. Perhaps he was doing what Max had hinted at and reporting back to Herr Hitler on the meeting. If only I had a camera in my possession, I could have taken a photograph and perhaps it could have been made large enough to read the contents of the letter. I'd obviously never make a proper spy. Not that I wanted to. My experience under the table had still quite unnerved me. I realized how incredibly lucky I was to have survived undiscovered. But Rudi's letter writing gave me a good idea. I could write a note to Darcy and have one of the other gardeners deliver it to him.

I wondered where I'd find writing paper and the obvious answer was Paolo's study. I was about to go in, when I heard voices inside. Men's voices, this time talking in animated Italian. That had to be Paolo and his uncle and I had no way of knowing what they were saying. Had the uncle been briefing his nephew on what they had discussed in the temple? I thought it unlikely. But something had clearly rattled one of them. I tried to catch the odd word, but they were delivered with such speed and force that I had to admit defeat and leave.

There was no sign of anyone else and I couldn't hear any other voices so I wasn't sure where to go next. As I wandered into the long gallery, I was pleased to find that coffee and cake were being served. A fire had been lit in the black marble fireplace, making the place feel quite cheerful. I went over to the table to help myself to coffee and cake and was about to take them to the sofa near the fire when a voice said, "So? You have recovered?"

And there was Paolo's mother, sitting in a corner, her knees wrapped in a rug and a cup of coffee in her hand. She eyed me with that birdlike stare. "You took to your bed with a headache," she said. "But here you are, up and about again. Well enough to walk in the grounds. My daughter-in-law was worried about you."

"I am quite recovered, thank you," I said. "It must have been the approaching storm that brought on my headache. I am susceptible to changes in the weather."

"I thought that was just old women like myself," the dowager countess said. "I feel every drop of rain in my bones. But I am glad you made such a miraculous recovery."

The way she stared made me feel that she suspected an ulterior motive had kept me from going to the island with the others and I realized, with a shock of horror, that she had also stayed home and had presumably noticed me searching frantically while she was tucked away in a corner chair. It occurred to me that perhaps she thought I was planning to help myself to one of the family treasures. I couldn't think of anything reasonable to say to her so I gave her a bright smile and took a sip of my coffee.

To my great relief I heard the sound of voices coming down the stairs and the Prince of Wales came in, with Mrs. Simpson's arm tucked through his. Clearly there was no more pretense that they were not a couple.

"Ah, coffee. What a good idea," Mrs. Simpson said. "Just what I wanted. You can pour me a cup, David."

If anyone at home in England had heard this they would have fainted with shock. Not only was she ordering the heir to the throne around but calling him by his family-only name and not addressing him as sir. But it didn't appear to have upset him. "Right-o," he said and went over to the serving table like a good boy.

Mrs. Simpson sat herself down on the sofa next to me. "And how are you, Georgiana, honey?"

"Much better, thank you. The headache is gone."

She nodded. "You didn't miss much. Some old villa on an island and a few walls. Frankly I think that Italy is clearly overrated. Give me the French Riviera any day, where the food is better and the streets are cleaner. I still can't believe that we came here when we had an invitation to join friends on a yacht in Monte Carlo. What an incredibly dreary group this is." She looked up as the prince handed her a coffee cup. "Don't tell me you are actually enjoying yourself here, David. Can we not make our excuses and leave? You've been called home on urgent family business? Your father's health has taken a turn for the worse? You'll think of something. I'll go and tell my maid to pack."

"Hang on a moment, Wallis," the prince said. "We can hardly walk out on a house party after one day. It simply isn't done."

"Honey, you're royal. You're practically a king, for God's sake. They're damned lucky to have you for even one day. They'll probably dine out on this for years. 'Do you know, the Prince of Wales came to stay with us once?' 'The Prince of Wales? Lucky you.'"

David came to perch on the arm of the sofa beside her. "I'll see if I can arrange a car to take you shopping tomorrow in Milan. Will that make you happy?"

"A car to take me to Monte Carlo and Bender's yacht would make me happy," she said. "But I guess a day shopping in Milan will appease me for a little while." She turned to me, right when I had just taken a bite of gâteau. "You must be bored out of your mind here, Georgie. No young people. No dancing. No music. No wonder you feigned a headache."

I still had a mouthful of chocolate cream and was attempting to swallow so I just gave her a smile.

"I don't know what Queen Mary was thinking when she wanted you to join your cousin at this place," she went on, now putting a hand on the prince's knee. "Did she assume there would be eligible men for you to meet? Well, I suppose there is that German count. He's quite a catch, I suppose, but I don't think there's any family money there. In fact, from what I've heard . . ."

I never did find out what she had heard, as my mother came into the room, followed by Max, chatting with Camilla.

"Oh good, you've found the coffee and cake," Camilla said. "I thought we should eat something as our picnic on the island was cut short and poor Georgiana only had broth for her luncheon. Aren't we lucky we made it back in time? Can you imagine being caught out in an open boat right now?"

As if to reaffirm this there was an almighty crack of thunder overhead. Mummy let out a little scream. The dowager countess crossed herself.

"Don't worry," Max said, putting an arm around my mother. "These storms in the mountains can be quite fierce but they rarely last long. And we're quite safe here."

"I just hate thunder," Mummy said. "I always have. As a child I used to hide under the bed."

"It is your delicate nature, *mein Schatz*," Max said, squeezing her shoulder affectionately.

Delicate nature, I thought, trying not to smile. My mother was as tough as old boots. I glanced across at her and tried to picture her married to Max, spending the rest of her life in Germany. Was that really what she wanted? If it were me, no amount of money and privilege would make me want to spend my life among people with whom I had nothing in common. Darcy and I would never be rich, but at least we would laugh together and teach our children to ride and hunt and gather conkers and play sardines in the castle. Just thinking these thoughts made me feel all nostalgic. To know he was so near and yet I couldn't speak to him was unbearable. Let's just get this over with and go home, I thought.

"Some cake, *Schatzi*?" Max asked my mother.

"Oh no, thank you, darling. I have to watch my figure," she said.

"Leave that to me. I like to watch your figure all the time," he said. Really his English had improved by leaps and bounds.

"Silly boy." She playfully slapped his hand, then came over to me, perching herself on the arm of the sofa beside me so that she and the Prince of Wales sat as bookends. "Are you feeling better, my darling?" She slipped an arm around my shoulder. "I was so concerned when Camilla said you had elected to stay home because you had one of your headaches. I know how terrible they can be. Utterly devastating. So were you successful?"

I glanced up at her, wondering how she dared to ask the question in public.

"Successful?"

"In getting rid of the nasty old headache, I mean?"

"Not entirely," I replied, giving her the answer I knew she was angling for. "I've tried to find—ways—of making it better, but as yet I haven't succeeded."

She nodded, understanding. "What a pity. So annoying . . . when these headaches strike. Then you must let your mama take care of you."

"You are fortunate to have such a devoted mother," Camilla said. "My mother wouldn't have turned a hair for anything less than a thunderbolt hitting me."

"Please don't speak of thunderbolts." Mummy shuddered. "Just listen to it growling away out there."

"It will soon pass, but it is suddenly chilly, isn't it? I'll have them light the fire in the dining room and maybe we'll have our after-dinner coffee here, rather than the salon. We should play cards. Paolo adores that and I gather you are rather a whiz at bridge, Mrs. Simpson."

"I do quite like a game of cards," Mrs. Simpson had to agree.

"I prefer roulette," Mummy said. "A game of chance. More exciting." She stopped talking abruptly as Rudi came into the room.

"What is it you find exciting, my dear Claire?" he asked, moving calmly and elegantly across the room to the food table. "I came in too late to hear your confession."

"A game of chance, Rudi. I enjoy a game of chance."

"So do you often win, at this game of chance?"

"Frequently enough."

"A lady after my own heart," he said, bringing his cup of coffee back to the group by the fire. "I also enjoy a game of chance and I also win most of the time."

I could feel the air between them was electric and wondered if the others in the room noticed it.

"We have no roulette wheel at the villa," Camilla said. "It will have to be bridge or whist, I'm afraid. Not as exciting. But we have enough for three tables."

WE FINISHED OUR coffee and cake and one by one people went up to change for dinner. I took my cue from the others and was about to go up the stairs when my mother popped out of a doorway and grabbed me.

"Well?" she hissed at me.

I looked around. Nobody in sight. "I did my best," I said. "I looked everywhere I could think of. I even started going through books in the library, but there are thousands of them. I tried to get into his room, but the door was locked. That must mean he has something to hide in there, mustn't it? Normal people don't lock their doors when they are staying with friends."

"Hardly friends, darling," she said. "I don't think he knows these people any better than we do, and frankly we are not friends with anyone here. I've no idea why Max insisted on coming unless it was to get on the good side of that dreary general. But Max isn't usually like that. He doesn't need favors. People ask favors of him."

"Anyway, I searched for you, everywhere I could think of except for Paolo's study. But if Rudi and Paolo aren't bosom friends he'd hardly hide photographs in there, would he?"

She was still holding on to my forearm, her long fingernails digging in. "What about that little pavilion place? I told you he goes out there sometimes, didn't I?"

"Only to smoke, I suspect. I did check it out and it smelled of cigar smoke. Besides, there was nowhere one could hide anything." Apart from under the table, I added to myself.

"Damn," she muttered, squeezing my arm even harder. "So what do we do now? How do we get into his room? Find another key that fits?"

"I tried mine and it didn't," I said. "I presume the maids must be able to get in to clean."

"Perhaps you could disguise yourself as a maid," she said.

I gave her an exasperated look. "Honestly, Mummy, do you think the servants wouldn't notice if I went down to the butler and asked for the key to clean Rudi's room?"

"I'm feeling desperate, darling," she said. "I have to do something. We have to do something. Couldn't you climb up to his balcony?"

"Not being a cat burglar, the answer to that is no. The wall looks quite smooth and there is no creeper like there is up to my balcony. Besides, if he's locked his door he will surely keep his French doors shut."

She gave a big, dramatic sigh. "I don't know what to do. I had such high hopes you'd find something."

My mother had always had the knack of making me feel like a hopeless failure. This was beginning to rankle. "I managed to find a way to stay behind and search for you," I said. "I did do everything I could, you know."

Another dramatic sigh. "Yes, I'm sure you did. But I'm so close to facing ruin. The end of happiness."

"Are you sure the photographs are as bad as you think they are?"

"Oh yes, darling. Frightfully bad. Absolutely scandalous. You'd blush if you even had to look at them."

"Then the only answer I can see is to confess to Max, claim that Rudi tricked you, got you drunk, drugged you, and it was the only time you've been unfaithful to him."

I could see her considering this, then she shook her head. "I couldn't. I simply couldn't. It would break Max's heart. Somehow we have to get into that room. You wouldn't like to creep down to the servants' quarters in the middle of the night and see if you can locate the duplicate key, would you?"

"Frankly no, Mummy."

"Then I'll just have to do it myself," she said and swept up the stairs, every part of her body showing indignation.

Chapter 18

Monday, then Tuesday, April 23rd
At Villa Fiori

Golly, this day seems to have gone on forever. All I want to do is to go to bed, lock my door and sleep. But I have to stay awake in case the storm dies down and Darcy comes to visit.

Gerda appeared with another dress for me—this time midnight blue and backless. When I protested that I couldn't possibly wear another of the contessa's dresses Gerda shook her head. "But you cannot wear the velvet that you brought with you. It is ruined, I think. I told the contessa and she quite agrees that you must look elegant in front of your cousin and his lady friend."

So I allowed myself to be made elegant and glamorous again. If Darcy could see this, I thought as I stared at myself in the mirror. Dinner that night was another rich, elaborate affair with wild mushroom soup followed by lake fish, venison and tiramisu, then rounded off with fruit and cheeses. Mummy made a big effort to be bright and witty at her end of the table. Mrs. Simpson was silent, sullen and clearly bored at hers.

"Camilla, Wallis would like to go shopping tomorrow," the prince said. "Is there any way we can have a car to take us into Milan?"

"Of course," Camilla said. "I'll come with you, if you like. I know where the best shops are. Is it leather you are looking for?"

"Leather, gold, anything to cheer me up," Mrs. Simpson said.

"The more expensive it is, the more she brightens up," the prince said.

I sat quietly, observing and trying to cut my leg of venison without shooting it off the plate, but I noticed two things. One was that the priest had not joined us for dinner tonight, so we were no longer thirteen. That had to be a better omen, didn't it? And the other was that when the prince made a joke Klinker had smiled. So he did understand English after all. I wondered if he was perhaps the one who had been sent by Herr Hitler to keep an eye on all the other Germans.

We had coffee and liqueurs in the long gallery, which had warmed up nicely by now. Then Camilla had card tables set up at intervals. The prince and Mrs. Simpson were invited to play with Camilla and Paolo. The general and Klinker got my mother and Max. I hoped they didn't notice that my mother was known to cheat. That left Rudi, me, Uncle Cosimo, the dowager contessa and the priest, who came to join us. Almost immediately the dowager announced that she considered playing cards to be sinful. She glared at the priest and then of course he had to say that he wouldn't be playing either. That left three of us. It was suggested that we played three-handed whist, but Uncle Cosimo preferred pinochle. I had no idea how to play that, so I bowed out, leaving him to play against Rudi.

I sat for a while looking at the fire, feeling sleepy, then when they were all occupied, I slunk out and went up to bed. It had been a long and stressful day. The storm had still not abated. I could hear the rain drumming on my patio and the wind rattled the shutters. For a fleeting instant the room was lit with a lightning flash. There was no way that I could expect Darcy to come to my room tonight. He'd be drenched and would risk being struck by lightning if he climbed to my balcony. I'd just have to wait until morning to try to meet him.

I went to the little writing desk, found paper and envelopes and wrote him a note, asking him to meet me as soon as possible as I had something important to tell him. I didn't dare say what this was, just in case it got into the wrong hands. But I did write *Urgent* on it. I was just about to get undressed when I sneezed. Golly, I hope today's soaking was not going to give me a cold, I thought. When I looked around for my handkerchief I realized I had left my evening purse downstairs, where we had had coffee. How annoying. I wondered if I could creep down to retrieve it without anyone noticing me.

As I opened my door another door nearby closed, just down the hall from me. I froze, standing in my doorway, as someone moved silently along the hallway, keeping to the edge, as if not wanting to be seen. At first I thought it was one of the maids, then she came closer to the lamp at the far end and I saw that it was Camilla. And I realized that she must have just come out of Rudi's room.

I gave her enough time, then I followed her downstairs. I was curious to know whether Rudi had been in his room as well, but he was still seated at the card table, engrossed in his game with Paolo's uncle. What's more, Camilla was now back at her table, calmly playing bridge. Or at least she seemed to be calm, until Paolo said, "Why did you play the king, Camilla? You know that they must have the ace!" in an exasperated voice.

"I'm sorry. I must be rather tired tonight," she said.

Nobody paid any attention to me as I found my purse and carried it back up the stairs. So she had crept into Rudi's room when he wasn't there. Why was that? And how did she get in? I wondered if he had left his door unlocked for her and if she had maybe left him a note telling him what time she might be paying him a visit. When I thought of the stiff and upright Camilla it all seemed rather improbable. But it did let me know that if she had found another key, then maybe I could too.

Drat my mother, I thought. There was nothing I wanted to do less than burglarize Rudi's room. I had just started to undress when there was a tap at my door. I realized I had failed to lock it and braced for the intruder, but it was Gerda who came in, carrying a cup and saucer.

"You should have rung for me, my lady. I did not realize you had turned in for the night until one of the maids said she had seen you going up the stairs. See, I have brought you an herbal tea. So good for clearing the head after a headache."

"Thank you," I said as she put it on the desk beside me. I sniffed it dubiously. I had never been a fan of herb teas and this one did not look inviting.

"You should drink while it is still hot," she said, urging me to pick up the cup.

I took a few sips to please her. It tasted as disgusting as it looked.

"The contessa always asks me to make this when she has had one of her sick headaches," Gerda said, standing sentry until I finished the cup. "Good. Now I will undress you."

She did this with rapid efficiency and quickly had my nightdress over my head and me tucked in bed. Outside the storm rumbled and clattered. I thought of Darcy and wondered if he was all right in his funny little stable-house. I have to confess I felt a bit uneasy myself. I must have inherited my fear of storms from my mother, because we certainly had our share of them up on the bleak Scottish moors when I was growing up. But I curled into a tight little ball, wondering if I would be able to sleep at all and wishing the storm would go away.

The next thing I knew, someone was standing by my bed. I must have gasped and tried to sit up.

"It's only me, my lady," said a calm voice.

It took a moment for the figure to swim into focus and for me to realize that it was broad daylight.

"Your morning tea, my lady," Gerda said. "The weather is still not favorable, I regret to say. I think you will need your tweed skirt and jumper again. If you wish to drive into Milan with the contessa and Mrs. Simpson I think you should get up soon."

"Why, what time is it?" I asked.

"Almost nine o'clock," she said. "I expect the storm kept you awake for much of the night. We have bad storms where I grew up in Austria, but this was quite as loud and fierce as any I have experienced."

I sat up and took a sip of tea.

"Shall I run your bath, my lady?" she asked.

"Oh yes, please," I said. Today I really did have a headache from sleeping so late. And from the unfamiliar amount of alcohol the night before. I decided I should get dressed then take a brisk walk outside to sweep away the cobwebs, and to find a way to deliver the message to Darcy.

When I was bathed and dressed I went downstairs and heard voices coming from the lake view room. So others were already at breakfast. I remembered then that Gerda had asked whether I wanted to go shopping in Milan with Mrs. Simpson. That was the last thing I wanted to do. There is nothing more depressing than to go shopping in expensive boutiques with someone who has an unlimited amount of money when one can afford nothing. But I hoped that most of the other guests would decide to go with her. That way I had less chance of being seen with Darcy. I decided I had better make my intentions clear before I went for my walk so I joined the party in the lake room. The prince and Mrs. Simpson were sitting in the window, the German military men on high-backed chairs,

Paolo with his mother and uncle in one corner, Camilla standing by the table, spreading jam on a roll. Only my mother, Max and Rudi were absent. At least I wasn't the last one down.

I muttered a good morning and went over to the table, helping myself to a croissant.

"We're going into Milan in a little while, Georgiana," Camilla said, turning as I approached her. "You'll be able to amuse yourself, I hope. We would naturally invite you to join us, only there's no more room in the car."

"That's quite all right," I said.

"I could stay behind if young Georgie wants to go with you," my cousin David said, giving me a friendly grin.

"Oh no, sir, that's really fine," I said. "I'm not a big shopper."

"And I want you with me, David," Mrs. Simpson said firmly. "I need your opinion on things that I buy. You know I like to look good for you and I value your opinion."

"Wallis, I tell you something looks nice and immediately you say it's terrible and you discard it," he replied, still laughing. She gave him a warning stare. I couldn't help feeling sorry for him, and worried too. If this relationship was to last it was clear who ruled the roost. And if he became king, would she expect to marry him and become queen? Impossible, I thought. The Church of England would never let him marry her. But she could still be his mistress, still be the power behind the throne. I just prayed that King George went on living for many, many years.

I had just finished my roll when my mother came in, looking stylish in a royal blue two-piece and jaunty matching hat. "I hope we won't get blown away," she said, making it clear that she was going shopping too. "And I hope the road between here and Milan is passable."

"I don't think there should be any problems unless there are downed trees," Paolo said. "There are quite a few branches down on our land I noticed this morning. A lot of work for the gardeners."

"About time you gave them something to do," his mother said with her usual critical stare. "Why do you employ so many men when there is usually so little to do? They stand around leaning on rakes all day. Or smoking behind the bushes. A disgrace. In my day we expected people to work."

"I think the grounds always look splendid so the gardeners must be doing a good job," Camilla said. "And as for employing lots of people, times are hard here. At least we're giving employment."

"I may go out and walk in the grounds myself," I said. "Have a lovely day in Milan."

"I hate to leave you alone, but I'm sure you will find something productive to do." My mother gave me a knowing stare. "And what should I buy for you in Milan, my darling?"

This was a new, solicitous mother. I was tempted to give her a long list, but I smiled and said, "Anything you think would look good on me would be very nice. You have such good taste. As you know, I have almost no fashionable clothes."

"I thought you've looked pretty good both evenings so far," Mrs. Simpson said. "Quite stylish. I was surprised."

"That's because the contessa's maid is a genius," I said quickly.

"You'll need an umbrella if you go out walking," Paolo commented, staring out of the window at the gray and angry lake. "It's still raining and it looks as if there is plenty more to come."

Oh dear, I thought. Did that mean that Darcy would not even be out on the grounds today?

"I'm used to the rain in Scotland," I said.

"Oh God," my mother echoed. "Don't remind me. Those years at that bloody castle seemed to be endless rain and wind. How it howled down those dreary hallways. The happiest day of my life was when I fled southward."

"Abandoning your only child." The words came out before I could stop them.

Mummy looked up, her eyes flashing. "Darling, you had a nanny and you were too young to miss me. I'd have made a terrible mother if I'd been unhappy all the time. And look at us now—how well we get on together." She flashed her brilliant smile at me, but I read it quite clearly. Drop the subject, her look said.

I went up to put on my raincoat. I had noticed umbrellas in the hall stand. I passed a maid carrying cleaning supplies, starting to clean the bedrooms now that we were all up and about. She stopped and dropped a curtsy as I passed. I took my raincoat out of the giant wardrobe, went downstairs and was about to select an umbrella when there was a distant growl of thunder. I hesitated. I didn't mind walking in the rain, but the prospect of walking in a thunderstorm, holding an umbrella, among big trees, certainly wasn't one I relished. But the need to find Darcy overrode all difficulties. I'd retreat if the storm came closer, I decided as I picked a large umbrella and went through the front door. The wind from the lake met me full in the face and raindrops peppered me, threatening to snatch the umbrella from my grasp. I almost turned back. It occurred to me that the others would think I was quite batty to choose to be outdoors in such weather.

As I walked out onto the grounds the destruction of the night's storm was very much in evidence. Branches were down, flower beds had been flattened and tulips were lying in sorry rows. Massive fronds had fallen from the palm trees beside the driveway. I heard the sound of voices and made for them. One gardener, an old sack draped over his clothing, was pulling a barrow while two others threw debris into it. And one of the two was Darcy.

They stopped as I approached them. I tried to think of a plausible way to get Darcy away from the others and decided to do my Queen Victoria imitation.

"You men," I said. "There is a branch across the path where I wish to walk. So dangerous." I paused then added imperiously, "A branch. Dangerous. Do any of you speak English?"

"I do, my lady," Darcy replied. "I'm the gardener from the estate in England."

"Good, then follow me," I said. "It is not a big branch, but it is blocking the path."

The other gardeners gave Darcy a look of commiseration as I stalked ahead of him, well away from the work that was going on. When there were several large hedges between us I turned and grinned. "Sorry about that," I said. "It will be the last time I boss you around."

"I doubt it." He grinned back. "But I've a bone to pick with you. You came up to me yesterday with something exciting that you had found, so I thought it was important enough to risk climbing up to your balcony with that storm going on. I got soaked to the skin, almost struck by lightning, and then I found you'd locked the shutters and the windows. I tapped several times, but obviously you didn't hear me over the noise of the storm."

"Golly, Darcy, I'm so sorry," I said. "I deliberately didn't put out the signal as I didn't want you to risk making that climb in a storm. I thought that even you wouldn't be foolhardy enough to climb up an ironwork balcony with lightning around. And I must have been sleeping deeply not to hear your knock."

"You must have fallen asleep immediately," he said. "I saw the light go out in your room and came right away."

"I'm sorry," I said again.

"I survived." He gave me a brilliant smile. "Only a little wet."

"Anyway, we shouldn't waste any more time. I've a lot to tell you." I pulled Darcy under my umbrella, half sheltered by the wisteria that spilled from a wall. "I have found out what all these people are doing here. And you won't believe what I overheard yesterday in that little marble pavilion." I lowered my voice even more. "It's really dangerous, Darcy. It seems there is a conspiracy . . ."

The end of this sentence was cut off by a loud scream, coming from the house. A woman was screaming and screaming. Not the sort of scream that would come from seeing a mouse, but the sound of absolute terror. I looked at Darcy. "I'll tell you later," I said. And I ran toward the house.

As I came in through the front door I heard sounds of running feet, raised voices, someone shouting, "Get a doctor," and another voice saying, "Too late for that."

The voices were coming from upstairs. I felt panic rising in my throat as I dropped the umbrella and ran up the staircase, fearing that the screams had been my mother's. She had the most powerful voice of those present. So I was relieved when I bumped into her, emerging from her bedroom, already wearing her dark mink coat and matching hat.

"What on earth's going on, Georgie?" she asked. "Has Rudi been at the maids, do you think? I wouldn't put it past him, odious man."

My eyes went instinctively to Rudi's door. It was open. I went toward it. Several people were standing in the doorway. Looking between them I saw Paolo with his arms around a thin, dark scrap of a maid. She was shaking all over and still sobbing. Then my gaze went across to the bed. Rudi lay there, or at least I presumed it was Rudi. It was hard to tell as part of his face had been blown away. The gun still lay in his dead right hand.

Chapter 19

Tuesday, April 23, 1935

We all stood there, frozen like statues, staring in disbelief. The only sound was the gentle sobbing of the maid. Of course it had to be my mother who broke the silence. She gave a dramatic gasp. "I can't believe it!" she exclaimed. "Not Rudi. He was so fun-loving, so full of life. He had so much to live for. Why would he do a thing like this?"

Paolo turned to her, his face deathly white and his eyes still wide with shock. "Sometimes people hide their inner pain with outward jollity," he said. "Perhaps none of us really knew him. We only saw the debonair and carefree man he wanted us to see." He made a gesture to sweep us from the room. "Come. I think we should leave. This is not a suitable sight for ladies. I must summon the doctor to write a death certificate."

While he spoke I had been staring with horrified fascination at Rudi. I had seen dead bodies before, but I suppose one never gets used to the sight, and this one was particularly horrible. Blood had congealed on his terrible wound, indicating that the deed had been done several hours before. But I had heard nothing, I thought. Surely someone in the next room would have heard a shot? I was trying to come to terms with the Count Rudolf I had witnessed, taking his own life. It seemed incomprehensible. If anyone thought a lot of himself it was Rudi. Thoughts flashed through my head: Maybe he had just learned he had an incurable disease. Maybe he had learned that he had lost his fortune or even was about to be arrested, given his behavior. But then he had shown no signs of distress the night before. Could a telegram have arrived in the middle of the night with bad news for him? Not that it mattered now. He was dead.

One by one the others stirred themselves as if waking from a dream and shuffled out of the room. I continued to stare at the body. Something was not right. Apart from his clear love of life, I was seeing something that worried me. I tried to pinpoint what it was. Something I was observing. I took in the blood-soaked pillow, the blood spatters on the wallpaper behind the bed and on the carpet, then Rudi's lifeless hand, still holding the pistol, slumped above it. And unbidden a picture came into my mind. Rudi sitting in the long gallery writing a letter—a letter I couldn't read because it was in German script. And he had been holding the pen in his left hand! Yet the gun was now clutched in his right.

As the room cleared out Paolo went over to the bed and bent to take the gun. "Don't touch it!" I shouted, surprised at the force of my own voice. "We should leave the room immediately. This is a crime scene."

Paolo looked at me in surprise. "But this poor man took his own life. I know it is a crime in the eyes of the church, but I hope Father Francisco might still give him a blessing."

The others froze in the doorway and stared at me. I felt my cheeks going red, but I said, in what I hoped was a calm voice, "I don't think he killed himself, Paolo."

"What do you mean?" he asked. "His door was locked. The gun is still in his hand. How can you suspect that anyone else was involved in this?"

"I can see the gun in his hand," I said. "But it's his right hand. I saw him holding a pen yesterday, writing with his left hand."

I heard a little gasp from one of those who had come back into the room. "That's right," Mummy said. "He was left-handed. I remember remarking on it once. We were talking about left-handed people being devious. And I remember how he chuckled." She put her hand to her mouth and gave a little sob. "He chuckled," she repeated.

Max put an arm around her shoulder. "Come away, *Liebling*. Do not distress yourself any further."

"Oh, Max, I'll never get that sight from my mind. Never. Take me away." Mummy allowed herself to be steered out of the room again. Paolo, Camilla, the German general and the Prince of Wales were still all staring at me.

"So what you're suggesting is that this was murder, Georgie?" my cousin said in a shaky voice.

"I'm saying he would not have shot himself with his right hand. I think we should summon the police."

"Oh, do you really think that's a good idea?" Paolo said. "You do not know our local police here. We are legally not part of the town of Stresa, but if I call in the Carabinieri they are a useless bunch of bullying peasants from the south. They could not solve a crime if the murderer was standing in front of them, handed them the gun and confessed. Unfortunately the local Polizia Municipale will not be much better, I fear. Why can we not call it a suicide and have done with it? Nothing we can say or do can bring the poor fellow back to life." He looked at Camilla. "You don't want this, do you, *cara mia*? Your guests subject to interrogation? Your home torn apart by peasant boys?"

The Prince of Wales cleared his throat. "Look here, Paolo. If this man was not killed by his own hand, then it means that there is possibly a murderer amongst us. We can't sweep this under the rug."

"Which rug should we sweep this under?" General Spitz-Blitzen asked, looking confused. "The rug in this room? No, I agree with His Highness. This matter must be brought to the authorities. There must be truth and justice."

Paolo sighed. "Very well," he said. "I will call in the Municipale. But don't say I didn't warn you."

He pushed past us and walked from the room.

"We should close the door and make sure nobody goes inside," General Spitz-Blitzen said. "Perhaps you could put one of your footmen to guard, Contessa?"

"What? Oh yes. Yes, of course. Good idea." Camilla sounded quite distraught. "Let's all go downstairs. I'll have Umberto bring us some brandy. I'm sure we could all use some after this shock."

The prince put an arm around her shoulder. "Buck up, old thing," he said kindly. "Stiff upper lip and all that."

She gave him a weak smile. "You are very kind, sir. Yes, we must all show a stiff upper lip. It's just that . . . I can't believe this has happened in my house, to one of my friends." And she stumbled down the hall like somebody sleepwalking.

I still stood in the doorway, looking around the room. I was dying to go in and check whether the French doors to the balcony were locked, although I couldn't see how anybody could have climbed up without a rope. It looked like a typical man's room. The room of a man who was orderly and had good taste. Silver-backed brushes and shaving gear lay neatly arranged on the dressing table. His clothes from the night before had been put away. His shoes were neatly beside the bed, as were his carpet slippers. His dressing gown lay across a chair. Otherwise there were no signs that the room was occupied. No papers, no books, no photographs. Then I noticed something: on the floor, a few feet from the bed, was a white feather. How strange, I thought. I was tempted to go and pick it up, when a voice spoke behind me.

"What happened to the maid with the key?" It was General Spitz-Blitzen. "We must certainly lock this door until the police arrive, do you not agree, Lady Georgiana?"

"What?" I turned to look at him. I hadn't realized he was still standing there. "Oh yes. Definitely. We should lock the door."

I moved out of the room.

General Spitz-Blitzen continued to look at me. He stepped closer, although we were now alone in that hallway. "You have an observant eye, Lady Georgiana. But I think it is not always wise to be too observant."

I looked at him in surprise. "You yourself said that truth and justice must prevail."

He nodded. "I did, and I believe it. But I am also thinking that somebody in this house has committed murder for some unknown reason and tried to make it look like a suicide. This person may not be happy that you have been observant."

"Golly," I said. "You are warning me to be careful."

He nodded. "Exactly. This person who killed may start to wonder what other clues you have observed."

He went over to the door and closed it firmly. The clang echoed down the hallway. "I think maybe I should summon Klinker to stand guard. He is a good, reliable man. One can count on him."

I looked around. "Where is Klinker?" I asked.

"I believe he went for a walk in the rain, as you did," he said. "He prizes his physical fitness highly. Our Führer encourages us to develop a healthy body."

I looked at his own rather corpulent stomach and kept silent.

We went along the hall and then down the stairs together. As we headed for the lake view room to join the others I heard a light tapping of heels and Mrs. Simpson appeared from the back of the house. “What on earth was all that noise about a while ago?” she said, looking around in annoyance. “Some female having hysterics? And where is everybody? I’m ready to depart for Milan now.”

Chapter 20

Tuesday, April 23
At Villa Fiori

This whole business gets more horrible by the minute. I wish I had never come here! I have to find Darcy right away.

Mrs. Simpson was not pleased to find that nobody would be driving into Milan that day.

"How inconsiderate of the guy to go and kill himself in a house where we are staying, David," she said as I escorted her through to the lake room. "I just hope there won't be a scandal. Why don't we pack our bags and hightail it out of here before the press arrives?"

The prince frowned. "Oh, I don't think that would be right, Wallis. There is some suggestion that his death might not be a suicide. Young Georgie here pointed out that the gun was in his right hand when the chap is known to be left-handed."

Wallis Simpson shot me a venomous glare, as if I had been personally responsible for spoiling her day's shopping. "Young Georgie seems to find herself mixed up in crimes, or imagined crimes, all too often," she said. "It's about time she got married and concentrated more on sex and babies."

There was a horrified gasp from Paolo's mother, sitting in her armchair beside the unlit fire.

"Anyway, we can't go anywhere before the police arrive so I'm afraid we're stuck. And really, look at the weather. It would be a beastly day for shopping. You'd get your fur wet and you'd be miserable," the prince said.

At that moment the butler appeared bearing a decanter and brandy glasses. This seemed to cheer everyone up. I took the moment when they were all occupied to slip away. Although I would have welcomed a glass of brandy with the other guests I had to tell Darcy what had happened. I had forgotten that I was still wearing my damp mack. My umbrella still lay where I had dropped it beside the front door. I looked around to see if anyone was watching, then I went out again. I wondered if Darcy had returned to his task with the other gardeners and had just passed the swimming pool when I heard him whisper, "Georgie. Over here."

He was standing beside that little octagonal pavilion. I went over to him.

"What was it?" he asked in a low voice.

"One of the guests has been murdered," I said. "Count Rudolf."

"Murdered? Rudolf?" He looked stunned.

I nodded. He opened the door and indicated I should follow him into the little pavilion. If anything it was less appetizing than it had been the day before. It still smelled of stale smoke and damp and I shivered as we stood there. I suppose the shock was just beginning to take hold. I tried to stay calm and composed as I told him what I had just witnessed: the locked door, the maid finding Rudolf with half his face blown away and the gun still in his hand.

"In his hand?" Darcy said. "Then it was suicide."

I shook my head fiercely. "That was what the murderer wanted us to think," I said. "But he made a mistake. Rudolf was left-handed. The gun was in his right hand."

"And who spotted that?"

"I did," I confessed.

He looked at me. "Sometimes you may be too observant for your own good," he said.

"Funny, that was what the German general said."

"He threatened you?" A flash of anger crossed Darcy's face.

"No, on the contrary, he was concerned for my safety. He was hinting that a murderer might wonder what else I had seen."

"I must get you away from here now," he said. "Can't you tell them that you've received a message from your sick friend and you are wanted back with her immediately? You could still go to Belinda's place and stay with her, couldn't you?"

A glimmer of hope flashed through my mind. Back with Belinda. Away from all this unpleasantness and intrigue. Then I shook my head. "We can't leave, Darcy. Rudolf has been murdered. If I run away I'll immediately look like a suspect. And besides, someone in that house is a killer."

"I'm not actually surprised someone killed Rudolf," he said. "He did like to sail close to the wind. A jealous husband, no doubt."

Of course when he said that I thought of Max. Mummy must have confessed to him and Max had taken revenge on Rudolf. But it didn't seem like Max's sort of crime. He was a straightforward sort of chap. Would he have been devious enough to have found a way to make it look like suicide and to successfully lock the door from the inside?

"I wonder," I said. "The only husband is Paolo and he was so shocked, he looked as if he was about to be sick. There are two would-be husbands—Max and the Prince of Wales—but I can't see either of them . . ."

"Need not have been staying here," Darcy went on. "A wronged husband could have followed Rudolf, found out where he was staying, crept in at night or climbed up to the balcony."

"He'd have had to be a darned good mountaineer," I said. "There is no handy creeper going up the wall like mine."

He nodded. "You were about to tell me something when we heard the screams."

"Of course. Yes, I was." With all the shock I had almost forgotten. "I overheard a conversation yesterday. In this very room. You'll find this hard to believe, Darcy." And I related exactly what I had heard.

"Crikey," he said, proving that I was not the only one with an unsophisticated vocabulary. "So that's what it was, that's why they are all here . . . trying to get the prince in on a secret pact with the Germans and Italians. I'm not surprised they tried to rope him in. He's shown himself to be impressed by Herr Hitler and all things German."

"But he's not even king yet," I said. "King George may live for years yet. And even if David were king, he has no real powers, does he?"

"Except that the people love him. If he came out and said that our future lay with Germany, they might well believe him."

"Golly," I said. "Do you think Germany is going to be a real threat?"

He nodded. "Yes. Yes, I'm afraid so."

"So what do we do now? Will you report this back to London?"

"In due course. The more urgent matter is killing Rudolf. Was he at this meeting yesterday?"

"Yes, yes, he was; but he didn't join in, other than translating from English for the young German officer, Klinker."

"I see."

There was a silence during which I heard the rain drumming on the roof and peppering the thin windows. The storm had picked up in intensity again. Darcy had been staring out past me, at the rain-soaked gardens. Suddenly he looked at me abruptly. "How on earth did you overhear this? You weren't foolish enough to follow them and eavesdrop outside the window, were you?"

I gave a nervous grin. "Much worse than that. I was under the table."

"What?" Darcy really looked shocked now. "Are you crazy?"

"It wasn't my idea, I promise you," I said. "I had been walking in the grounds. I came in to look at this little temple or whatever it is and suddenly I heard voices and saw men heading for the door. I didn't want to be caught, feeling foolish, when I was supposed to be in bed with a headache, so I did the first thing that came into my head and dived under the table."

Darcy shot me an exasperated look. "Why not just look up in surprise and say, 'Oh hello. I just came out here for some peace and quiet,' or something like that?"

"It would have been more sensible, I agree, but I had no idea they were going to have a meeting in here. All sitting around the table. Their feet inches away from me. It was awful, Darcy."

In spite of himself he had to smile. "Only you could get yourself into a situation like that."

"And at one point I wanted to sneeze. Luckily I managed to stifle it."

"Luckily, as you say. There were some ruthless people in that room, Georgie. You might not be alive now if they'd known you were there."

A thought just occurred to me. "You don't think that Rudolf's death could have anything to do with this, do you?" I gestured to the table. "You said he was well in with Hitler and . . ."

I broke off as I heard my name being called. I glanced at Darcy. "I have to go. It won't do to be caught in here with a gardener."

He nodded. "I'll come up to your balcony tonight. Don't lock the window this time."

"All right."

"And take care of yourself. Stay with other people. Lock your bedroom door."

"That didn't do much good for poor Rudolf," I said and for a horrible second I thought I was going to cry. He had been an unpleasant man but nobody deserves to die like that.

"Georgiana?" the voice echoed out again. I glanced out the door. Max was crossing the lawn, half hidden under a big umbrella.

"I have to go," I said again. Darcy kissed his finger then put it to my lips. "Don't say anything to anyone," he said. "Play the innocent until I've had a chance to think this through. You know where to find me if you need me."

"Which cottage is yours?"

"Third from the right," he said and almost pushed me out the door as Max approached.

"Ah, there you are," Max said. "Your mother was asking for you. She was worried that something might have happened to you. They were searching the whole house."

"I'm sorry, Max," I said. "I didn't mean to make anybody worry. I was just so upset by what I saw that I wanted to be on my own. I didn't want anyone to see me crying."

He held his big umbrella over both of us and put a big arm around my shoulder. It was only then that I realized I had left my own umbrella in the summer house. "Do not cry, little Georgiana. I will take good care of you, I promise."

His tone of compassion and gentleness caught me by surprise and a lump really did come into my throat. Until then I had had no feelings for Max. Frankly I couldn't see what my mother saw in him, apart from his godlike physique and his money, that is. I supposed those two things were enough for most women.

"You are very kind, Max," I managed to mumble. "Mummy's lucky to have you." And I let him steer me back into the house.

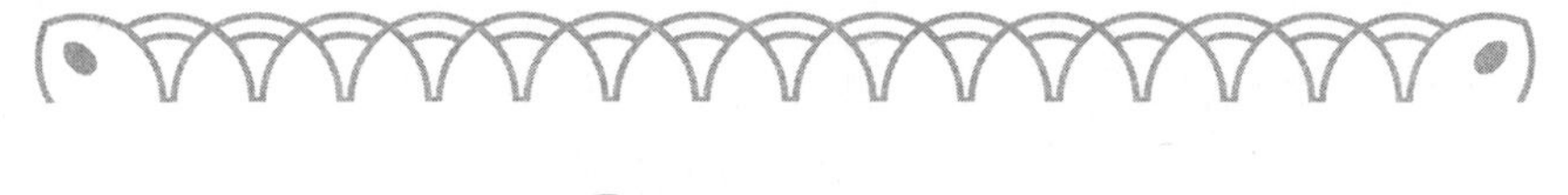

Chapter 21

Tuesday, April 23
At Villa Fiori

I could hear the murmur of voices coming from the lake room. I told Max I needed to change out of my damp clothes and went up to my bedroom. One of the footmen was standing outside Rudolf's door, clearly not relishing the task of being so close to a dead body. He had been staring in the other direction, and when I appeared behind him he jumped a mile and acted as if he was prepared to defend the door against all comers. Then he gave me a weak and embarrassed smile as I went past and into my own room. In that uncanny way of hers Gerda appeared almost immediately.

"Lady Georgiana, you have been outside? This is not wise in such weather and at such a time."

"I was upset," I said. "I wanted to be alone."

She nodded. "There is talk of nothing else in the servants' hall. This poor man. So tragic, to take his own life. I observed him and he seemed quite gay and full of life. But one never knows. Naturally you were upset. Should I bring you hot milk?"

"No, thank you. I think I should go and join the others, but I need to change my clothes and shoes."

"Let me remove them for you." She took off my shoes and made tut-tutting noises.

"One should not go out walking in such weather," she said. "So much mud will spoil the leather."

I didn't like to say that my brogues had been subjected to quite a lot of mud during their lifetime and were far from new.

"No matter. I will clean," she said. "And your jumper is quite wet around the collar. I hope you do not catch a chill."

In seconds she had a blouse down from its hanger, my jumper removed and the blouse buttoned for me as if I were a small child. It was useless to resist. Gerda was a force to be reckoned with. I wondered if Camilla had ever regretted hiring her in London, when her former maid was knocked down by that bus. But then Camilla had grown up with money. Perhaps all real lady's maids were so horribly efficient.

"Queenie," I whispered with a sigh. What I wouldn't give to see her bulky person waddling toward me with a vacant grin on her face and to hear her say "Whatcha, miss." Which probably shows how much Rudolf's death had affected me.

When Gerda had dried and styled my hair for me I was sent back downstairs while she whisked my shoes away, presumably to work a miracle upon them. The butler had served coffee to follow the brandy and I drank some gratefully, cupping my hands around the warmth of the coffee cup and feeling the hot liquid spread warmth through my body. I think I was still shivering. Nobody seemed to feel much like talking. Mummy had been idly turning the pages of an Italian fashion magazine, clearly not focusing on what was on them. Paolo's mother was saying her rosary, her lips moving silently over the beads. Mrs. Simpson pouted as she stared out of the window, puffing on her cigarette while David looked anxiously at her, as if he was terrified he had been responsible for upsetting her. Outside the tall windows the lake matched our mood—sullen and gray, with the mountains on the other side obscured behind a veil of mist.

Mummy now seemed to realize I was back. "Oh, here's my darling daughter, safe and sound," she said. "I was so worried that something had happened to you. But clever Max found you."

"I just needed to be alone," I said. "It was rather horrible, wasn't it?"

"It was. Especially for those of us who are of a sensitive nature." Her gaze went across to Mrs. Simpson. "In fact, I think I might want to go upstairs to lie down. I'm still feeling quite faint in spite of the brandy. Will you take me to my room, darling?" She held out her hand to me.

"I can take you. Let Georgiana have her coffee," Max said.

Mummy shook her head in dramatic fashion, making the curls bounce. "No, my darling. Right now I need my own little girl. My little treasure."

She had never called me her little treasure, not once in twenty-four years. But she got up and clutched at my arm like a drowning woman. As she dragged me toward the door she whispered, "The pictures. If they are in Rudi's room we have to find them before the police do."

"But someone is guarding the door," I whispered back.

"We must distract him. I'll turn on the full force of my charm and you slip inside. Otherwise . . ."

We had not even reached the stairs when the sound of a furiously rung bell announced the arrival of a police car.

"Too late," Mummy wailed. "Now all we can do is pray for a miracle."

We heard tires crunching on gravel and the butler walked toward the front door. Mummy and I reluctantly rejoined the others in the sitting room. We heard voices at the front door, then the butler appeared again. "The police have arrived," he said in Italian even I could understand. A short chubby man pushed past him and swept into the room. His thinning black hair was parted in the middle on top of a round face. His neck bulged over the edges of his tight uniform collar. He looked incredibly pleased with himself.

"Buongiorno," he said, giving a nodding bow. "I came immediately. I am Assistant Chief Romeo Stratiacelli of the Stresa Municipale." He rolled the *r* on "Romeo" almost as if he was an actor delivering a line. Even I could understand the Italian words because he delivered them so forcefully and with such dramatic gestures. "I come because this is a delicate matter, a matter that cannot be entrusted to the Carabinieri."

Romeo, I thought. The most unlikely Romeo I'd ever seen. And I had a sudden desire to giggle. Nerves, I suppose. Paolo stood and addressed the man, introducing each of us in turn. Camilla was sitting beside me.

"At least he's the assistant chief," I whispered to her. "Someone high up. That's good, isn't it?"

She shook her head. "No, it's terrible. Assistant chief is almost the lowest rank in the police force here. Only one rank up from agent, which would be our humble bobby at home. I don't think he'll have had any detective training." She stopped to see the assistant chief staring at her, realized that she was now the subject of the introduction and nodded politely.

"Will you be asking for assistance from Milan, Assistant Chief Stratiacelli?" she asked him. "An inspector, perhaps? Or a superintendent?"

"That will not be necessary, Contessa," he said, reverting to Italian. "I myself can handle this simple matter. I and my team. I have brought with me the esteemed *dottor* Falco, who will examine the body. And my men will examine the room for clues and take the fingerprints of everyone in the house. Do not worry. By the end of today we shall have this unpleasant business sorted out."

I didn't quite get the gist of that one, but Camilla translated for me. "Odious little man," she muttered.

"And your instructions are as follows," Stratiacelli continued. "Until I have solved this unspeakable crime, nobody is to leave this house until I give my permission. Nobody is to telephone to the newspapers. Nobody is to approach the room of the deceased. Is that clear?"

Paolo translated. "Most of our guests do not speak our language," he said to Stratiacelli. "Do you have any facility with English?"

"Ingleesh? I 'ave a little," he said. He turned to us. "No leave 'ouse. No go to room of dead mans. *Capiscono?*"

Paolo's uncle cleared his throat. He had been sitting, silent and brooding, in his usual chair. "Assistant Chief, I should remind you there are some very important people present in this room. The heir to the English throne. A trusted general of Herr Hitler. And I myself enjoy the confidence of our beloved Mussolini. Any mishandling of this case would be reported to him, I can assure you."

The assistant chief turned a little pale, and swallowed hard, making his stiff collar bounce up and down, but in the bulldog manner of small men went on pugnaciously, "Me, I do not care if you are the Holy Father himself. A murder is a murder and justice is justice, whether it be in the backstreets of Napoli or here in a palace." He turned to Paolo, ignoring Paolo's uncle. "Now, Count di Martini, please have me escorted to the scene of the crime."

The moment we heard his footsteps going up the marble stairs Camilla went over to her husband's uncle. "Uncle Cosimo, can we not telephone Milan and have them send someone else? This man is a fiasco, and I've always found small men who think a lot of themselves are dangerous."

Uncle Cosimo shrugged expressively, then put a hand on her arm. "Give him enough time to shoot himself in the foot, eh? Which he will most certainly do rapidly."

Camilla came to sit beside me again. "It's only just beginning to sink in that somebody killed Rudi. Someone in this house. It seems impossible." And she looked around the room, from one face to the next.

"Everyone is capable of murder, given the right circumstances," Paolo's mother muttered darkly, looking up from her rosary.

There was another awkward silence. I too looked around the room. My mother certainly had a good reason for wanting Rudolf dead. And if Max had found out what he was doing, he'd also have a good reason. And why had Camilla been sneaking out of Rudolf's room yesterday evening? If Rudolf was a blackmailer, who knew what he had found to use against the other occupants of the room? And yet, I thought, these were powerful people. Surely they would hire a lesser mortal to do their dirty work for them. One of them could have thrown Rudolf out of the speeding boat yesterday.

I looked up as we heard the tap of feet coming back down the stairs. Assistant Chief Stratiacelli returned, followed by Paolo.

"You people have called me here under false pretenses," he announced in Italian. Paolo translated. "This man was not murdered. He took his own life. Did you not see that the gun was still in his hand?"

"We did observe the gun," Paolo replied, "but it was pointed out by one of our guests that the gun was held in his right hand and that Count Rudolf was known to be left-handed."

The little man looked at us with a smirk on his face. "Have you never heard of people being ambidextrous?" he asked. "Some people they have the facility to write with one hand, to shoot the gun with the other hand. There. We solve the problem, do we not?"

I could see relief cross the faces of those in the room.

"So, now," he continued, "the body will be removed. My doctor will examine it to determine the time of death. My men will see if there are any other fingerprints on his gun. If not, we can conclude that no crime has been committed, except against God." He switched to speaking English. "So no worry. All is well. This poor man took his own life. May God have mercy on his soul."

With that speech he strode out of the room.

Chapter 22

STILL TUESDAY, APRIL 23
AT VILLA FIORI

In the middle of a difficult session and trying not to think what might possibly happen.

For a while nobody spoke. Then Mummy said in a tentative voice, "I suppose it is possible that he was ambidextrous. People are, aren't they?"

"Some people are," Camilla agreed.

Mrs. Simpson stood up. "Good. Well, that's settled, then. Unpleasantness over." She glanced at the gold Cartier watch on her wrist. "And still plenty of time to go into Milan. Claire, honey, are you still up for it?"

The Prince of Wales looked a little stunned. "I say, Wallis, there has been a death in the house. And the police chappie did say we were not allowed to leave without permission."

"That was when he thought it was murder, David. Now that he's decided it's a suicide, we're all off the hook and free to come and go as we please."

David cleared his throat. "I just think it would be bad form to go shopping at this moment. Give the wrong impression, you know."

"I think it would give the right impression. Show the press that his death was nothing to do with any of us." She started to cross the room.

"Why should it have anything to do with any of us?" Camilla asked sharply. "He was only a casual acquaintance, after all."

"You invited him, Camilla, honey," Wallis Simpson said smoothly.

"I don't think I did," Camilla said. "In fact, I'm not even sure why he was invited. Certainly not a friend of mine. Paolo just told me some Germans were coming and I had the maids make up rooms."

"Uncle Cosimo told me he wanted some friends from Germany invited," Paolo said.

"Rudolf was a friend of yours, Uncle Cosimo?" Camilla asked.

Cosimo shrugged. "I invited my good friend the general. He brings his own friends."

General Spitz-Blitzen stood up abruptly. "That young man was not a friend of mine. If anything I would say he invited himself when he found out who would be on the guest list. I brought only Klinker with me, who as my aide-de-camp naturally accompanies me everywhere. Actually, I am becoming worried about Klinker. Has nobody seen him? He has been gone a long time."

It just dawned on us that nobody had seen Klinker. I could tell what was going through other heads in that room—that Klinker was responsible for Rudolf's murder and had fled back to Germany. Wonderfully convenient.

"Did he mention where he was going?" Paolo asked.

"Just out for a walk, I believe," the general replied. "He is a very fit man. He prizes his fitness highly, you know."

"I will have the gardeners search the grounds," Paolo said. "If he has gone beyond that, up into the hills, then we will just have to wait."

"Is it possible that he left in a hurry?" Mummy asked sweetly. When the others turned to look at her she said innocently, "It does seem coincidental, doesn't it? That someone is killed and Klinker is nowhere to be found. The train from Stresa does have a good connection to Basel and then into Germany."

General Spitz-Blitzen's face turned beet red. "You cannot believe that Klinker would do such a thing," he said. "He is a man of honor, of the highest integrity. That is why I selected him for my aide. And besides, what possible motive could he have for killing Count Rudolf? He had never met the man before we arrived here."

"Calm down, General," Mrs. Simpson said in that lazy drawl of hers. She was now leaning against the doorpost, and took another long puff on her cigarette. "Anyway, I thought we all agreed that good old ambidextrous Rudi shot himself." She looked around the room. "And for God's sake let's do something rather than sitting around here like a bunch of ninnies. If David is going to be a spoilsport and not let me go shopping, there has to be some other form of entertainment. What do you suggest, Camilla?"

"Cards, perhaps? Or we could set up bowling or badminton in the ballroom if you like." Camilla still looked uncomfortable.

"Bowling in the ballroom. How delightful," Mrs. Simpson answered in such a sarcastic tone that the Prince of Wales stood up too and said hurriedly, "That sounds like it could be fun. Come on, Wallis. Buck up. Give it a try, what?"

He went over to join her and took her arm. As he led her from the room she said, clearly enough for us all to hear, "I can't think why you dragged me to this dreary place, David. I've been bored since the moment I got here. Let's leave right now. We can be back at the Riviera in time for dinner." Her voice grew fainter as they went down the long hallway.

"I'd quite like to leave too," Mummy said. "We could go back to our villa, Max, since the house party seems to be breaking up. What do you think?"

Max was frowning. "I do not think we should go anywhere yet, *mein Liebling*. We should not desert the count and countess in their hour of need. It is at times like this when friends should stick together, *ja?*"

Camilla shot him a smile. "Very kind of you, Max. I'm sorry I'm being such a lame hostess, but frankly Rudolf's death has completely shocked me. I mean, one never expects . . . in one's own house . . . does one?"

Paolo came over to her and put an arm around her shoulder. "Don't worry. It will all be sorted out soon, I promise you. Come on. Let's get the games in the ballroom started, shall we?"

"Are you coming to play with us, Georgie, darling?" Mummy said. She held out her hand to me and pulled me to my feet. "You go ahead, Max," she said. "I want to have a comforting word with Georgie. She is clearly still upset." She held me back with a grip of iron. "What's that, darling? Of course you are feeling queasy. It's only to be expected," she said, her theater voice projecting down the hallway. "A young girl like you should never have to witness anything as horrible as that. I feel quite queasy myself. Why don't you go and have a lie-down? I'll take you up to your room." As the last of the other guests disappeared down the hallway she whispered, "Quick. They'll all be occupied in the ballroom. This would be a good time to see if the police have taken the body away and to search that room."

"Mummy, you can't," I whispered back in horror. "Besides, it's all right now. They think he shot himself. They won't be searching for clues."

"All the same, someone will find the pictures eventually and I'd much rather have them back in my possession before Max can see them."

"At least he can't blackmail you anymore," I pointed out.

"That's true," she said.

For a second it did cross my mind whether she might have been the one to shoot him. Then I had to smile. My mother was horribly squeamish. I couldn't picture her holding a gun to a man's head and firing, and frankly I didn't think she was bright enough to plan a murder and make it look like a suicide. Such a crime took a skilled and devious person. I allowed her to walk me along the upstairs hallway.

"Who sleeps in these other rooms?" I asked.

"We have this one close to the stairs," she said. "Then the Prince of Wales and that woman have the big suite in the middle, then Rudi and then you. I believe the door at the far end leads to Paolo and Camilla's quarters."

"Yes, I think it does. My maid always appears from that direction," I said. "But what about the others, the general and Klinker?"

"In another wing, I believe, on the other side of the staircase. And I've no idea where Uncle Cosimo and the dreadful mother go at night. Or that priest. To hang by their toes in the belfry, I expect. Don't they give you the creeps?"

"They do," I agreed. "And what do you think about Klinker, by the way?"

"I'm not quite sure what to make of Klinker. Do you think he's actually human and not an automaton? I haven't heard him say a word or even change his facial expression since we arrived."

"I saw him smile once," I said. "A sort of little secret smile."

"I expect he's Hitler's spy, sent to keep an eye on the general, or on Max," she said. "I wonder if he did shoot Rudi."

"If so, why would he flee and thus point suspicion at himself?" I asked. "He'd made it look like a suicide. All he had to do was to stay put and act calmly. Instead of that he is nowhere to be found."

"Perhaps he's also been knocked off," Mummy said happily. "I expect we'll find the body stuffed in a fountain or something."

Before we could reach Rudi's room the door at the end of the hall opened and Gerda came out. "Lady Georgiana, is something wrong?" she asked. "You are not feeling well?"

"She is naturally upset," my mother said. "I thought she should lie down for a while."

"I suggested this when she came in from walking in the rain," Gerda agreed. "It is not wise to subject the body to stress when the mind has already been shocked. I will take care of Lady Georgiana, have no fear. You are free to join the rest of the party."

"No, I don't want to lie down," I said firmly. "I really don't. I don't want to be alone at the moment. I'd rather be with people."

"As you wish," Gerda said. "You only have to ring for me and I will be there."

She turned and went back through the double doors at the end of the hallway.

"Now!" Mummy hissed to me. She made a beeline for Rudi's door. She was only a foot away from it, with her hand on the handle, when it opened and a young policeman emerged. He looked as shocked as Mummy did to find a strange person standing inches from his face.

"Signora?" he asked and then rattled off something in Italian.

"Sorry. Don't speak Italian," Mummy said. "English lady. I lent Count Rudolf one of my books and I wanted to retrieve it from his room before it is lost. My book. Gave to count. Want back. Understand? Might I go in?"

This subterfuge was in vain. The young man clearly spoke no English. He shushed her away, closed the door and turned the key firmly in the lock. Then he walked away down the hall.

"Drat," Mummy said. It was mild for her, given the circumstances.

"I don't suppose we could find the key that the servants use?" Mummy suggested.

"I really don't think you could slip into the servants' quarters unobserved in the middle of the day. Besides, if you gained access to his room and turned the place upside down looking for those photographs and they decided to take fingerprints, think what that would look like."

"Then let's just pray that it is called a suicide and nobody does anything more. But to be on the safe side, I think Max and I should slip back to the safety of Switzerland. Such an orderly country, isn't it? So clean. And so kind to one's money. Boring as hell, but safe."

It occurred to me that I could do the same. Excuse myself and go straight back to that nice little room near Belinda in the safety of Switzerland. After all, I had no reason for being here. I had recounted to Darcy what I had overheard. And I certainly wasn't about to get involved in solving Rudolf's murder. But then Darcy was still here and I wasn't going to abandon him. Maybe he had learned all he needed to know and could quietly melt away as well. I'd have to wait until tonight when he came to my room to make plans.

We arrived at the ballroom to find that a long runner had been laid and indoor bowling was taking place. It was strangely eerie in there with the tall velvet curtains half drawn back and the far corners of the room still in shadow. The clack of ball against skittles echoed from the high painted ceiling while Roman statues glared down on us disapprovingly. Nobody seemed particularly enthusiastic.

"Ah, here are Georgie and Claire now," Paolo said, trying to sound cheerful. "We should make teams."

"Oh goodie. Teams," Mrs. Simpson said dryly.

Paolo had just finished dividing us into two teams. I found myself with the reluctant Mrs. Simpson, the general and Uncle Cosimo, hardly a combination likely to win anything. I had just picked up the ball to have my first bowl when Umberto, the butler, appeared. He made an announcement in Italian.

"Damn," Paolo said. "It's that policeman, back again. Let's hope he's come to tell us all is completed, Rudi shot himself and we can get on with our lives."

Assistant Chief Stratiacelli came into the ballroom even before Paolo had finished speaking. The rain must have picked up because he was still wearing a cape over his uniform and left a trail of drips across the parquet floor. The butler hovered behind him, trying to divest him of the cape, but without success.

"So here you all are," Stratiacelli said, opening his arms expansively. "Having a good time. No doubt celebrating that you have managed to fool the poor local policeman. But you have underestimated Stratiacelli. You think you can fool me. But Stratiacelli is thorough. He misses nothing. You find nobody better in Milan or even in Rome." Although this was in Italian his gestures made the gist quite clear.

"What are you talking about?" Paolo asked. "Is something wrong?"

"Is something wrong?" the policeman mimicked. "One of you knows what is wrong. The gun this man held in his hand has not been fired recently. However he died, it was not with a bullet from this gun."

Chapter 23

Still Tuesday, April 23
In the ballroom at Villa Fiori

The plot has thickened. Oh dear.

"The gun was not fired?" Max demanded when this was translated for him. "Then please tell me how half his face was blown away."

"No, you please to tell me," the assistant chief said. "Since one of you, or maybe more than one of you, clearly knows. This is now a murder investigation. My men will go over the victim's room for any telltale clues. They will search the whole house. You are please to go to the room at the front where I first met you and to stay there until I give you permission to move." He looked at the rest of us and switched to English. "Go now. Stay room. Nobody must leave. I will find who has done this evil deed. Stratiacelli will find who tries to trick him."

"Give us permission?" Uncle Cosimo demanded. "Do you know who you are addressing? Need I remind you that in this room you have a close confidant of our beloved Mussolini, a senior adviser of Herr Hitler, and none other than the Prince of Wales himself."

Stratiacelli shrugged. "As I told you before, Count di Marola, a murder is a murder. Someone in this house is guilty and I aim to find out who. Now, please. My men will escort you to the front of the house and there you will stay until you are summoned. No use of telephone and nobody is to leave the villa."

"I suspect some of the bedrooms may be locked, Assistant Chief," Camilla said. "Some of my guests choose to lock their doors."

"Then you will please provide me with the necessary keys. I presume your servants have passkeys?"

"Yes, of course there is a passkey," Camilla said. She looked across at the butler, who was still hovering behind Stratiacelli. "Umberto, please make sure the assistant chief has access to all the rooms."

"Of course, Contessa." He gave a dignified nod. "This way, Assistant Chief."

We were ushered back into the lake room. The sky was brightening a little, clouds were breaking and a shaft of sunlight shone onto a tall black cliff across the dark waters. It was most dramatic. Almost like a Romantic painting.

"At least the weather is clearing up," Paolo said, still in an attempt to remain cheerful.

"What is happening now?" his mother demanded as we trooped back into the lake view room. She had not moved from her customary place. Neither had the priest.

"The policeman has returned. Apparently the gun in Count Rudolf's hand had not been fired. He is now searching the house and we have been instructed to remain in this room."

"But it is almost time for luncheon," the dowager countess said in a horrified voice. "You know how important it is to my digestion that I eat my meals at the correct time. You must tell this silly little man." She looked across at Paolo's uncle. "Cosimo, you must telephone to Rome. Tell them what fiasco is happening here."

"We have been forbidden to use the telephone at the moment, Angelina," he said.

"Then you must speak to him, Father Francisco," she said imperiously. "Tell him he is not allowed to treat aristocrats as if they were a herd of sheep. He will surely listen to a man of the church."

"The church may not interfere with the affairs of the state, as you know very well, Contessa," the priest said, looking up from his prayer book. "It is written in our constitution."

"When has that ever stopped the church from interfering before?" she said in scathing tones. "You are all weaklings. I shall approach him and tell him myself."

She attempted to stand up. Paolo put a hand on her shoulder. "No, Mamma. You may well make things worse. This man is enjoying his moment of power. And he has every right. There has been a murder in this house. The murderer must be found. So I beg you for patience. I expect it will all sort itself out soon enough."

"Well, I, for one, do not wish to remain here a single minute longer," Mrs. Simpson said. She was pacing angrily, like a caged panther. "David, you must let your father know that we are being held here against our will. Or if not your father, the British ambassador in Rome."

"I can hardly do that if we can't use the telephone, Wallis," the Prince of Wales said. His voice was high and taut. I suppose he was just realizing the implications of being caught in this situation and what his father might make of it.

But I found myself watching Mrs. Simpson. She hated being thwarted in anything, that was true, but was it possible that she had a bigger motive for making a hasty getaway? Rudolf was known to be a blackmailer. Was it possible he had found out something about her—something she wouldn't want my cousin to know? Something that might finally damn her chances of being married to a king one day? I didn't think she'd have any qualms about shooting a sleeping man and she would also be clever enough to make it look like a suicide.

Camilla was also pacing. "Perhaps I should order some sandwiches in this room, if we are to be caged up here long," she said.

"I don't know what this man thinks he will find," the general said, also in a tense and clipped voice. "If someone has the wit to exchange guns, then the real weapon will be hidden or disposed of, you can be sure."

"What does not make sense to me," Paolo said, his handsome forehead wrinkled in concentration, "is why not shoot him with his own gun, if it was available? Why go through this complicated charade?"

"Perhaps he had a gun but no bullets to go with it," Mummy suggested. "Or perhaps he had hidden the bullets where they couldn't be found. People do hide things, you know."

She glanced at me and I knew what she was thinking. Were the police at this moment turning over Rudi's room and had they yet discovered the photographs? I wished Darcy were here with us. I was still shocked and it would have made all the difference to know he was here beside me. At least he was within reach, I told myself. At least I'd see him tonight.

We heard footsteps going up and down the stairs. We heard noises of furniture being moved.

Nobody spoke. Even Mrs. Simpson had stopped pacing and now stood, staring out of the window at the lake. Perhaps she was working out how she could get to one of the motorboats and drive herself to Switzerland. There was no sound except for the rhythmic ticking of the ormolu clock on the mantelpiece. It seemed we were all holding our breath and waiting for doom to fall. I looked around the room—which one of them? It was unlikely that an outsider could gain access to a bedroom in a house full of servants. It was unlikely that a servant would be involved in the murder of his or her master. So it was one of us. Someone in this room . . . Except that Klinker still had not returned. That was something to tell the assistant chief when he came back into the room.

At last we heard a steady footfall coming toward us. All eyes focused on the door. But it was not the policeman. It was Umberto, carrying a tray.

"It is past your customary time for luncheon, Contessa," he said. "I thought you might need a little sustenance."

On the tray was a carafe of white wine, glasses and a stack of sandwiches.

"Well done, Umberto," Camilla said. "Help yourself, everybody."

"I don't know how anyone can feel like eating at a time like this," Mrs. Simpson said.

But Paolo's mother was already making a beeline for the plate. "Ah, smoked salmon," she said. "My favorite." And took several. The priest was right behind her. I waited my turn then took a couple, although I also found it hard to swallow. I kept glancing across at Mummy then expecting the policeman to come downstairs waving the photographs triumphantly for all to see. We had finished the food and wine and the clock had chimed two before we heard more footsteps. Stratiacelli came into the room, a triumphant grin on his face. He was carrying a morocco leather train case.

"To whom does this belong?" he asked. Actually he said, "Who this belongs?"

"Why, it's mine," Mummy said, sounding surprised.

"Yours, signora?" He was still smiling as he placed the train case on a side table and clicked it open. He removed the top layer then held up a pearl-handled revolver. "And who does this gun belong to?"

"That's also mine," Mummy said. She sounded flustered now.

"You have a gun?" I blurted out before I realized that it was wiser to stay silent. "You carry a gun around with you?"

"I've never actually fired it, darling." Mummy gave a nervous little laugh. "Max insisted I have one for protection when he is away on business. There are still communist agitators in Berlin, you know."

"You say you have never fired it?" Stratiacelli said. "Then it must surprise you to know that it has been fired recently? And I think we find that the bullet that went through that poor man's head is the size that fits this gun?" He didn't actually say it as elegantly as that, but we all understood what he was getting at.

"But that's not possible," Mummy said. "The gun has never left my train case and my case has never left my room. Tell them, Max."

"This is ridiculous." Max stood up. "What possible motive could this lady have for wanting to kill Count Rudolf? She hardly knows him. We have met maybe one or two times at a party in Berlin. This is all. One does not plan the death of a total stranger."

"As to her motive we do not know it yet," Stratiacelli said. "Maybe it will become clear when I interrogate each of you. You claim you are innocent. Who else knew of the existence of this gun?"

"Why, only Max, I suppose. I never mentioned it to anyone else. To tell you the truth I had even forgotten that I had it with me. I had stuck it into my traveling case when we left Berlin because one never knows about brigands on mountain passes."

"So nobody else knew of it except this gentleman. That seems to point to your guilt, signora."

"Oh, come on," Mummy said in an exasperated voice. "I am not stupid. If I had fired the gun and killed somebody, do you think I would have put it back in my train case? Of course not. I would have tied a rock to it and thrown it into the lake, or at the very least stuck it into the middle of one of the bushes, where it wouldn't be found for ages."

There was a silence while Stratiacelli digested this. "Maybe," he said. "Or maybe not. Perhaps you are sure everyone will think this man killed himself and there will be no police inquiry."

"Do we know the approximate time of death, Assistant Chief?" Paolo asked.

"It was before midnight, so the good doctor tells me," Stratiacelli said.

"There you are, then." Max brushed his hands together. "Until midnight this lady and I were both sitting in our room, awake and talking."

"Awake and . . . talking?" Stratiacelli put an insinuation into this.

"That is correct," Max said.

"You are this lady's husband, *mein Herr*?" Stratiacelli asked.

"They are not married," Paolo's mother remarked from her chair beside the fireplace. "There is much sin in this house, even before the murder. Is that not so, Father Francisco?"

The priest looked up and nodded solemnly.

"So you share a room, *mein Herr*, but you are not married?" Stratiacelli asked sweetly.

"We are engaged to be married," Max said in an annoyed voice.

"Actually that was what we were talking about," Mummy said. "We were discussing plans for our wedding this summer and whether it would be better to hold the ceremony in Berlin or at our villa on Lake Lugano."

"And Claire thought that Lugano in summer would be more pleasant than Berlin, where it gets rather hot," Max added.

"That's right," Mummy said. "And then we heard the downstairs clock chime midnight and we said we had better break off the discussion and go to sleep. So we did."

It took a moment for Stratiacelli to process this as it was translated for him. Then he said, with a sneer in his voice, "You people—I don't understand. Your morals are not my morals. You think the changing of bed companions is a game, yes? So who knows which of you was in this man's bed last night, eh?"

"How dare you." Paolo's uncle stood up. "That is enough. You insult my guests. You question their morals. You have overstepped your rank and I shall now make a telephone call to Rome."

"If you attempt to make a telephone call, I shall have you arrested and thrown into jail," Stratiacelli said. "I see now that this is a conspiracy. Perhaps you all know who killed this man and you think you can stay silent and keep the truth from Stratiacelli. But let us see how silent you remain after a few days in a prison cell."

"You would not dare!" Mrs. Simpson said. She strode across the room and stared into Stratiacelli's face. "This is the Prince of Wales. The heir to the English throne. If you dare to suggest that he has been involved in a crime, if you dare to take him to jail, you will find that England declares war on Italy. I would not want to be in your shoes when the British fleet sails into Genoa harbor to rescue the prince."

Stratiacelli clearly hadn't understood most of this rapid outburst, but he got enough of it to make him turn pale.

"Naturally the Prince of Wales is beyond reproach," he said rapidly. "I must go by the facts. By the evidence before my eyes. The evidence will tell me all I need to know. And what I have so far is a dead man, a gun that has not been fired and another gun that has. What am I to conclude from that? That the second gun put an end to this man's life. And the owner of this gun must be my first suspect. So, now we check for fingerprints on the guns. My men will take the fingerprints of everybody in this house and we will see which fingerprints appear on both the guns."

"Actually yours do now, Assistant Chief," Camilla said, pointing at the gun in his hand. "And presumably so do those of your man who found it."

The policeman looked down at his hand. "Ah so. Yes. You may be right," he said, hastily putting the gun down on the table.

"You may well have smudged or destroyed any prints that would have been there before," Camilla said. There was a note of triumph in her voice. "We may never be able to prove who fired that gun."

Stratiacelli looked a little worried and embarrassed. Then he drew himself up to his full five foot four. "Do not worry, Contessa. Stratiacelli will not rest until this case is solved and the murderer is brought to justice," he said. "My men will now take your fingerprints."

"And what about our luncheon?" Paolo's mother demanded. "All we have had to sustain us is a few little sandwiches. When you are my age you need proper meals at regular times to sustain health."

"You may eat when the fingerprints have been taken," Stratiacelli said. He looked out of the window. *"Mamma mia,"* he said. "There is a strange man creeping around the outside of your house." He rushed into the foyer and called up the stairs, "Bernardo! Giancosimo! Down here immediately. Apprehend the man creeping through the bushes!"

Chapter 24

Tuesday, April 23, still being interrogated

Things are looking bad for my mother. Surely she wasn't stupid enough to have killed Rudi?

Footsteps clattered down the stairs and I heard the crunch of feet on gravel outside. My heart was racing. It had occurred to me that the man could well be Darcy, trying to see what was happening in the house. If they caught him and brought him in here, how would he ever explain what he was doing and how would I ever explain that I knew he was here? I waited, hardly daring to breathe. We heard men's voices and then footsteps coming back into the foyer. I had an overwhelming desire to come out and see for myself. We heard one of the policemen speaking, then Stratiacelli's voice. Then the assistant chief came back into our room, followed by two young policemen, holding between them a struggling Klinker. Klinker was covered in mud and soaking wet and looked very miserable.

"Do any of you know this man?" Stratiacelli demanded. "He

was caught sneaking outside your house and has refused to answer my men's questions."

"That is because he speaks no Italian." The general had risen to his feet. He glared at Klinker, who stood there, his eyes darting around nervously. "*Mein Gott*, Klinker. What has happened to you?"

Klinker turned to face the general and let out a rapid string of German. The general said, *"Ach so."* He smiled, then addressed Stratiacelli. "This is my adjutant, Lieutenant Klinker. He went for a walk up the mountain early this morning. When he came down, he found that the small stream he had crossed had become a raging torrent because of the rain. He tried to find a way around, but there was none. He found a place where a crossing may have been possible by using a tree branch that extended across the water. The branch gave way. He fell into the raging waters and was swept downstream. He nearly drowned."

Camilla stood up. "Lieutenant Klinker, I'm so very sorry. What an awful ordeal. Let me have someone run a bath for you and get you out of those wet clothes immediately. And I'll have brandy sent up to your room." Then she must have remembered that we were in the middle of an interrogation. "If that is permissible, Assistant Chief? I cannot let one of my guests catch pneumonia."

"Very good. You may allow one of your servants to take care of this man."

Klinker shook his head and said something in German.

"He says he does not wish to cause any inconvenience. He was trying to find a back way to gain access to the house so that he was not seen in this embarrassing condition. But he is quite capable of taking care of his own needs."

"Oh no, Lieutenant Klinker," Camilla said. "It will be no trouble to have one of our footmen look after you. You've had a horrible experience." She started to usher Klinker to the door.

Stratiacelli motioned to one of his officers. "Go with them, Bernardo. Keep watch at all times."

He waited until the little procession had left. "Now we return to our business," he said. "The matter of fingerprints. Do not move. My man will be with you shortly."

And he left us.

"Impossible, annoying little man," Mrs. Simpson said. "Paolo, we must telephone the British consul and have His Highness taken from this place before the press gets wind of the murder." She turned to glare at me. "And why you had to notice the gun in the wrong hand and couldn't have left this as a convenient suicide I can't think, Georgiana. Look at the trouble and annoyance you've put us through now."

Frankly I was beginning to think the same thing. Rudolf had not been my favorite person. He had been blackmailing at least one person in this house, probably more. He was probably also Hitler's spy. So why should I have cared that someone took his life? I suppose it was that wretched Rannoch upbringing that instilled a sense of duty and honor at all times. "I'm sorry," I managed to mumble. "I did what I thought was right at the time."

"And now you've got your poor mother into deep trouble," Mrs. Simpson went on. She was clearly enjoying this part. "I don't know how she's going to get out of this. Not if that little man has his way. Do they have the guillotine in Italy? Or the firing squad?"

Mummy gave a little gasp of fright.

"Wallis!" the Prince of Wales said. "That was quite inappropriate."

"Sorry, honey. Just trying to lighten the mood."

"Hardly going to lighten it by relating the various ways I could be executed," Mummy said angrily.

"Don't worry, *mein Liebling*. I will make sure you are safe," Max said. "If necessary we will take one of the speedboats and whisk you to Switzerland."

A young policeman came in, looking horribly embarrassed. *"Mi scusino, signori,"* he said and opened his fingerprint kit on one of the tables. One by one he took our prints and then made a getaway as fast as he could, murmuring, *"Grazie, signori. Grazie."*

"Well, that's finished," Paolo's mother said. "Now for luncheon. Father Francisco, you may escort me." She waited for him to take her arm and they left the room.

"I suppose we may join them," Camilla said, glancing at Paolo. "I've no idea whether the servants have been allowed to prepare a meal or whether they too have been questioned by the assistant chief."

She headed for the door. The others followed. As I went to follow I was dragged back by a grip of steel on my arm. Mummy held me as the others disappeared through the door.

"Georgie, you've got to help me," she whispered. "If they find those photographs I'll hang, or be shot by a firing squad or whatever they do here. I'm done for. You're the only person who can save me."

"I don't really know what I can do," I said. "I have already searched in the obvious places. He may have stuck the photographs into a book in the library, but I can't go through all those volumes, and neither will the police. They are not looking for photographs."

"They must be in his room. They must be," she insisted. "We could go up now, while the others are at lunch. The police must have finished dusting his room for fingerprints."

"Are you out of your mind?" I hissed back at her. "If we are caught in his room, searching for something, do you not think that might make Stratiacelli even more convinced that you are guilty?"

"Then you go for me," she said. "He doesn't know you are my daughter. If you're caught you can just say you were curious, or you made a mistake and went into the wrong door."

"Mummy, I don't think one enters the room of a murdered person by mistake."

"Then think of something, please. For God's sake, Georgie. It may be now or never."

She was clinging to my arm as if she was a drowning person and

I was a tree limb. And she was shaking. What could I do? "All right. I'll give it a try," I said.

She hurried down the hall, calling out brightly, "Max, darling. Wait for little *moi*."

I climbed the stairs, one by one, each step feeling heavier and heavier. The upstairs corridor seemed to stretch out forever. I reached Rudolf's room. The door was slightly ajar. I pushed it open cautiously, one inch and then one inch more. The room appeared to be empty. I took a deep breath and stepped inside, tiptoeing over the carpet that covered most of the floor. I noticed that white feather still lying a foot or so from the bed. There was a strange and unpleasant smell. A burned odor, not only that of gunpowder but of something else I couldn't quite identify. I also caught a whiff of the smell of blood and the smell of death. The bed was now empty, the body having been removed, but the pillow was dark brown with dried blood and blood spatters decorated the pink wallpaper above the brass bedstead. I had an urge to rush over to the French doors and let in some good fresh air.

But I knew I might only have a few moments. I looked around the room. If I were Rudi, where would I hide something I didn't want found? Certainly not in one of the drawers of that armoire beside the bed, nor the vanity. There was a similar wardrobe to mine on the right side of the room. That looked big enough to hold a multitude of secrets. I had no idea how big the photographs were: if they were ordinary snapshots they could be in the pocket of any piece of clothing. I shook my head in despair. An impossible task. But I had promised my mother that I would do my best and a Rannoch never goes back on her word. I had to start somewhere: under the mattress, maybe? That should be my first search as the bed would obviously be stripped in the near future. I stared at that dried blood with distaste and took a deep breath, willing myself to do it.

As I took a step toward the bed a figure rose up from beyond it. I opened my mouth, but I was so terrified that just the ghost of a scream came out. I stepped backward, lost my balance and careened into the armoire. The vase that had been on it teetered and started to fall. I made a grab at it, but it was too late. The vase crashed to the floor. The person who had risen up from behind the bed looked equally terrified. It was Camilla.

"Georgie! Oh, my God. You scared the daylights out of me," she said. "What on earth are you doing in here?"

"I suppose I could ask the same question of you," I said, trying to speak and breathe normally. "You were presumably not kneeling on the floor to say your prayers to Mecca."

"I was looking for something," she said. "You too?"

I nodded.

"Letters?" she asked.

"Photographs."

"We only have a few minutes. Let's cooperate," she whispered. "You take that half of the room and I'll take the other."

"I have to pick up the pieces of that vase first," I said. "Someone may have heard it falling. It made an awful crash."

"Here, let me help." She came around the bed and we scrabbled on the floor, picking up china. Luckily it had broken into several big pieces.

"We must get rid of these before . . ." Camilla whispered. We both froze as we heard the sound of voices coming up the stairs. "Quickly, into my room," I whispered.

We dashed to the door and were just opening the door of my room when Stratiacelli's voice echoed down the hallway. "Where are you going, ladies?"

We stopped and turned to face him, horribly conscious of the sharp shards of the vase in our hands. "Into my room," I said. "I wanted to get a handkerchief, but I was afraid to come upstairs alone so the contessa was good enough to come with me."

Stratiacelli came closer. I slipped the bits of broken china into my skirt pocket. "This room is yours?" he asked.

"Of course," I said. "You may see for yourself if you like."

"Next door to the dead man's room?"

"That's right."

He came closer and went into my room, prowling around. While his back was turned I saw Camilla tuck her pieces of vase behind a pillow on the bed. Stratiacelli looked up unexpectedly.

"But on the night of the murder you heard nothing? No gunshot?"

"I know. I thought that was strange too," I said. "I'm sure the walls are thick in an old house like this, but a gunshot is a loud noise, isn't it?"

"It is. Even a small pistol like the one that killed this man makes a loud sound. You were in this room before midnight?"

"Oh, I was sound asleep by eleven," I said.

"You are a heavy sleeper?"

"Not usually, but I must have been extra tired. And we did have a lot of wine with dinner. I'm not used to it."

"Ah," he said. "And this man who died. Count Rudolf von Rosskopf. You were acquainted with him?"

"I only met him when I arrived here two days ago," I said. "I have never been to Germany and I don't usually move in smart society."

"You are not also an aristocrat? A companion, maybe?"

"Signor Stratiacelli," Camilla said in a shocked voice, "this young lady is related to the King of England. She is cousin to the Prince of Wales."

"I see. But you do not meet other aristocrats? I thought you people play together, no?" he asked, the hint of a sneer on his face now.

"I have no money," I said. "My branch of the family is penniless. I am about to marry a man who is also penniless. I only came to this party because the queen knew I was going to be in Stresa and thought it would be a treat for me to be in such exalted company."

Camilla had to translate this for him.

"Ah," he said again. "I see."

"Lady Georgiana is very upset by this business, Signor Stratiacelli," Camilla said. "She is delicate by nature. I think we should let her lie down for a while, don't you?"

"Very well," he said. "You may rest, Lady Georgiana. I hope my men do not disturb you when they finish taking fingerprints from the next-door room."

He bowed and retreated.

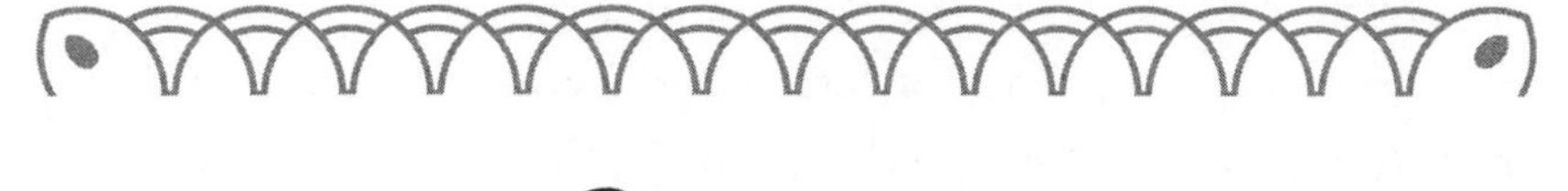

Chapter 25

Tuesday, April 23, around 2:30 p.m.

Just had a lucky escape.

"Let's just hope it is only fingerprints that they find," Camilla said as the door was closed, leaving us alone.

"That was close," I said, removing my hand from the folds of my skirt and holding out the pieces of broken china. "Where can we hide this?"

"Don't worry. I'll tell Gerda the policemen knocked it over and have her take the pieces out to the trash." She managed a little smile of conspiracy.

It was just beginning to dawn on me that Camilla was a suspect in Rudi's murder. It was her house, after all. She could come and go as she pleased without anyone noticing. And it seemed that she had a motive. I remembered that she had sneaked up to Rudi's room earlier that night. And it might have been her I overheard having a tense conversation in his room too.

"Camilla, was Rudolf blackmailing you?" I asked.

Her face went white. "How did you know?"

"You were searching for letters, you said. You were taking a tremendous risk, going into the dead man's room while the police are still in the house, so I figured it must be very important to you."

"Very important?" Her voice had an edge to it. "A matter of life and death." She sank down onto my bed. "Oh, Georgie, it's been so awful. A nightmare."

I sat beside her. For a while she stared at her hands. One of them had a small cut from those sharp edges of china. We watched as blood oozed from it. Then she said, "I did a foolish thing. Something I shall regret for the rest of my life."

"You let Rudolf seduce you?" I asked.

She looked up and nodded, glad that she hadn't had to spell it out herself. "So stupid of me. But you know how things are with our sort of people. We were at a big party in Monte Carlo. Very glamorous. I—well, I've never been the glamorous type. You remember me from school. One of the plain county-set girls, right?"

I could hardly say yes, so I said, "I don't think any of us could have been called glamorous or sophisticated at school."

She nodded. "I couldn't believe my luck when Paolo started courting me and then asked me to marry him. It was like a dream come true. I mean, he was handsome. He had the title. One of the oldest families. Anyway, he had to return to Rome suddenly and he left me with the friends in Monte Cosimo. We went out on a yacht. Mostly people I didn't know. Rudolf started paying attention to me. I was flattered because there were some beautiful women there. We drank a lot. Then he came to my cabin. I had drunk much more than usual and I wasn't able to fight him off."

"He forced himself on you?" I asked, shocked.

"Well, no. That's the worst part. I started to fight him off, but the more he went on, the more I found myself giving in, actually enjoying it. In the morning I was horrified at myself. I had to get away as quickly as possible. The yacht was docked in Monte Carlo.

I wrote Rudolf a note, telling him I could never see him again and please not to contact me, then I slipped ashore and went home. And I thought that was that."

She looked up again, willing me to understand. "Then the letters started arriving. Rudolf had my note, actually incriminating myself, confessing to the night I had spent with him, and he was going to show it to Paolo if I didn't send him a large sum of money."

"So you paid him?"

"I have some private money from my family. I sent him what he asked for, thinking that would take care of it. But of course it didn't. He wanted more and more. And the problem was that I couldn't risk letting Paolo get his hands on that note."

"You don't think he'd understand that you were drunk and that Rudi took advantage of you?"

She shook her head. "Paolo's family is very strict on infidelity. It might be a last straw in deciding that I was no longer suitable to be his wife. You see, I can't have children. We've been married three years with no baby on the way so I went to be tested and . . . well, I had a burst appendix when I was twelve and apparently that has ruined my chances. I think Paolo was shattered by the news. He's an only son. The title would die out with him. And so what better excuse to divorce me for infidelity and marry an Italian girl who can give him lots of babies?"

I took her hand. She gave me a sad little smile. "Perhaps he loves you for the person you are, Camilla. And now there is every chance that you are free. Rudolf's secret has died with him."

"God, I hope so." She gave a long sigh. Then something occurred to her and she looked up at me. "Was he also blackmailing you?" she asked. "Did he also force himself upon you?"

"He tried to on the train coming here," I said. "But no, I'd never met him before. It's my mother he's blackmailing."

"Golly." Camilla looked surprised.

"In her case he had a hidden camera and took pictures. Her

situation is like yours. Max is quite prudish and the photographs were, shall we say, risqué? She's been living in fear since she found he was a fellow guest at this party. What on earth did you invite him for?"

"I didn't!" Camilla exclaimed. "I nearly died of fright myself when he showed up on the doorstep. Apparently Uncle Cosimo had told Paolo he wanted to host some Germans—good for Italian/German understanding, he said. I had no idea that Rudolf would be one of them."

"Let's just hope that the police don't search that room too well," I said. "I did look through the rest of the house to the best of my ability, but I think he must have kept things in his own room. The door was locked when he went out."

"Yes, I know. I tried it too."

"You must have access to the servants' key," I said. "Why didn't you take that?"

"It's not that easy. Signora Follini, our housekeeper, keeps the duplicate keys on her belt," she said. "She takes them to bed with her at night. She hands them out when servants ask for them. I suppose I could have just demanded the key, but I couldn't think of a good reason. And there was never a moment when I wouldn't risk being seen."

"I saw you coming out of his room yesterday evening," I said.

"Yes. I did manage to get in there once. I'd tried a few times, but this time he left his door unlocked. I did search in all the likely places, but I only had a few minutes while my hand was dummy so I had to get back to the table."

"If you couldn't find anything in the likely places, there's a good chance the police won't find anything either," I said.

"A good chance, yes," she said. "Let's just say a little prayer, shall we?"

"Get your tame priest to pray for you," I said, before realizing that this might not be the thing to say to a die-hard Catholic.

But she actually laughed. "Yes, he's pretty dreadful, isn't he? He gives me the willies, frankly. But he comes with the house. Rather like a dog you can't put down. He and Paolo's mother. That's why I'm glad I'm not here too often."

"You must miss your family," I said. "Do they come out to visit you often?"

"Never," she said. "I think I told you that my father is of the impression that abroad starts at Calais and anywhere abroad is utterly bloody. Give him his hounds and his pheasants and his pigs and he's quite happy. And Mother is the timid sort who would never travel alone. So I see them maybe once a year."

I looked at her with pity. Here was someone who had everything—palaces, an ancient title, respect, oodles of servants and a handsome husband—and she was lonely. Then I thought that Darcy and I would muddle along on little money and be blissfully happy.

"I suppose we should join the others for luncheon," she said. "They will wonder what has happened to us."

Before we could leave the room there was a light tap on the door and Gerda appeared. "Ah, Contessa," she said, hesitating in the doorway. "I was told that Lady Georgiana was not feeling well and went to lie down. I wondered if I could bring her something."

"Very kind of you, Gerda," I said. "But thank you. I think I feel well enough to join the others for lunch. It has been something of a shock for all of us today."

"Naturally," she said. "One does not expect a death in the house. It is always shocking, especially for those with sheltered upbringing. Myself I saw death during the Great War."

"Did the war come to Austria?" I asked. "I hadn't realized that."

"I volunteered to go as a nurse," she said. "I was only eighteen, but I felt I should do something to help the suffering."

"Very commendable," Camilla said.

"One does what one has to," she said. She gestured to the floor beside the wardrobe. "I took care of the mud on your shoes, my lady. I think they look a little better than they did."

A little better! The shoes were gleaming as if they were brand-new. "You're a genius, Gerda," I said.

She actually almost blushed. "You are most kind, my lady. So if you do not need me, I will go back to pressing the contessa's evening dress."

She bowed and walked out.

"Golly," I muttered involuntarily. Camilla shot me a look that completely echoed what I was feeling—that Gerda was a little scarily perfect. We walked down the stairs together in silence. In the dining room a simple luncheon had been prepared: grilled pike from the lake with parsley potatoes, followed by ice cream and biscotti. We ate in near silence. Nobody felt like talking and most of us didn't feel like eating either. My mother pushed her food around her plate, glancing up nervously at me from time to time. Klinker, now in clean clothes again, looked exhausted and ate methodically. Only Paolo's mother and the priest tucked in with obvious enjoyment.

After lunch my mother announced she was going to lie down. I decided I couldn't wait a second longer. I had to see Darcy. The storm had passed and the sky was now a brilliant blue, with a few streaks of white cloud clinging to the mountaintops. A perfect excuse to go out for a walk. I had just reached the front door when I heard a voice behind me.

"Where do you go, signorina?" It was Stratiacelli.

"I thought I'd take a stroll through the gardens, since the weather has brightened up," I said.

"Really?" He had that same smug smile on his face. "Did I not say that all were forbidden to leave the house without my permission?"

"I don't see any harm in letting me go for a little walk," I said.

"No harm? The innocent young lady who has never met the murdered gentleman before."

"That's true," I said.

"And yet her fingerprints are all over his room. On his door. On the armoire beside the gentleman's bed." He had his head on one side, giving me an inquisitive look.

Golly. I swallowed hard. How could I come up with a good answer to that one? Then Camilla called to me. "Is something wrong, Georgie?"

"Signor Stratiacelli won't let me leave the house because he says my fingerprints were in Rudolf's room," I said.

"Well, of course they were." Camilla came up to us. "Perfectly simple, Assistant Chief. When Lady Georgiana arrived I asked her which room she would prefer. I showed her the room that Count Rudolf eventually occupied and the room she finally chose."

"That's right," I said. "I was originally assigned to Count Rudolf's room, but I wasn't comfortable there as it had a masculine feeling to it. So the contessa let me switch to the room next door."

Stratiacelli frowned as he tried to understand this. Camilla obliged by translating into Italian. "I see," he said. "And you have no connection to the gentleman at all?"

"I told you. I met him for the first time when I arrived here." I was just praying they hadn't managed to find out we were on the same train. Nobody knew that except for my mother and Camilla.

"One of the servants tell me you were seen coming down the stairs together, arm in arm and looking very friendly. Perhaps he tried to become even more friendly. Perhaps you did something with him that you later regretted. Perhaps he forced himself on you. The signora had told you that she had a gun and you decided to take revenge."

"A good story, Assistant Chief," I said, "except that I was never friendly with Count Rudolf. It's true he did try to turn his charms on to me, but I rejected them. And he held my elbow to come down the stairs so that I did not fall in a tight evening dress. And for your information, I am still a virgin. I am saving myself for my marriage this summer."

To my amusement Stratiacelli looked a trifle embarrassed. "All the same," he said, "nobody may leave this house for any reason until I have apprehended the murderer."

"I think we may be here for a long time," I muttered to Camilla as Stratiacelli stalked off again. "Golly, thank you for saving me, Camilla. That was quick thinking."

"We have to stick together at this moment, Georgie," she whispered back.

Chapter 26

Tuesday, April 23
Late afternoon at Villa Fiori

Still haven't managed to see Darcy.

It was a long afternoon. We sat in the lake view room, watching the steamers sailing up and down the lake and waiting. Every now and then one of us was summoned to be interviewed by Stratiacelli. Mummy remained in her room all afternoon. I had some time to think: Was it possible that she had actually killed him? She had the means. She had the motive. And I knew that she was ruthless. Nobody gets to the top of her profession as an actress and then marries a duke without a streak of ruthlessness in her nature. I didn't think she'd have the nerve to put a gun to Rudi's head and pull the trigger, but then I couldn't be absolutely sure.

And then there was Max. He also knew about the gun; in fact, he was the one who insisted she carry a gun to protect herself. What if he had somehow found out about Rudi's fling with my mother and subsequent blackmailing? I could see him killing to preserve her honor. But he was a straightforward sort of chap. I didn't think he'd go through the whole charade of switching guns and trying to make it look like a suicide. He'd have thrown Rudi overboard when they were in the speedboat, or he'd have taken a potshot at him when they were in the grounds.

So who did that leave? Camilla was the obvious one. I couldn't bring myself to ask her if she had killed him when we were together in my room. Again she had a strong motive—the strongest. Her whole marriage and future were at stake. And she knew where there was a duplicate key, and could well have found out that Mummy carried a gun in her luggage. But could she have sat with me so calmly and discussed his blackmailing her? And of course the ultimate reason that she was not the murderer: if she had shot him she would have had all the time in the world to search his room. She'd have had no need to be crawling around on his floor when I found her.

But then there was Paolo. Had he somehow found out what Rudi had done to his wife and taken his own revenge? I realized he had been very quiet since the murder had been discovered. Was he lying low? Then I shook my head. I had seen his face when the dead man was first discovered. His face had shown utter shock and terror.

I didn't for one second believe that my cousin David could shoot anybody at close range. Just not the type. Mrs. Simpson, on the other hand, had the sangfroid and ruthlessness to calmly pull a trigger and make it look like a suicide. I thought how happy the king and queen would be if she was hauled off to an Italian jail. But I didn't see how they would ever prove anything against her. She'd also be the type to have wiped everything meticulously clean of fingerprints.

That left the Germans and Uncle Cosimo. Would they have any reason to get rid of someone who was probably sent to be Hitler's spy and keep tabs on them? That episode with Klinker was interesting. I wondered if he had been somewhere in the morning and the wet and bedraggled appearance had been arranged to give him a good alibi. But if he had killed Rudolf, why not take the next train back to Germany, rather than face the investigation here? Then something did cross my mind: Klinker was the general's aide. He went everywhere with him. Was it possible that they had more than a friendship? I had heard that even the toughest of men could have leanings in that direction. And if Rudolf had found out about it, he would not have hesitated to blackmail the general. That sort of information would undoubtedly cost him his job, his reputation. And they were both experienced with firearms.

Which led to the white feather. I knew that during the war white feathers were a symbol of cowardice, given to those who did not join the armed forces. Was it possible that Rudolf was killed because he had displayed cowardice in some way? Blackmailers are certainly the worst sort of cowards.

If only I was allowed out of the house, I could find Darcy. It seemed others were feeling the same way about being cooped up and idle.

"Really, David, I don't believe this," Mrs. Simpson said. "You have got to telephone the British ambassador in Rome. Have them send a car for you immediately. Any moment now the press will catch wind of this and we'll be besieged with newsmen. And you know what your father will say about that!"

"Wallis, the police chappie did say that we were not allowed to use the telephone," the Prince of Wales said.

"You're the damned heir to the British throne, for God's sake," she snapped. "A jumped-up little policeman from the back of beyond can't tell you what to do. If you won't call the ambassador, I will."

She got up. The prince grabbed her wrist. "Absolutely not, Wallis. It wouldn't be the right thing to do at all. Just be patient. I'm sure by tomorrow we will all be free to leave."

"Why don't they just arrest Claire? It's obvious she did it, isn't it?"

"Do you think so?" I asked. I had been sitting silently until now. "My mother is not stupid, Mrs. Simpson. Like you, she is a survivor and opportunist."

There was a hissed intake of breath from Mrs. Simpson. "Now see here," she began, but I went on.

"If you had just shot somebody and taken the trouble to switch guns and make it look like a suicide, would you put the real weapon back in your bag where it could be found?"

"Perhaps she thought that it would be called a suicide and nobody would do any searching," Mrs. Simpson said in a peeved voice. She hated to be crossed in any way.

"She could easily have gone out into the grounds and hidden the weapon, or tossed it into the lake," I pointed out.

"But then Max would notice she no longer had the gun with her," Mrs. Simpson said, triumphant at having scored a point. "And being the correct and upright guy that he is, he'd probably report it to the police."

"And she could say her gun had been stolen," I countered. It was like verbal Ping-Pong. Actually I was jolly proud of myself. When I first met her I had been completely tongue-tied.

"At least they should let us go outside," the German general said. "The weather is now fine. It is not healthy to sit here all day."

"I agree," David said. "Surely that wretched policeman could station one of his men at the gate if he was worried about our making a bolt for it."

We stopped talking as we heard footsteps coming across the marble foyer. It was Umberto, the butler, and he carried a silver salver.

"A note for the lady Georgiana," he said. "Delivered by hand."

From Darcy, I thought and almost snatched it from the tray. Then I saw it wasn't Darcy's bold, black script. I opened it and saw it was from Belinda.

My darling Georgie,

I took your advice and I'm back at my little house in the village. You suggested I could move back home and you could look after me. I'm sure your house party must be nearly at an end and frankly I couldn't stand it in that place a moment longer. All those rules and dreary food and nuns giving me disapproving looks, and worse still, praying over me and for my lost soul. Of course I'll have to return when the birth is imminent, but in the meantime I can't wait to be back with you and we can laugh and eat and drink what we want to. Even smoke if I want to, which has been strictly forbidden there! I'm sending this note with Francesca's granddaughter who speaks a little English. She's been told to wait outside for a return note from you. Let me know how soon you can be here.

Love,
Belinda

Oh crikey, I thought. What am I going to do now?

"Bad news, Georgiana?" Camilla asked.

"Not at all. Just unexpected. The sick friend I came to visit really misses me and wants me at her side. I'll have to write and tell her that I'm not allowed to leave here just yet. Could I possibly have some writing paper?"

"Of course," she said. "Paolo, could you take Georgie to your study and set her up with a pen and writing paper?"

Paolo stood up and smiled at me. "Come with me, Georgie."

I thought how strained he looked, utterly drained, and how nice he was. And again I found myself wondering if he had found out about his wife's being blackmailed and taken things into his own hands. And with his sort of family honor, he was now being eaten up with guilt about what he had done. I wished that Stratiacelli would hurry up with his search for fingerprints and could now conclude who actually had committed the murder. I followed Paolo along the mirrored corridor and into his study at the far end. It was a dark room, its window in the deep shadow of a colonnade outside. Paolo cleared off his desk and put paper and an inkwell in front of me.

"I will leave you in peace," he said.

"Thank you," I said. "You are most kind. This business must have been a terrible shock for you."

"It was," he said. "Never did I think that a murder would take place in my house. And what is worse is to know that somebody among us committed that murder. What if they never find out the truth? What if that silly little man arrests the wrong person? I feel so helpless."

"We all do," I said. I looked around the room as I spoke and I noticed that the window leading to the colonnade was, in fact, a French door. I could get out without being seen! I gave Paolo a sweet smile. "I won't be long," I said. "And I can find my own way back to the others."

He took the hint and left. I wrote quickly:

Dear Belinda,

What a shock to find you have returned home. I hope it was the right thing to do at this stage, as you were being well looked after, although I'm sure it was boring. I'll try to join you as soon as possible, but I can't say when that will be. One of the guests at the house party has been murdered and we are currently all under suspicion and not allowed to leave the premises. Until I can be let out maybe Francesca's granddaughter can do some shopping and bring in some food for you. I'm sorry. This is really quite upsetting and I can't wait to leave. Take care of yourself.

Your friend,
Georgie

I tucked the note into an envelope, then I slipped out through the French door, finding myself in a colonnade that ran the full length of the back of the villa. I crept along it and caught sight of

Francesca's granddaughter, Giovanna, standing outside the servants' entrance on the far side. I called to her and she ran up to me.

"Here." I handed her the note. "It tells the signorina why I can't come today. You help her, all right? You get food for her if she needs it? Bring messages?"

"Okay. I do," she said and gave me a bright smile before running off.

I looked around wondering where I might find Darcy and whether I'd get into trouble if Stratiacelli looked for me and I was nowhere to be found. On the side of the house where I was now standing there was a kitchen garden and beyond it an orchard, olive trees and even a chicken run. Darcy had promised to come to my room tonight, but he must be dying with curiosity to know what was happening inside the house. I hesitated, torn between wanting to find him and finding myself in serious trouble with the assistant chief. I set off, darting toward the first row of shrubbery and then planning to make my way around to the gardeners' quarters. Then I heard a whistle. Surely it came from a human and not a bird. I looked around in the direction it came from and Darcy's head poked out from behind the henhouse.

"Georgie, over here." He beckoned.

I slipped into the kitchen garden, between the rows of beanpoles, and reached the olive trees that bordered it. Then I dodged around until I came to the chicken run. Darcy was standing behind the henhouse at one end of their enclosure. The chickens rushed over to me, clucking madly in the hope that I had come to feed them. I just prayed that nobody heard this ruckus. I looked around and saw that we were hidden from view of the main villa.

He grabbed me as soon as I reached him. "Are you all right? I've been hanging around as close as I dared to the house all day, hoping to find out more."

"I'm fine," I said. "Although all of our nerves are on edge. It's like waiting for doom to fall. We are not supposed to leave the house."

"So they haven't found out who shot Rudolf yet?"

"No. There's a highly inept policeman from Stresa. I think we're all under suspicion although the gun that shot him belonged to my mother."

"Your mother? Surely the policeman can see that she had no motive. Why would she want to shoot Rudolf?"

I decided to tell him the truth, or at least part of the truth. "Actually he was blackmailing her."

Now he really looked surprised. "Blackmailing her? About what?"

"He had got his hands on a rather revealing photograph he threatened to send to Max," I said, deciding to skirt around the whole story. "He was blackmailing at least one other person in the house."

"Was he really? I always knew he wasn't quite straight, but I never thought he'd sink to blackmail. No wonder he lived so well. Ah well, that's okay if someone he was blackmailing decided to kill him." He looked relieved. I stared at him, confused.

"Why is that okay? Is one justified in shooting a man who is blackmailing?"

He gave an uneasy chuckle. "No, I didn't mean that." He glanced around, although we were quite alone. "Look, I really shouldn't tell you this, and you are not to repeat it to anyone, but Rudolf was one of ours."

"What do you mean? You told me he was Hitler's spy."

He nodded. "He was. He was also a double agent."

"Crikey," I said. "He was working for the British government?"

He nodded again. "He was very useful to us, reporting what was going on in Berlin. That's how we heard that something was going to happen in Stresa and why I was sent here."

I stared at him. "So someone found out he was a double agent and got rid of him."

"Highly possible."

"Especially as he was present at that meeting," I said, my brain now putting thoughts into order. "Then that would be either the general or Klinker, I suppose. But how on earth did either of them know that my mother carried a small pistol with her?"

"She might have mentioned it?"

I shook my head. "No. She had completely forgotten it was in her luggage. Apparently she had never used it, but Max made her carry it to protect herself when he wasn't around."

"Max did?" Darcy paused and I read his train of thought.

"You think Max is the real German agent here?"

"Why else would he be invited to take part? Or did he get himself invited because Herr Hitler wanted him to get rid of Rudi?"

"Oh golly," I said. It made all too much sense. Persuading Mummy that she needed the pistol to protect herself. Easygoing, amiable Max. Was that a cover for a ruthless man? I knew he owned factories and had made millions. A man does not achieve that kind of wealth without being ruthless. Poor Mummy, I thought. Would he save her if she was arrested for the murder?

"I'll ask London what they know about Max," Darcy said. "And the general and Klinker. Are there other Germans in the house?"

"No, only the two army chaps and Max," I said. Then I added, "Camilla's horribly efficient maid comes across to me as more German than Austrian. Aren't Austrians supposed to be fun-loving and friendly? She is stiff and rigid, although of course she is a maid."

Again his eyebrows went up. "German-speaking maid, eh? What's her name and where did she come from?"

"Her name is Gerda. Let me think. What did she say her last name was? Oh yes. I believe it was Stretzl. Gerda Stretzl. Yes, that was it."

"Faithful retainer? With the family for years?"

"No, actually, she only came to Camilla a couple of months ago. But she comes with impeccable credentials," I added hastily. "She was formerly with the wife of a cabinet minister. She didn't say which one, but the woman committed suicide, I gather. And Camilla's maid had just walked under a bus, so it was ideal for both of them. She's rather frightening, Darcy. Horribly efficient. Actually makes me long for Queenie."

Darcy chuckled. The chickens squawked again, still hoping to be fed, and I glanced toward the villa, horribly conscious of the passing of time.

"I must get back. They'll be looking for me," I said. "I wish you were in the house with me."

"That might not be a bad idea," he said. "I'd feel happier knowing I was on the spot, should anything happen."

"What do you mean, should anything happen?" I asked uneasily.

"I mean that you overheard that conversation."

"But nobody knows."

"You think nobody knows. What if somebody suspected?"

"Nobody suspected," I said uneasily. "And whoever killed Rudi would have no reason to fear me."

"All the same," he said, "I think I'd be happier if I was in the house with you. I think I'll make an unexpected appearance. I'll say I had business in Milan and decided to pay a surprise call upon my beloved."

"Oh yes," I said, my spirits rising at the thought of Darcy in the house with me. "What a lovely idea. Maybe you'll be able to work out which one of them shot Rudi. I'm certainly in the dark so far."

"I have to go into Stresa and send a couple of telegrams first," he said. "So I may be a while. I might not even get any answers before the morning."

"How are you going to get out if they won't let anyone leave?"

He grinned. "The way I got in to begin with. Climb from the wall onto the roof of the gardeners' cottages. Simple. Then when I'm ready to make my appearance I'll go around to the main gate and demand to be admitted."

"Surely they won't deliver replies to your telegrams to the gardeners' quarters?"

He smiled as he shook his head. "No, I'll have to go to the post office to collect them. So I may not put in an appearance here until tomorrow morning. You should be safe with all the policemen in the house at the moment. I've been watching them coming and going."

"Unless the assistant chief makes an arrest and leaves in triumph."

"Stay with the others," Darcy said, "and lock your door when you go to bed."

"I will. Although I really don't fear for myself," I said.

"I'll try to take you away from here as soon as possible." He touched my cheek.

"I have to go back to Belinda," I said. "I just received a message from her. She did a bolt from the clinic where she was staying and is now back in her own little house and wants me to look after her."

Darcy raised an eyebrow. "You're too good to that girl," he said. "She takes advantage of you."

"Yes, I think she does," I said, "but I do feel for her. It must be awful to be in her position right now."

"She did bring it upon herself," he said. "She was very free with her favors."

"Which I believe you took advantage of once," I pointed out.

"Did I? I've quite forgotten. It can't have been memorable." He managed a little grin.

"I have to go," I said. "I'll see you soon."

He blew me a kiss, then slipped between the trees and was gone.

Chapter 27

Tuesday, April 23
Evening at Villa Fiori

Darcy is going to come and join us at the villa. I feel so much better!

I let myself in through the French door. All was quiet. As I made my way down the hall again I glanced back and was horrified to see a trail of muddy footprints behind me. Oh Lord! When I had spotted Darcy I hadn't stopped to think that the ground was sodden from that rain. I looked down at the shoes that Gerda had so beautifully polished and saw they were now caked with mud again. What's more, there were a few chicken feathers stuck to them. Oh, I'm going to be in deep trouble this time, I thought. I found the nearest chair, sat down and took off the shoes. Talk about leaving clues behind me, I thought grimly as I stared at the telltale footprints. Now everyone will know I've been outside. Unless I act quickly! I sprinted up the stairs and into the nearest bathroom. I grabbed a towel, ran down again and started wiping up the mud. Unfortunately this just had the effect of smearing mud across the white marble. Hopeless. I was just praying that one of the servants would appear to clean this up before Signor Stratiacelli saw it, when I heard a voice.

"Lady Georgiana Rannoch, what are you doing?"

I looked up to see Stratiacelli looming over me. Oh golly. My mind went blank. What was I doing?

"What am I doing?" I repeated, as I sank down onto the marble, trying to hide the muddy smear and the dirty towel beneath my skirt.

"That is what I asked."

"I dropped my earring." I tried to look nonchalant and unruffled as I sat on the damp towel. "I was looking for it."

It was too much to hope that he wouldn't notice the rest of the footprints. He did. "And where have you been?"

"Writing a note to my friend who lives nearby," I said, giving him what I hoped was a breezy smile. "I had promised to visit her today, but of course I had to tell her I was not allowed to come."

He looked at the muddy shoes and the trail of footprints. "You had to go outside to write this note? Against my orders?"

"Not to write the note," I said. "The girl who brought me the message from my friend was waiting outside for my reply. I had to give it to her and I'm afraid I stepped into a muddy patch." When he said nothing I added, "You can ask your agent at the gate, if you like. He will tell you that a little peasant girl came with a note for me, and left carrying a note from me."

He took a while to digest this rapid outburst in English, then said, "Please return to the sitting room with the other guests. I have an announcement to make."

"But my shoes . . ." I indicated them, looking muddy and forlorn on the shiny floor. Gerda was going to be so displeased.

"Leave the shoes. This is more important."

"I can hardly come into the sitting room in my stockinged feet," I pointed out. "It wouldn't be correct."

"Very well," he said. "You may change your shoes, but return immediately."

I swooped up the shoes and towel, fled up the stairs and looked around for a place to hide my muddy shoes where even Gerda wouldn't find them. As I looked at them I noticed that the small feathers stuck to the mud were white, which was odd because the chickens I had seen had been rust colored. More white feathers. Could there be any connection? Did the white feather on Rudi's floor mean that someone had actually come in from the outside and brought a feather stuck to the mud on his shoes as I had? An outsider after all? I remembered how hard it had been raining that night. Did that also mean that the carpet might be wet in places? And the butler was up and around until midnight. Might he not have heard an intruder?

I knelt down and shoved the shoes as far as I could under the bed, then hastily put on my indoor shoes and came down to find everyone seated in the lake view room, eyes all focused on Stratiacelli. My mother had now joined them and looked decidedly hollow and frail.

"My investigation has reached an impasse," he said. "There were only the fingerprints of the dead man on the gun that was not fired. On the pistol of this lady"—he pointed to my mother—"there are no fingerprints at all. It was wiped clean."

"Except for your fingerprints, Assistant Chief," Mrs. Simpson pointed out happily. "Remember you picked it up and showed it to us?"

"Ah yes. Of course. My fingerprints," he said, his face flushing. "But apart from mine . . ."

"So how do we know that your prints didn't cover any telltale hint of a print that might have been left?" Mrs. Simpson went on sweetly.

I could tell he couldn't quite master this amount of English.

"Whoever committed this crime took great care," he said. "The pistols were wiped clean. No fingerprints in the man's room, except for those of the household, and of the young lady." He turned to give me a hard stare, perhaps hoping that I would break down and confess.

"The young lady?" my mother demanded. She frowned at me. "Georgie, you were in his room?" She was doing a good job of acting the indignant mother.

"I've already explained this to the assistant chief," Camilla said calmly. "We were in the room together when Georgie first arrived."

"So I have to ask myself," Stratiacelli continued, "who wanted this man dead? So far none of you has told me anything. I believe you know more than you say. No matter, I have plenty of time. I shall keep you all here until one of you confesses."

"Now see here," Mrs. Simpson said, standing up. "You can't keep us here."

"If you prefer I could have you transferred to the jail in Verbania," he said with a satisfied smile.

"Don't be ridiculous," Paolo's uncle said. "You cannot throw aristocrats in a common jail. Il Duce, Mussolini, will not be pleased when he hears of this and he most certainly will."

A hint of fear crossed Stratiacelli's face. "I can tell that some of you are innocent of this crime," he said.

"At least the Prince of Wales must be allowed to return to Britain. He has official duties waiting for him." Mrs. Simpson took a step toward him.

"I do not believe that the prince is responsible for this death," Stratiacelli went on. "But perhaps he knows something and remains silent. At this moment all of you are suspects." He held up his hand when Mrs. Simpson tried to object again. "When I was a young agent, I was told to always start with the facts. What do we know? We know that the pistol that killed this man was owned by this lady." He pointed to my mother. "It was found in her luggage. So I should conclude that she is responsible. The simple thing to do is arrest her now, take her to the jail."

"Max, don't let him take me away." Mummy grabbed at Max's sleeve.

"Of course not, *mein Liebling*," Max said. "I shall send a telegram to Herr Hitler himself if you dare to threaten this lady. I have already told you that she and I were talking together until midnight. We were together every moment from ten thirty onward. So I have no idea how anyone managed to steal her pistol, but it must have been done when we were playing cards that evening."

"I do not think that the court would find you a reliable alibi for this lady's actions," the policeman said. "That is my problem. You say you all went to bed. The house was quiet. Nobody heard the shot, which I find very surprising. But nobody has an alibi that can be confirmed."

"Our butler is usually the last to bed. He checks the windows and locks the front door when we have all retired," Paolo said. "He might well have heard something or seen something. Have you asked him?"

"I have questioned this man," Stratiacelli said. "And he tells me one interesting fact. He saw one of the gentlemen wandering around in his night attire."

"Which gentleman?" Paolo's uncle demanded.

"The young German officer." Stratiacelli turned to stare at Klinker. Klinker looked to the general to translate what had been said. When he heard he didn't appear to flinch. He replied in German to the general.

"He can explain that easily," the general said. "He tells me that he could not sleep so he came downstairs to see if anyone was still in the kitchen to make him some hot milk. When he found the kitchen in darkness he did not like to warm his own milk, but retreated back to his room."

"What time was this?" Stratiacelli asked.

Again we paused for translation.

"After midnight. He heard the clock chime."

"And he did not hear a shot or see anyone?"

"Nobody."

I was watching Klinker intently. If someone had been sent from

Berlin to get rid of Rudolf, he would be the most likely person. Going downstairs for a glass of milk was a lame excuse.

"What we all seem to have forgotten," Paolo said, interrupting my train of thought, "is that the door was locked. How could any of us have gained entry to Count Rudolf's room?"

Aha, I thought. That's why Klinker was going to the kitchen. He had been looking for the passkey. But surely he couldn't have found it. I glanced up to see Klinker watching me. I was not going to be stupid enough to share what I was thinking until Darcy was in the house. I would play the innocent but if the moment was right I would see if I could get Klinker to confess. I gave Klinker an encouraging sort of smile. He returned it with a half smile of his own. If only I was a vamping sort of girl I would know how to seduce Klinker and lure information out of him, I thought, and had to grin at the prospect of vamping anyone.

Stratiacelli showed no sign of leaving. Neither did the men he had stationed around and outside the house. I wondered if they would even let Darcy in if he arrived on the doorstep. I wondered about the telegrams he had sent to London and what answers he might receive. There was no point in wondering to whom they had been sent. Darcy was annoyingly silent about for whom he actually worked and what he actually did. Of course I had my suspicions, but . . .

Eventually we all went up to change for dinner. Stratiacelli thought this unnecessary and suspicious until Paolo's mother told him in no uncertain terms that aristocrats always changed for dinner, no matter what the circumstances, and the mere matter of a murder was not going to shake her out of her routine. She was a force that even Stratiacelli could not withstand. He smiled weakly and said, "Very well, but do not think of trying to use the telephone. My man will guard it at all times. And do not think of escaping from the house."

Mummy waylaid me in the upper hallway. "You go ahead, Max," she said. Then she whispered, "Did you get a chance to go into his room?"

"I did, but I had to escape in a hurry. I can tell you that the photographs are not hidden in any easy place. I haven't looked under the mattress. The bed is pretty disgusting. Soaked in blood."

Mummy crept down the hall and tried the door of Rudi's room. "Damn. Now it's locked again. And that awful little man threatened to take me away and lock me up."

"He won't do that, I'm sure," I said. "He was just trying to scare you into confessing or else to see if anyone else was rattled."

"Who do you think did it?" Mummy whispered. "You're quite good at this sort of thing usually."

"I really don't know," I said. "Klinker was seen wandering around. Nobody else was, apparently."

"Why on earth would Klinker want to shoot Rudi? Had he been blackmailing him too, do you think?"

"It's possible," I said. "It's too bad Klinker speaks no English. I'd be willing to have a chat with him and see if I could get anything out of him."

"It's a pity it can't be Mrs. Simpson," Mummy said. "I'd love to see her locked away. So would the king and queen and half the country."

"I don't think it can be her," I said. "The Prince of Wales is a bit of an idiot sometimes, but he's true-blue when it comes to honesty. He'd say if she left their room after they went to bed."

"Perhaps he fell asleep and she tiptoed out," Mummy said, quite enjoying this now.

"Mummy, you're terrible." I had to laugh. Then I grew serious again. "Mummy, you don't believe it was Max, do you?"

"Max? What possible motive could he have?" She sounded shocked.

I didn't mention the Hitler's spy connection. "Maybe he found out Rudi was blackmailing you and decided to take care of him."

She frowned, then shook her head. "But his alibi is as solid as mine. We really were talking together until midnight." She glanced up the hallway. "We should go and change, I suppose. There's Camilla's grim-faced maid. Is she looking after you as well?"

I saw then that Gerda had emerged from Camilla's suite and was standing at the head of the hallway, watching us.

"Yes, with frightening efficiency," I said. "Did you bring your maid with you?"

"Didn't bother, darling. I never do if it's only for a few days now. Max has become remarkably adept at doing up buttons and things, and of course he adores undressing me." She gave a cat-with-the-cream sort of smile. "But Camilla's German girl did clean my shoes when we first arrived." She sighed. "I'd never have come if I'd had an inkling anything unpleasant like this would happen. Frankly I wish we could just slip away and borrow a motorboat. In half an hour we'd be in Switzerland where they couldn't touch us."

"But then you could never come back to Italy again."

"Wouldn't bother me. The food and clothes are better in France," she said. "Although I have to admit the shoes are nice. And the handbags."

"But presumably Max might want to do business in Italy in the future. And you'd have this hanging over you, which wouldn't be pleasant."

She sighed. "I suppose so."

I put a tentative hand around her shoulder. "Don't worry, Mummy. I'm sure we'll get to the bottom of it soon. As a matter of fact, Darcy is nearby and working on it for us."

Her face brightened at this. "The dear boy is here? That is good news. Ah well, now I can go and change in peace."

I suppose I should have been annoyed that she thought more of Darcy's detective skills than of mine, but I too was vastly comforted knowing he was within reach and working on the case. I went into my room, where Gerda had already laid out the black evening dress.

"All is ready, my lady," she said. "Oh, and I cleaned those shoes you got so muddy again. Really, may I suggest you borrow Wellington boots if you have to go outside in the mud."

How did she find them? I managed a smile. "You are amazing, Gerda," I said. "The contessa is so lucky to have you."

"No, I am so lucky to be employed by her," Gerda said. "I just do my duty, but she is a good employer. And after this year's tragedy, I am lucky to find another job so quickly."

As she spoke she helped me out of my day clothes, making small disapproving noises at the dried mud on my skirt. Then she styled my hair, attached my rubies and brushed rouge onto my cheeks. "All finished, my lady," she said. "Go down and have a good dinner. Do not let the distressing events in this house put you off your food. This is not your worry. And ring for me when you come to bed. I will bring you another herbal tea to help you sleep."

She gave a small, bobbing curtsy and left me staring after her. Because something had just struck me. She had brought me an herbal tea last night and I had slept so soundly that I had to be woken at nine o'clock. So soundly that I had not heard Darcy tapping on my window. So soundly that I had not heard a shot in the next room. For the first time I realized it was highly possible that I had been drugged.

Chapter 28

Tuesday, April 23
At Villa Fiori

I stood in my room, staring at my reflection in the mirror on the wardrobe door, digesting this fact. Darcy had pricked up his ears as soon as I mentioned Gerda. I realized that Stratiacelli had questioned all of us, but perhaps he had overlooked the servants. Now that I examined it, the timing of Gerda coming to this job was fortuitous: Camilla's maid unfortunately stepping in front of a bus at the same time as Gerda's former mistress had commited suicide in a bathtub. Had the murder of Rudolf been planned for some time?

It occurred to me that Mummy had called her "that German girl." Was it because she didn't realize she was Austrian or had Max spoken to her and detected her accent was not from Austria? And Mummy had said that Gerda had cleaned her shoes. A perfect chance to snoop and find the little pistol. I shook my head. Maybe I was reading too much into this. Perhaps it was because she was so horribly efficient. She might well turn out to be exactly who she said she was—a first-class lady's maid. And someone else might have had an opportunity to slip something into a drink that Gerda had innocently prepared for me.

I hoped that Darcy's telegrams to London might reveal something. Otherwise I wondered how we would ever come to the truth.

I could see the strain showing on other people's faces as we sipped aperitifs before dinner. Stratiacelli had announced that he was going home for the night, but his men would remain, one guarding the telephone in the front foyer, and others stationed at the outside of the house so that nobody was allowed to leave. Conversation was monosyllabic. I think we were all conscious of that policeman standing a few feet away. I was alert and listening for any noise that might indicate Darcy had returned from Stresa and had come to join us. But there was no sign of him as the gong summoned us in to dinner. This time I found myself sitting beside the silent Klinker. I thought about why he was here, about his disappearance and reappearance earlier today. Had he really fallen into a swollen mountain stream? If not, where had he gone? And why? I decided to take a little chance.

"Would you pass me the salt, Herr Klinker?" I said.

"Gern," he said and handed it to me.

I gave him a secret little smile. "Ah, so you do understand English. I thought you did."

"Understand, *ja*. Not speaking," he said. "I remain silent so I do not make error in speech."

"It sounds pretty good to me," I said. "Better than my German."

"If you are to visit Berlin, it is soon getting better, I think," he said, struggling to find each of these words and pronouncing "visit" as "wisit." "I hope you wisit Berlin one day. I show you our city."

"That would be nice," I said. Another encouraging smile.

"Gut," he said and went back to attacking his roast beef.

I decided to press on a little further. "You are quite recovered from your shock today?"

"Shock?"

"You fell into the river."

He gave an embarrassed grin. "*Ach.* Was not so bad. Just a little slip and I got wet."

"You're very brave." I wondered if I was overdoing it. "You must have been glad to be away when we discovered the count's body. It was very distressing."

"Yes. I am sure. Most distressing."

"Did you know him, before this?"

He shook his head. "I am only soldier. Not part of Berlin society. This here for me, very grand."

"It is quite grand, isn't it?" I said. "My family lives in a castle, but it is quite simple inside."

"Simple I like." He nodded and returned my smile.

We were getting along famously. I just wished I knew how to lead the conversation from here. "More wine, Lieutenant Klinker?" I asked, reaching for the carafe.

"Bitte."

I poured, trying not to grin at the thought of myself getting a man drunk and then wringing a confession from him. Then my thoughts quickly sobered again. If he had shot Rudolf himself or been part of a conspiracy to shoot him, then he was a dangerous and ruthless man. Tread carefully, Georgie. I wanted to bring up his nocturnal wandering looking for hot milk last night, but I couldn't think of a way to phrase it without making it sound like an accusation.

I think the food was good, but in reality I didn't taste any of it. I just wanted Darcy to arrive and this whole sorry business to be over. Frankly if Klinker had shot Rudi, if Gerda had aided him, I didn't see how it could ever be proven. In the end we might all leave Stresa not knowing what had really happened. Dinner ended with fruit and cheese. Camilla rose from her seat and we women followed suit, going through to the long gallery where coffee was being served around the fire while the men enjoyed their cigars and brandy.

"What an awful day." Camilla sighed as she sank into an armchair. "I feel as if it's been going on forever."

"You feel like that?" Mummy said. "Think how I feel. That man has practically accused me of shooting Rudolf."

"It was your gun, honey," Mrs. Simpson said dryly. "He was only jumping to the easiest conclusion."

Mummy turned a withering gaze onto her hated rival. "Can you see me standing two feet from a man's head and blasting his brains out? I mean, really. You must know I faint at the sight of blood. If I were going to kill anyone I would poison his drink so that he died in a nongory fashion."

We all laughed at this, breaking the tension just a little. There was a tap on the front door. My heart did a little flutter. Darcy had come. All would be well. I waited, holding my breath, until one of the policemen came into sight. He bowed to Camilla. "Contessa," he said then rattled off a string of Italian.

Camilla nodded and took a letter from him. "For you, Georgie," she said. "A note from your friend you couldn't visit today."

She handed me an envelope. It did indeed say, *From Lady Georgiana's friend at the clinic.* But it wasn't Belinda's handwriting. I opened it, intrigued, and inside I recognized Darcy's bold script. *Still waiting to hear details from London,* he had written. *May not get to the villa until the morning. But one thing to pass along. No Gerda Stretzl registered with the Austrian Embassy in London. And—home secretary reported his wife's death as suspicious. Be very careful tonight. Lock your door. Place a chair behind it.*

"Good news?" Camilla asked.

"What?" I looked up. "Oh, just that my friend was really disappointed I couldn't come to visit her today. She hopes I'll be able to get away tomorrow." I stuffed the note back into the envelope and put it into my evening bag. I'd have to make sure that Gerda didn't get a chance to see that!

We finished our coffee. The men came through to join us, Uncle Cosimo suggesting we play cards again. This was met with little response.

"Oh, come on, buck up," the Prince of Wales said. "We must do something. We mustn't let these chaps see that they are getting us down. How about a party game? Charades?"

"You are too bloody cheerful, David," Wallis Simpson said. "Of course nobody feels like charades. I suggest we all go to bed early. And lock our doors!"

"Really, Wallis," the prince said. "You don't think we're in any danger, do you?"

"Until we know who killed Count Rudolf and why, I can't rule out that we might be in danger too," she said. "It could be a deranged servant, bumping off the aristocracy one by one."

"Hardly that," Paolo said. "Our servants here have been with the family for years."

"What I want to know is how one of us managed to get into his room," Mrs. Simpson went on. "They say his door was locked and the maid had to get a key to open it. We wouldn't know where to find a spare key, would we?"

"Our housekeeper has them in a ring on her belt," Camilla said. "Guards them like a dragon at all times. Sleeps with them under her pillow, so we're told. So no, I don't think any of us could have found a key."

"Sometimes it is possible to turn a key from the outside with pliers," the general suggested. "Might that have happened? Or one can push out the key onto a sheet of paper and pull the paper through under the door. So there are ways."

"In which case how could one put the key back on the inside and lock it again?" Paolo said. "Not so easy."

"True," the German general agreed. "That is indeed a puzzle."

"Could someone have climbed up to his balcony? Or across from Georgiana's balcony?" Max suggested.

"Have you seen the wall?" Camilla replied. "It's smooth marble. Even a good rock climber would not make it up to that balcony."

"And there is too big a gap to my balcony," I said.

"Such a puzzle," General Spitz-Blitzen repeated. "Let us hope that our little policeman requests help from detectives in Milan so that we may come rapidly to the truth. This waiting is not good for the nerves, or the digestion." And he gave a loud belch.

I watched him take a big gulp of brandy. He seemed completely at ease. And he was suggesting that detectives be brought in from Milan. Not the words of a guilty party, surely?

"We have to do something," my cousin insisted. "We simply can't go to bed this early. No dancing, I suppose?"

"I don't think we feel like dancing, sir," Mummy said. "But I wouldn't mind playing a hand or two of whist. Take our minds off things."

"Splendid," Paolo said. "Let's get tables set up. Claire and Your Royal Highness against Camilla and Uncle Cosimo. Mix things up, eh? That leaves myself and Max and Mrs. Simpson and Georgiana?"

"Oh, not me," I said. "I'm hopeless at card games."

"I should enjoy to play," said the general. "I will take the young lady's place."

"Jolly good," Paolo said, beaming as if he had pulled off a coup. "Two tables, then. My mother will have gone to bed. Father Francisco despises card games. That leaves just you and Klinker, Georgie." He looked around, frowning. "Strange. I thought we had enough for three tables."

"That was when Rudolf was alive," Camilla pointed out.

"Oh yes. Right." A somber mood fell upon us. We shifted uneasily on our seats, all thinking, presumably, how easy it was to forget that a death had occurred in the house.

"Get out the cards then, Paolo," Camilla urged, ushering people to card tables. I hesitated, rather wishing I had agreed to play. I had no wish to be alone at the moment, and certainly no wish to go up to bed before the others. As the games started I wandered through to the lake view room and stood looking out across the lake. A full moon had appeared beyond the distant mountains and was painting the water with silver streaks. Lights twinkled on the far shore. It all looked very peaceful and romantic. I sighed, wishing I was far away from this house, somewhere safe, with Darcy.

"It is beautiful, is it not?" said a voice behind me. I hadn't heard anyone come into the room and turned to see Klinker, looking rather handsome in his dress uniform. His blond hair glistened in the moonlight.

"Very beautiful," I said.

"Like you," he said. "You are very beautiful. Fine Aryan girl. Like the girls at home."

"Thank you," I said. "My ancestors are German."

"Ja?" he said. "What part of Germany?"

"Saxe-Coburg, I believe, and what was Queen Mary? She was Princess Mary of Teck before she married, wasn't she? I've no idea where Teck is."

"Queen Mary? You are of the royal family?"

"Yes, my father and the king were first cousins."

"*Mein Gott.* I had . . . no . . ." He searched for the word. *"Ahnung?"*

"Idea?" I filled in for him. "Yes, I suppose I don't look very royal."

"Oh, but *ja*. Fine royal girl." He had moved quite close to me. "May I ask . . . I would like very much, permission to give you . . . kiss?"

On any other occasion I would have told him I was engaged and he was being fresh. "You want to kiss me?" I asked.

"Please? This I would like."

The concept of vamping flashed through my head again. We were, after all, only a few steps away from the rest of the party. Quite safe.

I pretended to be shy. "All right," I said.

He took me in his arms. I felt his buttons and medals and braid dig into me. His lips were cold and unappealing and he pressed them against mine. I was reminded of being kissed by Prince Siegfried of Romania, whom Belinda and I had nicknamed Fishface.

Luckily he didn't open his mouth or try to force mine open. He just kept his lips locked onto mine and breathed hard. His hand stroked my hair, then caressed my back. Then, to my surprise, I felt one hand grab my left breast. I pulled away.

"What are you doing?" I demanded angrily.

He looked shocked and embarrassed. "This you do not like?"

"Not with someone I hardly know."

"Please to forgive. I have not much practice with women. I read book. It is called *How to Make Love to Woman*?" He translated slowly. "It says number one: the lips. Number two: stroke the hair. Then the back. And number four: the chest. It says woman likes the chest to be grasped. Did I grasp too forcefully?"

I was trying hard not to giggle. "What is your first name? I can't keep calling you Lieutenant Klinker."

"It is Fritz."

"Well, Fritz, I don't think you can learn to make love to a girl from a book."

"No? In the German army we have books to learn most things."

"It has to come naturally. And slowly. Most girls don't like to be rushed."

"You mean I must take the bosom slowly?"

"I mean that a girl must get to know you and like you before she lets you touch her body. She must trust you and love you."

"I see." He looked crestfallen. "I am sorry I make mistake and offend you."

"I'm not offended," I said. "We all have to start sometime."

"In Berlin it is hard to meet nice women. We have not much time for such things in the army life." He gave me a wistful smile. "You are kind woman. May I ask—could we go to your room, perhaps? And I will try to do better this time. No grasping."

Until now I had been rather amused by the whole thing. I couldn't wait to tell Belinda. How she would laugh. But the mention of my room raised a red flag. Was he really the innocent young man he claimed to be or was he looking for a chance to lure me away from the other guests? Did he think I knew something and was a danger to him? Were he and Gerda working together?

"Oh no," I said. "I'm afraid that would not be proper. My royal relatives would certainly not approve."

"They need not know."

"My cousin is here. He would notice if I disappeared with you. Besides"—I gave him a smile—"I have a young man at home and he would not approve either."

"I see." He gave a sigh. "So you are already promised to somebody?"

"I'm afraid so."

"That is bad," he said. "All the nice girls are promised. Poor Klinker. He must remain unloved."

"I hope not," I said. "I'm sure you'll meet somebody soon."

He sighed again. "I think I go to bed, if you will excuse me."

"Don't forget to ask for your hot milk before the servants go to bed," I said.

Did I detect a sudden sharpness of glance? It was for the briefest of seconds, and he said, "I do not think I will need milk tonight. My walk on the mountain and fall into the river have made me tired. I shall sleep well." He faced me and clicked his heels together. "*Gute Nacht*, Georgie."

"*Gute Nacht*, Fritz," I said.

I watched him walk away, still not sure if I had nearly been sleeping with the enemy.

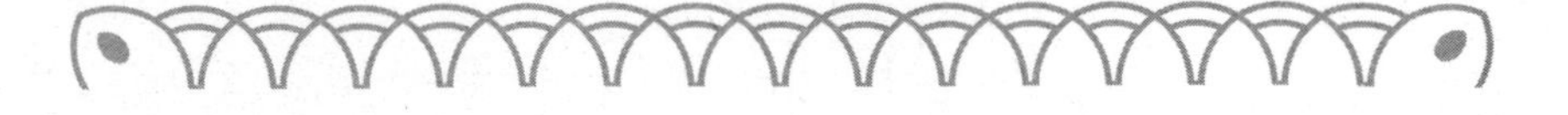

Chapter 29

The night of Tuesday, April 23
In the grounds of Villa Fiori

I don't know how I'm going to sleep tonight. Will that chair under the doorknob really keep out intruders? I wish Darcy would hurry up!

I went back to the others and sat, thumbing through magazines, until Mummy declared she was tired and wanted to go to bed. I think this was because she was currently winning. Mummy always liked to go out on a high note. The party broke up and I followed my mother and Max up the stairs. At the first landing the general gave a polite bow. "I wish you all a pleasant night," he said. He went up a flight of steps to the right while we went to the left. A long way from Rudolf's room, I thought. And if Rudolf was killed before midnight, then the butler was still up and around. There was a danger of being seen, as Fritz Klinker had been. Had he been on his way to shoot Rudolf when he was spotted? Or had he done the deed and was returning the key to its rightful place, wherever that was?

I found it hard to think of him as a cold-blooded killer, but one never knew.

I had scarcely reached my bedroom and had no chance to lock my door when Gerda appeared, carrying a cup and saucer. "Ah, my lady. I bring you the good tea again to help you sleep."

I looked at the cup. "How kind," I said, giving her a reassuring smile. "Perfect. Just what I need."

She tried to hand it to me, but I said, "Put it on the table beside my bed. I'll get undressed first. It looks too hot to drink yet."

"As you wish, my lady," she said. I sat at the vanity while she took off my necklace then helped me out of the dress. All the time my brain was racing. I had to believe that the drink was drugged again, but this time it might not be just to make me sleep, but enough so that I didn't wake up again. I tried to think of a way of not drinking it without giving away what I suspected.

"Thank you, Gerda," I said when she had put my nightdress over my head. "That will be all, I think. I have to visit the WC before I go to bed."

"Your tea, my lady," she insisted.

"I'll drink it when I come back, when I'm in bed," I said. "No need for you to wait."

"I shall return for your cup then?"

"Don't worry about it. You can retrieve it in the morning. I'm sure you need a good night's sleep. We all do after what we have gone through today."

She hesitated, then she said, "Very well. In the morning, then. But do not let it get cold."

"Of course not. Thank you, Gerda. I appreciate all you have done for me."

"You are kind, my lady," she said, and for a moment I thought she looked regretful. I watched her go, then I poured some of the liquid into my toothbrush holder, to be tested if necessary, and tipped the rest of it down the sink. I went to the lavatory at the end of the hall and saw no sign of Gerda when I returned. I locked my door and tried to move a piece of furniture against it, but the chests and armoires were too solid to be moved. So I did what Darcy had suggested and positioned a chair balanced under the door handle. If anyone managed to push the door open the chair would fall with a clatter.

I was still feeling quite jittery as I prepared for bed. Perhaps Darcy would come to my room tonight, I thought. I was going to leave the window unlocked, but then I remembered that an unwelcome visitor might also get in that way. This time I'd be awake if Darcy tapped. I went to remove the extra pillows from my bed. I like to sleep on my side with only one pillow and they had given me four. I paused, a pillow still in my hand. There had been four on the other nights. Now there were only three. Strange. Had the maid decided I didn't need so many and put one in my wardrobe, perhaps?

I went over to the wardrobe and opened it. It was rather an alarming piece of furniture—awfully good for playing hide-and-seek or sardines, but full of shadowy corners in the poor light of my bedside lamp. I hesitated to poke around inside, looking for that extra pillow. I told myself I was being silly. After all, I had grown up in a castle full of old pieces of furniture, not to mention suits of armor and even secret passages. These had never frightened me before.

"You see," I said to myself firmly, "it's just a large wardrobe. Built in the days when dresses and cloaks were much bulkier than modern dress. Nothing frightening about it."

I reached past my dresses to give the back of the wardrobe a reassuring pat and my fingers touched a cobweb. I reacted as one does, lost my balance and put out my hand to steady myself. The back of the wardrobe gave way under my touch. I pitched forward into darkness.

For a moment I lay there, too stunned to move. I had caught my shins on the lip of the wardrobe as I plunged forward and now they were throbbing horribly. Cautiously I got to my feet. I recoiled as something soft brushed my cheek. I reached out to touch it and identified a gentleman's jacket sleeve. And realized where I was. I was in the adjoining wardrobe in Rudolf's room. This must be a convenient way between the two rooms for those who wanted to practice bed-hopping without the risk of being discovered! My first thought was, Thank God Rudolf didn't know about this or he might have paid me a nightly visit.

My second thought was more somber and momentous. So this was how it was done! I saw it all clearly now. Gerda, and I had to believe now it was she, had drugged me so that I didn't hear her come into my room and reach Rudolf's room through the door at the back of the wardrobe. And . . . another thing fell into place. The missing pillow. Of course. She had used the pillow to muffle the sound of the shot. Hence the white feather on the floor, and the unpleasant burned odor I couldn't identify. It was burned feathers. She probably thought she had picked up all the stray feathers and then deposited the remains of the pillow in the chicken run, where a few extra feathers would never be noticed. Except she had seen the feathers stuck to my shoes and she now feared that I had figured everything out.

I scrambled back into my own wardrobe and attempted to close the door again, fumbling for a catch while all the time expecting to see Gerda opening Rudolf's side of the wardrobe with a gun in her hand. I told myself that the assistant chief now had both the guns in his possession, but there could be more guns in the house. And she could still have a knife or chloroform or even a scarf to strangle me and force drugs down my throat. And she was a powerful-looking woman. I was not sure I could fend her off. I looked around the room, wondering what to do. Should I try to escape right now, run down the hall and hammer on my mother's door? Or go down to the policemen stationed at the front door? But what if she was lying in wait? What if she leaped out of Rudi's door, dragged me in there and finished me off? What if it was a well-planned plot and there were indeed two or more of them? And my ultimate worry: what if Max was involved? I saw it was all too possible that someone in Germany had learned that Rudolf was a double agent, feeding information to England. They had been sent down from Berlin to get rid of him and make it look like a suicide.

Suddenly I wasn't sure whom I could trust. Camilla and Paolo, surely? But Gerda was Camilla's maid. And I had no idea about their private part of the house behind those double doors. Maybe just a bedroom and dressing room, or maybe a whole corridor with a room for Gerda nearby. She might well be lurking near the entrance.

Even as I was considering these things I heard the slightest of noises. A faint click, and I noticed my door handle move just a fraction.

"Yes?" I said imperiously. "Who is it? What do you want?"

There was no reply. No Gerda saying, "I'm sorry, my lady. I came to see if you were asleep," or something harmless like that.

Darcy, I thought. I must get to Darcy. I pulled off my nightgown and wriggled into a dark skirt and jersey. Then I put on those beautifully clean brogues and opened my balcony door as silently as I dared. I closed it behind me, not wanting to give away instantly the route I had taken. I half hoped to see him waiting below, to hear his voice whispering, "Georgie, I'm down here."

The garden was dappled with moonlight, but a wind had sprung up and branches swayed, making shadows dance. I stood waiting for a second or two longer, then made the decision. I'd have to go to his cottage. To get safely away from here. I looked down at the vine. I had certainly done some climbing during my formative years; in fact, Belinda and I had climbed over the roof and down the drainpipe to escape from school once. At least, she had done it more often, to meet ski instructors. I, being a good child, had dared to do it only once. That vine looked solid enough. It had been solid enough to hold Darcy. I took a deep breath and swung my leg over the railing, then the other, and fished around until a foot connected with part of a solid limb. Then I lowered myself inch by inch. Leaves brushed my face. Twigs scratched me. It seemed to take forever and at the back of my mind was the thought that she'd be waiting for me, or one of them would be waiting for me, at the bottom.

At last my foot touched the gravel. I stood there, in the shadow of the villa, trying to breathe quietly, looking around. The vast shape of the villa lay in darkness. No lights shone out of any of the upstairs windows on this side of the house. The wind sighed and rustled through the leaves and rattled branches. I hesitated, deciding. I could go around to the front and to the policemen who were supposedly stationed there. Or I could make my way through the grounds to Darcy. Surely he wouldn't have stayed the night in Stresa, waiting for more telegrams from London. He had to be close by or he couldn't have sent that note. I decided I couldn't risk going around to the front of the villa, just in case Gerda or one of her coconspirators was waiting for me, lurking in the bushes, before I got there.

None of them knew about Darcy, I told myself. Nobody would expect me to run to the gardeners' cottages. I sprinted across the stretch of open lawn until I reached the first of the topiary hedges. I darted behind it, then made my way toward the swimming pool. That little marble temple glowed in moonlight. I gave it a wide berth, just in case. . . . I was now in the wilder part of the estate, a section of open woodland, great trees, flowering rhododendrons. The wind was stronger here, coming straight off the lake without being blocked by the house. Branches danced crazily above me. Clouds scudded across the sky. One of them covered the moon and I was plunged into darkness. I pressed on, hoping I was still heading in the right direction, moving unsteadily over the uneven ground. Trees loomed up at the last second and I went forward like a blind person, my hands out in front of me.

I looked back, just in time to catch a glimpse of a flicker of light between the bushes. It went out almost instantly, but I hadn't imagined it. It had definitely been there, on the other side of the swimming pool. Someone with a torch was following me. I waited, hidden behind a big oak, and sure enough it flashed on again, then was quickly extinguished. Was it a signal to a second person? I stood listening, but any sound of footsteps was drowned out by the creaking of branches and rustle of leaves. I turned and kept going, moving from tree to tree, every now and then looking back to see if my pursuer was gaining on me. The moon came out briefly and I broke into a run, not caring if I was heard. Surely the edge of the estate and the cottages must be getting close now. I felt alone and so vulnerable. If my pursuer had a gun, I would be an easy target in the moonlight. Why, oh why, hadn't I opted for the policemen stationed on guard at the front of the house? It had seemed quite simple to find my way to the edge of the estate and the gardeners' cottages in the daylight. The ground ahead of me was rising gently. Was that right? I knew the whole estate sloped up the hill, with the terraces above the house rising steeply. But surely the land in front of the cottages was relatively flat, wasn't it?

The moon disappeared again and I waited behind a big bush to see if the flashlight was still following me. Nothing. Perhaps the person had given up and gone back to the house. Perhaps it was one of the policemen, I thought. Trying to apprehend an intruder. But perhaps it wasn't. It was a chance I couldn't take. Then I saw it again. This time it cut a big arc of light through the trees. The person was searching for me, no longer worried about being seen. At least I had my pursuer pinpointed. She, or he, was slightly behind me, but definitely closer than before, and below me. If he, or she, moved quickly, and the cottages were lower down the estate, closer to the road, I could well be cut off before I reached them.

I also remembered that there was a gravel forecourt outside the cottage area. My pursuer could wait until I came out into the open—if she (assuming it was Gerda) had figured out that I was making for the gardeners' cottages. Perhaps she just thought I was trying to find a way out of the estate. But a new doubt crept into my mind.

What if I sprinted to Darcy's front door, hammered on it, and he wasn't there? There was that worrying possibility that he could have stayed the night in town, waiting for that telegram in the morning. A picture flashed into my mind: me standing at the front door while my unknown assailant crept up behind me or poised a pistol to take aim. I stood, hidden behind my bush, in an agony of indecision. If Gerda, or whoever was following me, thought I was now trying to reach the edge of the estate, then wouldn't the most logical route be to double back to the villa as quickly as possible? Even if the front door was locked, there were supposed to be police guards somewhere around. And hammering on the door would wake somebody. Yes, that seemed less of a risk than trying to find Darcy's cottage right now. And if the person was carrying a gun, then it would be possible to shoot two of us. I couldn't risk that, could I?

I came to a decision. I would go up the hill first so that I could make my way around in a semicircle and approach the house without having to cross the open area beside the swimming pool and then the lawn and driveway. If I could reach the orchard on the other side, I'd have the cover of the kitchen garden, and then a short dash to the house. Surely nobody would expect me to take that route. As I started to move, the wind suddenly dropped, almost as if someone had turned off a switch. And the moon reappeared from a cloud. I felt horribly vulnerable and exposed. I stood still, listening. There was no sound, apart from the distant lap and hiss of waves on the lakeshore. All the time I stood still I imagined my pursuer creeping up silently on me, and the first time I would know of her presence would be the flash and explosion of a gun.

Then I heard a small noise of something moving, still slightly behind where I was standing, and lower down the hill, and, almost at the same moment, I saw a dark figure slink behind a bush, also lower down the hill but ahead of me, between me and Darcy's cottage. A second person was after me. I took the only course open to me. I started to go uphill, trying hard to move silently. The moon stayed out, highlighting every time I darted from bush to bush. The ground started to rise more steeply. I knew at the edges of the estate there was wilderness. Across the central portion were the terraces with their high hedges dividing them as they rose up the mountainside. If I could just reach them, I could sprint across to reach the villa with ease. Unless there was a third person, waiting to cut off my retreat, a little voice whispered in my head. I chose to ignore it. Every now and then I paused. Once I heard a twig snap behind me. In the silence of the night it sounded unnaturally loud, like a gunshot. It was bright enough now that the torch was not necessary so I had no way of pinpointing how close they were.

I gasped in horror when a white figure loomed out of the darkness ahead of me. I pressed my hand to my mouth to prevent me from making a sound. I froze, trying to calm my racing heart. Then I realized what it was: a marble statue of a Greek warrior, arm lifted and carrying a spear. One of the guards of the terraces. I stumbled up the last few yards and disappeared into the narrow walkway between high hedges. I had to move quickly. I broke into a run. I heard my feet crunching on the soft gravel underfoot. Statues appeared in niches, each one making my heart leap again. At first I thought my footsteps were creating an echo. Then I stopped and realized the worst: someone was running behind me.

Suddenly I had had enough. I was tired of running away. My Rannoch ancestors would not have fled from the field of battle. They stood and fought against impossible odds. I reminded myself that most of them had ended up being hacked to pieces, but that Rannoch pride still stirred in my veins. I ran until I came to the end of the terrace. Surely pursuers would expect me to run straight back to the villa. I looked around for a weapon. There was another marble figure guarding this entrance, but I was not strong enough to move a six-foot warrior. I heard the feet coming closer, moving fast now. Then I spied a small stone fountain—a basin with water bubbling up in the center and on one rim a stone frog. I tugged at the frog and felt it move. I wrenched harder and it came free, revealing that it was held on the basin with a metal spike. I felt it, heavy and satisfying, in my hands as I examined that metal spike and imagined driving it into someone's skull. Then I shook my head in horror. I was quite prepared to knock somebody out, but not to kill. I turned the frog so that the smooth stone of its back was ready to strike. I'd only have one chance. I had to make it count. And I took up my position behind the hedge, out of sight.

The last yards seemed to take forever. I stood holding my breath as the wind picked up again, sending the leaves above my head rustling and whispering and disguising the crunch of approaching footsteps. Then the person came into view. As I expected, he or she came to a halt, looking around and trying to find the quarry. I raised the stone frog as I stepped out behind my pursuer. As I got ready to bring the frog crashing down on a skull I froze at the last second. Gerda was about my height. And this person's head was some six inches taller and had dark, unruly hair. He stepped into moonlight and I recognized him the second he swung around and saw me.

"Georgie!" he exclaimed. "It is you! What's going on? I was keeping an eye on the house and I thought I saw you go past the swimming pool and . . ."

I put my finger to my lips. "Being followed," I mouthed and pointed back along the narrow pathway.

He nodded, understanding. Then he motioned me to stand on one side of the opening while he took up the other. Then he spotted the stone frog I was still holding. Put that down, he indicated with another gesture. I complied. We could hear footsteps running now, coming closer. The figure did exactly what Darcy had done: burst out of the terrace and then paused to look around. Darcy flung himself in a magnificent rugby tackle and brought the person crashing to the ground. In a second he was kneeling on top of his or her back and had twisted an arm. "Try to move and I'll break it," he said in a threatening voice.

"What do you think you are doing?" Gerda's voice came, half muffled, from the turf. "I am the contessa's maid. I was concerned about Lady Georgiana. Let go of me."

"So concerned that you tried to drug me," I said. "I have saved some of that tea for testing, by the way. And I know how you killed Count Rudolf. I found the door through the wardrobe."

"It doesn't matter anymore," she said. "I have done what I was sent to do."

Chapter 30

The night between April 23 and 24

Darcy shifted his position, keeping a knee in her back and her arm twisted up behind her. "Georgie, go for help," he said.

"Will you be all right with her?"

"Yes. Just go." His voice sounded ragged and tense.

I ran down the lawn, along the side of the house, to the front door. A policeman was sitting on a wicker rocking chair on the marble terrace, fast asleep. He jumped up, guiltily, when I aroused him.

"Come with me." I motioned. "Now. *Rapido.*"

Luckily he didn't question this. I think he was still half asleep. But he staggered after me and recoiled in astonishment when he saw Darcy kneeling on a person.

"This woman killed Count Rudolf," Darcy said in Italian. "Do you have handcuffs?"

He didn't.

"Take off your tie," Darcy said. The policeman did and Darcy swiftly bound Gerda's hands behind her back. None too gently cither. Then he hoisted her to her feet. She gave him a look of contempt. As they left I went to follow them, then spotted something shining in the moonlight. I picked it up with care and ran to catch up as they marched her back to the house, where the butler soon roused Paolo and Camilla.

"This man attacked me," Gerda said angrily. "He is mad. I saw Lady Georgiana leave the house and I was concerned for her safety. So I followed her."

"Who are you?" Paolo demanded, glaring at Darcy.

"I know who he is!" Camilla exclaimed, her face breaking into a smile. "You're cousin Darcy."

"The very one," Darcy said. "How are you, Camilla? I was in the area so I thought I'd drop in on my fiancée, only to find her being stalked by this woman."

"Who was trying to kill me," I said. "She'd already poisoned my drink tonight, but I tipped it away."

"Of course I wasn't trying to kill her." Gerda spat out the words. "Trying to protect her."

"With this?" I held up a long, thin-bladed knife. "She dropped it when Darcy tackled her."

"Well done, Georgie," Darcy said, giving me a smile. "I have received several telegrams from London about this woman. Not an Austrian citizen. And the home secretary, where she was employed as a maid, had expressed concern that she might be spying on him. Then his wife died, in highly suspicious circumstances, and Gerda disappeared—conveniently finding a job in Italy for her next assignment."

Camilla turned to face Gerda. "You pushed Monique under that bus, didn't you? My sweet little Monique who never harmed anyone. You're a monster."

Gerda merely smiled. "I am not weak like you. Like all of you. I despise weaklings. You wait until my country rules the world."

Soon Stratiacelli and more policemen arrived. Uncle Cosimo telephoned Milan and senior officers were on their way. Stratiacelli was told to do nothing until they arrived. Other guests were woken by the goings-on. General Spitz-Blitzen came down in a red-and-white-striped dressing gown that made him look like a child's spinning top. He seemed genuinely horrified.

"Of course I don't know this woman," he said. "Clearly she was sent by the Abwehr and, believe me, I stay well away from them."

"What about Klinker?" I asked. "Is it possible he was sent to help her with the assignment?"

"Klinker? But he seemed like such a simple boy."

"Has he been your aide long?"

"No, only a few months. But a good and willing worker. Go and ask him yourself. You will see."

A servant was sent to Klinker's bedroom, but came running back, babbling almost incoherently in Italian. It seemed Klinker was lying in his bed with his throat cut.

I turned on Gerda, as she sat, with a police guard on either side of her. "You killed Klinker? Why?"

Again that look of utter derision. "He proved to be a weakling. He was supposed to take care of you for me."

"You wanted Klinker to kill me?" I could hardly stammer out the words.

"He refused. He said he was not going to end the life of such a nice girl. He had fallen in love with you. A weakling."

I swallowed back a sob. Poor, sweet Klinker, trying to make love from a book. I wondered how he had found himself working with the German secret service. Had he volunteered or been coerced into it? Now we'd never know.

Darcy slipped an arm around my shoulders. "Are you all right?" he asked. "You've had a hell of a night. I should put you to bed right away."

I smiled at him. "Any other time I'd take you up on that invitation, but I don't think I'll be allowed to go to bed until the next lot of policemen get here and we have all given our statements. I just feel so badly about Klinker. He came across to me as a sweet boy. He tried to make love to me, but he hadn't a clue what to do."

"I hope you didn't encourage him," Darcy said.

"For heaven's sake, Darcy. I felt sorry for him."

"If he was working for the Abwehr, as he obviously was, then he was no sweet and innocent boy," Darcy said. "That was how he hoped to win you over and get you to a place where he could kill you."

"But he didn't," I said. I felt a tear well up and trickle down my cheek. "He was decent in the end."

High-powered policemen arrived from Milan. Gerda was taken away in a black Mercedes, looking defiant and triumphant to the end. Klinker's body was removed. When the first streaks of dawn showed in the sky the British consul arrived from Milan, to whisk away the Prince of Wales.

The prince came over to me as servants were trying to find room for all of Mrs. Simpson's luggage. "I say, Georgie, there is an aeroplane leaving Milan for London this morning. I'm sure we could squeeze you in, if you'd like to come with us. Not much fun going through another police investigation here and my mother would obviously be happier if I brought you safely home."

"It's very kind of you, sir," I said, "but I came here originally to be with a sick friend and I have to return to her the moment I am able."

He gave me a nod of understanding, then he said, "Look, we can dispense with calling me sir, except on formal occasions. We are cousins, after all. Why don't you just call me David? Wallis does."

"I know," I said. "Thank you, but behavior toward the royal family was ingrained in me at a young age. You'll always be sirs and ma'ams to me, however fond I am of all of you. Although I do confess that I call the little princesses by their first names. That will probably stop when they get older. I rather fear that Elizabeth may be a stickler for protocol."

He grinned. "Righty-o, then," he said. "If you don't want a lift, then we should be off. Glad to get away from this place, if you want the truth. Waste of our time. Don't know why we came here in the first place."

I do, I thought. Instead I said, "It was probably a valuable experience for all of us. It showed us that the Nazis can't be trusted, didn't it? When the time comes, we'll know which side we should be on."

"Yes," he said, thoughtfully. "I suppose we will. Pip-pip, then, old thing." And he went out to join Wallis Simpson, who was loitering by the motorcar.

As the car drove off, Camilla came to join me. "What a horrid experience this has been," she said. "I wish I'd never had the bally house party. I can't think why I agreed to it in the first place. None of these people are my friends." Then she corrected herself. "Except you, Georgie. You've been stellar. I hope we'll remain friends and you'll come and stay more often. Now that you'll be family, you'll have no excuse not to. In fact, if you and Darcy would like to use one of our houses for your honeymoon, we'll be happy to oblige."

"That would be lovely, Camilla," I said. "But we haven't got around to planning honeymoons yet. First we have to get our permission to marry."

"I'm sure there will be no problem with that," she said. We watched the prince's motorcar turn out of the gates. "You'll be leaving too, will you?" I detected a wistful note in her voice.

"I must go back to my sick friend," I said. "She was the reason I came here, after all. And Darcy says he has to return to London."

"If your friend is nearby, do come over to visit," she said. "Bring your friend if she's able to come."

"I don't think she is," I said. "But we have unfinished business before I leave, don't we?"

She made a face. "Oh golly. Don't we just. As soon as those policemen give permission my servants will be stripping Rudolf's bed and cleaning out his room."

"Then we'd better get to work now while nobody is paying attention," I said. "One last chance."

We headed rapidly up the stairs. Rudolf's room had been closed up and that unpleasant metallic dried-blood smell was still heavy in the air. Camilla glanced at me and pulled a face again. "If you're up for it, we'd better strip the bed and see if he hid anything under the pillows or mattress."

With utter distaste we peeled the blood-caked sheets apart. We lifted the mattress. Nothing. We went through the drawers and checked behind the paintings on the walls. Then, as a last resort, we went through his pockets. In the breast pocket of his dinner jacket we found Camilla's letter, neatly folded inside his white silk handkerchief. She gave a sob of relief when she saw it.

"I'm going to burn it straightaway," she said. "But where can your photos be?"

"We've searched this room thoroughly," I said. My eye was drawn to the old-fashioned black leather prayer book on the bedside table. "I can't imagine Rudi bringing a prayer book with him," I said. I had already been through it once and knew it contained only mass cards of deceased family members, but I picked it up again.

"I don't think that's his," Camilla said. "It's an old missal. We have some just like it in the chapel."

"The chapel!" I didn't wait a moment longer. I ran down, through the long hallway and into the little door that led to the chapel. At this early hour it was almost bathed in darkness, except for two tall candles that were lit on the altar. Strange shadows flickered and danced and I wondered if there was an electric light I could turn on. It was horribly unnerving, after a night of unnerving events. But I couldn't give up now. I searched around and found a low cupboard behind the pews, stacked with books. The first ones I removed looked more modern. I thumbed through them. Nothing. Then lower down I came upon a couple of older leather-bound volumes just like the one Rudi had borrowed. And as I thumbed through the first one a photograph fell out. It was too dark to see what the photo portrayed. I took the photo over to one of the candles and nearly dropped it in shock.

I had a pretty good idea by now of how a man and a woman made love. Or at least, I thought I did. But this was nothing like it. A wild jumble of arms and legs and my mother's face . . . Even though I was alone, I found myself blushing furiously. A rapid search of the other identical missal produced more photographs. Six in all. All equally shocking and disturbing. I didn't think I'd ever be able to look at my mother again without blushing. I rummaged through other books and just prayed that I had located them all. I wasn't going to wait a second longer. I lifted down one of the candles from the altar, held the offending pictures close to the stone floor and burned them, one by one, enjoying watching the treated paper curl and writhe like a snake in agony before it turned to ash.

I had just got rid of the last one, trying not to study it too closely, and had just stood on tiptoe to replace the candle when the door at the back of the chapel opened and Father Francisco came in.

"Buongiorno," I said. Trying to breathe normally.

He gave me a puzzled nod. "You come to mass?" he said in stilted English. "Not for one more hour."

"I was upset after last night," I said. "I came to pray."

"Bene." He nodded again. "Prayer is good. I also pray. Stay. We pray together."

"Oh no. I wouldn't want to disturb you," I said. "No, really. I must go." As he put out a hand to restrain me, I crept past him and fled. I wondered what he would make of the pile of missals I had left on the floor, or the little piles of ash near the altar. No matter. I was leaving. I wouldn't have to explain them. And as I left the chapel I suddenly pictured what might have happened if Paolo's mother had opened the wrong missal. And I had to grin.

Chapter 31

Wednesday, April 24, 1935

Finally leaving Villa Fiori. Never been so glad in my life!

During the time I was in the chapel the sky had brightened. Now I got my first look out of the east-facing windows toward the lake and saw the sun appearing between the peaks. The lake itself looked like molten silver and the first ferry of the day left a silver trail behind it. I stood, transfixed by the beauty and peacefulness of the scene, allowing myself for the first time in ages to enjoy what I was seeing. As I stood there I heard the neat tap of high heels on the stairs. I looked up to see my mother coming down them, looking delicate and serene in pale blue.

"Good morning, darling," she said. "Did you manage to sleep after that horrid day yesterday?"

I stared at her as if she was speaking a foreign language. "Have you only just woken up?" I asked.

"Well, yes. It is only seven. That's horribly early for little *moi*."

"Then you don't know?" I stammered. "You didn't hear all the commotion last night?"

"Slept like a log, darling. So did Max. Did something happen?"

"Only that Camilla's maid Gerda was arrested for Rudolf's murder," I said. "She killed Lieutenant Klinker too and she tried to kill me."

"Good God," Mummy said. "I never liked her. Po-faced, wasn't she?"

"And too perfect. I'm quite longing to see Queenie again," I agreed.

"So we are free to go, do you think?" she asked and a frown wrinkled that perfect forehead. "Although I don't see how I can leave not knowing . . ."

"All taken care of," I said. "The offending items went up in smoke. A pile of ash."

Relief flooded across her face. "Darling. You are a genius. If there's anything I can do for you in return . . . anything. We'll pay for your wedding, of course. Give you a lovely trousseau. Maybe I can ask Max to buy you a sweet little house somewhere. I'll never be able to repay you."

I let her hug me, overwhelmed by this display of affection, and was glad when Uncle Cosimo summoned me to be interviewed by yet another important policeman wearing a lot of braid. I told him everything, and mentioned that I had saved a sample of the tea that Gerda wanted me to drink because I suspected that she was going to drug me again or even kill me this time. He nodded when Uncle Cosimo translated all this for him, then he said something in Italian. Uncle Cosimo smiled and translated. "He says you are a brave and intelligent young woman. You will make some man a good wife."

"Thank you," I said. "I intend to."

And I went to find the man in question. Darcy had just returned from removing his belongings from the cottage, leaving no evidence that he had ever occupied it. The English gardener had just vanished and as far as the other gardeners were concerned, good riddance.

We ate a hearty breakfast, for once with eggs as Camilla thought we needed nourishing. Mummy and Max departed with lots of hugs and kisses and promises. I doubted if any of them would be fulfilled, but at least I'd remind her to pay for my wedding . . . if it was allowed to take place. I had put that worry aside while I was here, but now I'd fulfilled my part in the bargain. I had done what the queen had asked, and I could report back that Mrs. Simpson was still not free to marry her son. She could rest easy that . . . then I remembered why he had been brought here. Oh crikey! Should I tell them what I had overheard? Then I decided to keep quiet. Darcy would report to the men who mattered. The prince would be watched and advised accordingly. And would do the right thing, I hoped.

I went out onto the steps to wave good-bye to my mother. Just as they were about to get into their motorcar I remembered something. "By the way, Mummy, did you know that Granddad is getting married?" I said. In all the turmoil of the last days this worrying fact had completely slipped my mind.

Her eyes opened wider. "Married? To whom? Not that awful old bat next door who has been trying to get her hook into him for years?"

"The very one," I said. "Mrs. Huggins, or 'uggins, as she calls it."

"But we can't let that happen!" she said. "We can't have a creature like that in the family. She'll show up at your wedding with her hair in curlers and wearing a pinny."

"Surely it's up to him, isn't it? He's lonely, Mummy. He just wants company."

"She's lured him with her treacle puddings," Mummy said. "Well, it's going to happen over my dead body. Max!" she called as he loaded one of Mummy's many bags into the backseat. "I've changed my mind, darling. We're not going to the villa after all, we're heading straight for England."

And so I watched them go, wondering whether Mummy would get the better of Mrs. Huggins. I wasn't quite sure who would win.

When Darcy and I finally found ourselves alone he said to me, "Listen, I have to go back to London to report on all this."

"Of course," I said, trying to appear calm and businesslike.

"Hold on a minute." He put a hand on my shoulder. "I didn't say I had to go back immediately. I could go back tomorrow instead of today. I thought maybe you and I could find a little hotel somewhere on the lake and have some time together. It's very beautiful here."

Oh golly, I was tempted. But I shook my head. "I promised Belinda I'd go to look after her. Now that she's no longer at the clinic she'll need someone to do her shopping and cleaning."

"She doesn't have servants?"

"She had one, but the woman has gone to be with her daughter, also having a baby right now."

"Bugger Belinda," Darcy muttered. "How about us for once?"

I ignored the swearword this once. I did feel the same way myself. "Maybe it wouldn't matter if I left her alone for one more day," I said, already weakening. "And I suppose she could have Francesca's granddaughter run errands for her."

Darcy's face lit up. "There you are. Perfect. Shall we get going, then?"

I still hesitated, torn between duty and desire to be with my beloved. "I should perhaps just stop in to make sure she'll be all right. Maybe buy her some food, you know."

"All right," Darcy said. "We'll take your suitcase up to her house and just bring a small bag for tonight."

Those words made clear the implication of going away with Darcy for the night. We had been chaste until now. But we were going to marry soon. Did it matter that much if we didn't wait another couple of months?

"Yes, a small bag for tonight," I repeated.

We went up to my room and Darcy sat on the bed while I packed my suitcase. It was easy to pack because everything was in neat piles.

"I must say there were some advantages to Gerda," he said,

watching me. "Maybe we can find you another efficient maid when we are settled."

"Golly, no, thanks," I said, making him laugh. "I was terrified of her, even before I knew she was a trained killer."

We went to say good-bye to Camilla. She hugged me, a little awkwardly, and made us promise to come back and stay soon. And to invite her to the wedding. I took my leave of Paolo, his mother and Uncle Cosimo. I wondered what Paolo felt about his uncle and whether he knew of the sort of scheming that had gone on. I didn't think so. He seemed a likeable, straightforward type of chap. I hoped he and Camilla could be happy together and that he wouldn't be tempted to stray.

When I asked if someone could telephone for a taxi, Paolo offered to drive us up to Belinda's. I didn't quite know what to do about that—I'd have appreciated the ride, but I couldn't risk Paolo seeing Belinda, could I?

"Please don't bother," I said. "It's a lovely day. We can easily walk."

"No bother at all," Paolo said.

I glanced at Darcy. "He can't meet Belinda," I whispered. "Old lover!"

"Blimey," Darcy muttered. Paolo brought around the Maserati and our bags were loaded into the back. I think I held my breath all the way up the hill. This time there was no group of women outside the bakery. In fact, the village street was deserted apart from two old men who sat outside the café/bar, each with a glass of red wine in front of him—even though it was not yet ten o'clock.

"I'm afraid I can't ask you in," I said as he inched the sports car into the alleyway. "My friend is still quite ill and not up to receiving visitors."

"Don't worry," Paolo said. "I understand. I am merely the chauffeur."

He helped Darcy unload our bags. I prayed that Belinda

wouldn't open the door and come rushing out. I gave a big sigh of relief as the Maserati reversed into the street and drove away.

Darcy picked up my bag. "I'll carry it to the front door for you," he said, "then I'll wait on the street while you tell her our plans."

"You're not coming in?"

"You don't want me to come in with you," he said.

"Why not? Belinda would love to see you. She needs cheering up."

"But don't you think she'd be embarrassed, for a man to see her in this . . . condition?" he said. I had rarely seen him uncomfortable.

"Darcy, I think she'd like to be treated like a normal person, to be reminded of her old life at this moment. I feel so sorry for her."

"She did bring it upon herself," he said. "Her lifestyle was never what you might call prudent."

"This was different," I said, leaping to her defense. "The man told her he loved her and talked about their future together. She thought he intended to marry her. It could happen to any of us. To me, if we go to a little pension tonight and then you change your mind about marrying me."

"Absolutely not," he said, actually blushing. "I would never let that happen to you. In the first place, I would make sure, and in the second, we don't have to do anything you don't want to. I just wanted time alone with you."

I looked at him, melting. "Oh, Darcy. I do love you," I said. "And I want to spend time with you more than anything. But you do see my point. The man always walks away free as air and the girl's life is ruined. Belinda thinks that nobody will marry her now, that she's spoiled goods."

Darcy nodded, then finally said, "Come on, then. Let's get this over. This suitcase is beginning to weigh a ton."

I tapped at her front door. There was a long pause, then Belinda opened it. I gave a little gasp. She looked terrible. She was in her nightclothes, a purple silk dressing gown tied over her monstrous belly. Her hair was unbrushed and plastered to the sides of her face. She looked ashen white, almost gray.

"Oh, Georgie," she said. "Thank God you've come. I feel terrible. I don't know what's wrong. I think it must be food poisoning."

"Come on, let's get you to bed," I said. "Darcy's with me. What have you had to eat today?"

"Nothing. I haven't felt like food since I got here."

"I'll make you some tea. Do you have eggs?"

"Nothing really. The larder is bare."

"Then I'll send Darcy to get food. Go and lie down."

I led her into the bedroom, took off her robe, tucked her in and sent Darcy off for eggs, milk, bread and fruit.

"When did you start feeling like this?" I asked.

"As soon as I got here," she said. "I decided on the spur of the moment to escape from the clinic, so I packed my things and I had to almost run down the hill to catch the midday ferry."

"Belinda! You must be out of your mind."

"I couldn't find a taxi," she said, "and I couldn't ask them to summon one." She took a deep breath and said, "You don't understand. I hated that place. I was becoming so depressed there."

"It might have been boring and sterile but surely the best place to have a baby."

"Oh, I'll go back nearer the time, I suppose," she said. "I just couldn't stand another moment of doing nothing. Sitting there while those frightful nuns drifted around me, telling me what a sinner I was. The last straw was when they told me I'd not be allowed to know where my baby would be going. I chose that clinic because they arrange adoptions when necessary. But I thought, naïvely, I suppose, that I'd be able to choose a jolly peasant family and come to visit the little dear whenever I wanted to. Then I found out they take the baby away as soon as it's born. I'm not even allowed to hold her—in case I get attached, they said."

I looked at her with pity and she had tears rolling down her cheeks.

"I know it's for the best, but I thought I could keep this little house and pay someone in the village to take care of her and come to see her often. Much better, right? So I fled. And I . . ." She broke off, grimacing in pain. There were beads of sweat on her forehead.

"Belinda, you don't think you're in labor, do you?" I asked.

"But it's not due for at least two more weeks," she said, looking at me in fright. "And these are great waves of pain over my whole body. My back, my stomach."

"I'm not much of an expert, but it sounds as if you could be giving birth. That run down the hill probably brought things on."

She sat up, clutching my hand. "Oh God, Georgie. I can't have a baby here. There are no nurses or gas or anything."

"When Darcy returns we'll have him go for the doctor. He'll be able to tell what's happening. In the meantime I'll make you that tea."

I boiled a kettle. Darcy returned with milk and food, and I sent him out again immediately to find a doctor.

"You mean she's having the baby?" he asked, looking more worried than I had ever seen him. "Here? Now?"

"It very much seems like it," I said. "At least the doctor will be able to tell us."

"I'll go right away." He looked relieved not to be in the house with her, I thought.

I went back to Belinda and propped her up while she sipped tea. She had to stop halfway as another wave of pain swept over her. "This is awful, Georgie," she said. "If it's labor, remind me never to do it again. I'll never go near another man as long as I live. I'll join those nuns . . ."

I had to laugh and then so did she. "Oh, Georgie," she said, taking my hand. "I'm so glad you are here. I was so scared . . ."

"I won't leave you now," I said, giving a little inward sigh. "It's going to be all right."

"I wish you could have come earlier. Was there really a murder in the house?

"There were actually two murders."

"Two? You certainly seem to have an attraction for dead bodies." She managed a weak smile.

"It was all rather horrid and the local policeman wanted to arrest my mother."

"Your mother was there?"

"Oh yes. It was a jolly gathering." I grinned. "I couldn't wait to get away, even before the murder."

"I'm glad you're here now," she said. "How was Miss Cami-Knickers?"

"Rather nice, actually. I think she enjoyed having me there. She's lonely, you know."

"Lonely? How could one be lonely with that gorgeous Paolo? She doesn't deserve him."

She broke off talking again, rocking back and forth and groaning. I had never witnessed an actual birth, apart from a foal in our stables in Scotland, but I had heard about contractions and how they came closer and closer together. Belinda's, I deemed, were only a few minutes apart.

It seemed an eternity before Darcy returned, panting from having run. "There is no doctor in the village," he said. "I had to find someone with a telephone and I put through a call to the doctor in Stresa, but he is out on his house calls and his receptionist has left a message for him when he returns. But she has no idea when that will be. Some of his patients are up in the hills."

"Golly," I said. I lowered my voice, glancing back at Belinda's room. "I don't think we've got that long. She doesn't seem to have a clue, but I believe she's getting awfully close."

"To having the baby, you mean?"

"No, to swimming the Channel," I replied, exasperated. "Of

course I meant having the baby. She's having contractions every minute or so."

"So what are we going to do?" Darcy said. "Should I go back to the village and see if I can round up a couple of women who know about this sort of thing?"

"From what I've seen on films, you have to find clean towels and boil water."

"What for?"

"I'm not actually sure," I confessed.

He grinned. "A fine pair of midwives we are."

"We're the best she's got right now. Come on, let's get back to her."

"You don't need me in there." Darcy hung back.

"Honestly, Darcy. I thought you were fearless."

"Drug runners and gangsters and international spies are one thing, but a woman having a baby?" He shook his head.

"Oh, all right. Go and boil the water and find those towels," I said.

I went back to Belinda. She was lying back, now bathed in sweat. "Georgie, I think you're right," she said. "I think I might be having the baby now."

"Just cottoned on to that, have you?" I grinned. "Darcy's gone to boil water. I suppose we better take a look and see. . . ." I pulled back the bedclothes. "Oh," I exclaimed, rather shocked at what I saw. "Oh golly, Belinda," I said. "I hope the doctor gets here soon."

"When did Darcy say he was coming?"

"He didn't. The doctor is out on his rounds and could be anywhere. It may be just us."

"I keep feeling I want to push," she said. "That's bad, isn't it?"

"It means the baby is coming out," I said. "Which is good, I suppose."

I peeked under the sheet again and saw a little pink mound between Belinda's legs. As I watched, the mound revealed itself to be the top of a head, then a whole little head. I stared, horrified and fascinated. Darcy came in behind me. "The water has just boiled. What do you want me to . . . oh, my God!" he exclaimed.

"She's giving birth right now," I said.

"I can see that."

Belinda let out a primeval yell and the rest of the baby slithered out. Darcy and I stared at it, neither of us daring to touch it.

"Here's one of those towels you wanted," Darcy said.

"It's still got the cord attached," I said.

"Aren't we supposed to cut it or something?" Darcy asked. "I'm sure I read an instruction manual once. You're supposed to tie it with bootlaces and cut it."

"I'm not cutting anything," I said. "Let's wait a while, shall we?"

"I'm going to go and find those women," Darcy said and left rapidly. "Somebody ought to know what they are doing around here."

"Has it come out?" Belinda asked, trying to sit up. "Why isn't it crying?"

Gingerly I wrapped the little pink thing in a towel. Immediately it flailed its arms and let out a high-pitched cry. I looked at it in wonder. A tiny person. Just perfect. Waving little hands, and face screwed up in indignation. I wiped the face clean, looked at Belinda and smiled.

"It's perfect," I said. "A perfect little person."

"Boy or girl?"

I hadn't thought to look until now. I looked. "A boy. You have a little boy."

She looked crestfallen. "A boy? No. What can I do with a boy? I could handle a little girl. Look after her. But not a boy. I simply couldn't raise a son."

"Then you'd better take him back to the nuns, I suppose," I said.

"If only you and Darcy were married, you could raise him for me," she said.

"But we're not, Belinda, and thinking about this logically now, I'm not sure that starting married life with someone else's child is the best idea. If we couldn't have children, it would be a different matter . . ." I broke off, wondering why I had been so dense until now.

"What?" she asked, seeing my face.

"I think I might have a solution that would suit everybody," I said.

"What kind of solution?"

"I can't tell you now, but if it works, it would be good."

Chapter 32

Wednesday, April 24
At Belinda's little house in San Fidele

I broke off at the sound of shrill voices and several women crowded into the room. I backed away, as they obviously knew what to do. In no time at all Belinda and the baby were cleaned up and he was settled down happily in her arms.

"Look at me," she said. "Did you ever think I'd look maternal?"

"Wonders will never cease," I said.

Darcy took me aside. "You won't want to leave her, will you?"

I shook my head. "I can't, now. I hope you understand."

He took my hands. "I should be getting back to London anyway," he said. "Let me know when you're coming back."

I nodded, feeling tears stinging at the backs of my eyes at the thought that he was going and I didn't know when I'd see him again. "I never know where to write to you," I said.

"There's always Princess Zou Zou's house," he said, smiling down at me in a way that melted my heart. "And I'm sure she'd be delighted for you to stay there. She must have finished her round-the-world race by now."

"Yes, I hope so," I said. "I wish you didn't have to go. I wish I could come with you, but I can't."

He took me in his arms and kissed me. I felt the longing in that kiss. Not long now, I thought, and we'd finally be married and all this separation would be over. But then I reminded myself that he'd still be going away, never telling me where and for how long. It was something I'd have to live with, I supposed.

I watched him walk up the lane, then I went back in to Belinda. "I'll be gone for a little while," I said. "Don't worry, I'll hurry back."

Then I set off down the hill.

Camilla was surprised when I found her writing a letter in the long gallery.

"Georgie, you're back. Did you forget something?"

"No. I came back because I needed to talk to you. Can we take a walk where we won't be overheard?"

"Yes, of course," she replied cautiously. "Is this something about Rudi and the letter?"

"No, something quite different. Much nicer."

We went out to the gardens and walked in silence for a while. Then I told her the real reason I had come to Stresa. "My friend is of a good family," I said, "and of course she can't keep the baby. It just seemed—well, it's a little boy. And I thought of what you had told me. And I wondered . . . Paolo would have a son to carry on the title."

"I don't know what to say, what to think," she said. "I'm stunned."

"You'd have a chance to rear a child from day one," I said. "Just like your own baby."

I saw a glimmer of hope in her eyes. "It does sound wonderful," she said. "I'm not sure that Paolo would agree to it. He is from an old and proud family."

"You can only ask," I said.

"You're right," she said. "I can only ask."

We turned and walked back in silence, past the little octagonal pavilion, past the swimming pool. As we approached the house she turned to me. "This friend of yours—it's Belinda, isn't it?"

"Yes," I said, not being able to lie on such a solemn occasion.

"It's—it's not Paolo's child, is it?" Her voice wavered.

"You knew about Belinda and Paolo?"

"Oh yes. He told me how fond he was of her. I knew he'd have married her if she'd been a Catholic, and had a less damaged reputation."

"No, it's not his child. That was over a long time ago."

"I see. And the child's father?"

"An American. A cad. Promised her the moon and left her in the lurch."

"Poor Belinda," she said. "I always thought she'd come to a bad end. She took risks, didn't she?"

"Always," I agreed.

"I remember catching her climbing out of the dorm window." She smiled.

"That was one of the lesser risks she has taken," I said. "But she didn't deserve this. She was sure he planned to marry her."

"Could I come and see the baby?" she asked.

"Not today. She's just given birth and I'm sure she's exhausted. Also she won't want to see anyone when she's not looking her best."

"I understand. And I'll have to talk it through with Paolo first. He may not want to. Men are funny about adopting. But she's nearby, is she?"

"She's in San Fidele, just up the hill."

"How amazing. And we never bumped into each other."

I didn't say that Belinda had taken good care that they never met. I went back to her and found her and the baby asleep. A few days later Camilla came to visit. I had prepared Belinda in advance, but even so the meeting was an awkward one. Camilla took the baby and held him, gazing down at him with wonder. "So tiny," she said. "And so perfect."

And so it was arranged. Camilla and Paolo came to see the baby and instantly fell in love with it. At least Camilla did and Paolo didn't seem to object. The baby and a nurse went down to Villa Fiori. I stayed with Belinda for a few days, looking after her until she had regained her strength and until Francesca returned. Belinda had decided to stay on for a while in the little house. So that she could get some dress designing done in peace, was how she put it. I suspected it might be that she didn't feel ready to come back to society in England yet, but also so that she could visit her child. I didn't think this was the wisest thing. Would she be brave enough to face Paolo just to catch a glimpse of her baby? And if she saw him growing and looking adorable wouldn't the yearning to keep him become stronger? I didn't express these thoughts; instead I said, "You must come back to England soon, Belinda. I'll want you to help me get ready for my wedding. You must design my wedding dress, you realize."

"Yes," she agreed. "I'll come back soon."

On the night before I was due to return to England we sat out on her terrace, watching the lights across the lake.

"I did the right thing for him, didn't I?" she said.

"Of course you did. He'll be raised in a noble family with adoring parents. You couldn't have planned a better future for him."

"Yes," she said. "Yes, of course. Actually I'm glad it was a boy, Georgie. If it had been a girl, I would have been tempted to keep her and that would have made my life so complicated."

"It's all for the best, Belinda. Of course you are going to feel some regret at this stage. After all, you carried him around for nine months. But now you are free to get on with your life."

There was a long pause and then she said, "It's ironic, isn't it? I was really in love with Paolo and now he has my baby and I come away with nothing."

"You come away with a bright future," I said. "Your grandmother has left you enough money to launch your dress designs, or to travel, or to do what you want to."

"I wonder if I'll ever find happiness, the way you and Darcy have," she said in a wistful voice.

"Of course you will. Just be a little more careful in future."

She looked at me and laughed. "That respected aphorism: If you can't be good, be careful; and if you can't be careful, keep your knees together. Right?"

"Absolutely." I laughed with her.

THE TRIP BACK to England, on the first of May, went smoothly. I arrived at Victoria Station to blustery rain. Now I really know I'm home, I thought. I telephoned Princess Zou Zou's residence and found that she had returned, Darcy had already been to see her and she was dying to see me. So I had a place to stay in London until I decided what to do next.

ZOU ZOU GAVE me a lovely warm welcome and had a pretty little room on the top floor all ready for me. "Far enough away from the rest of the house in case Darcy comes to visit," she said with a knowing wink.

The next day I paid a courtesy call on Queen Mary. The Mall and Buckingham Palace were being decked out for the Royal Jubilee and flags fluttered around me in a stiff breeze.

"I hear that your stay in Stresa did not go exactly as planned," the queen said as I took a seat beside her.

I wondered for an awful moment whether she had heard about Belinda, but she went on, "A German spy was murdered at the very house in which you were staying, so I'm told. How very disagreeable for you."

"It was, ma'am. But I'm happy to report that a certain American lady is still officially married to her latest husband."

"I'm very glad to hear it," she said.

"Although she is in the process of filing divorce papers."

She sighed. "Of course she is. But I wonder what made my son attend that particular gathering, then. They didn't sound like his kind of partygoing crowd."

"I got the impression he wished he hadn't accepted the invitation," I said. I had debated with myself whether I should say anything at all about the meeting I had overheard. I could hardly say, "Your son appears to be very pro-German, which might be a problem one day." Because Queen Mary, the king and myself all came from a German background. Finally I had decided against it. The British government knew what had taken place. That would have to suffice.

I had more important things to think about. I was just debating how to broach the subject when she said, "Oh, and about your proposed wedding . . ."

"Yes, ma'am?" I asked.

"I understand that Parliament will see no problem with accepting your withdrawal from the line of succession. We can start to plan a summer wedding for you."

"Thank you so much. That is good news." If it had been anybody other than Queen Mary, I would have hugged her. But one does not hug a queen.

Historical Note

There is no historical evidence that the meeting in this book ever happened. But the international conference between Italy, England and France to discuss ways to combat the Nazi threat really did take place in Stresa in 1935. When I read that, I thought it was strange as Mussolini was a big fan of Hitler and a fellow Fascist. So immediately I thought, I bet there were other meetings going on behind the scenes. And I knew that the Prince of Wales was also impressed by Hitler, so I thought, "Why not?"